PRAISE FOR *CECE RIOS AND THE DESERT OF SOULS:*

"An astonishing and moving tale infused with spirit and unforgettable magic. I loved Cece from page one!" —**J.C. CERVANTES**, *New York Times* bestselling author of the Storm Runner series

"*Cece Rios and the Desert of Souls* is the kind of story you don't want to put down. Flush with incredible world building, mucho español throughout, and an unforgettable cast of brujas, criaturas, and humans, this book reminds us that our greatest strengths can sometimes be found in the unlikeliest of places." —**PABLO CARTAYA**, award-winning author of *The Epic Fail of Arturo Zamora*

"Pokémon meets *Coco* in a spirited and moving adventure, the perfect balance of Mexican American, Mesoamerican, and fantasy elements. Cece's world is at once familiar and tantalizingly strange, peopled by beautifully crafted, well-rounded, and vivid characters." —**DAVID BOWLES**, award-winning author of *They Call Me Güero*

"In *Cece Rios and the Desert of Souls*, Kaela Rivera puts her stamp on familiar Mexican folktales, brujas, and gives us a brave and loyal hero all kids can look up to." —**ZORAIDA CÓRDOVA**, award-winning author of *Labyrinth Lost*

"A new Narnia full of desert heat and danger, *Cece Rios and the Desert of Souls* mixes familiar myth, inventive magic, and vivid characters to capture readers. Always refreshing when a book trusts its heroine to question the foundations of her world without losing hope and to face her fears without hardening her heart." —**ANNA MERIANO**, author of the Love Sugar Magic series

"If you're a fan of mythology and beautifully written fantasy stories with tons of heart, you're going to love Kaela Rivera's splendid debut novel about friendship, sisterhood, and the lengths we'll go to save the ones we love." —**RYAN CALEJO**, author of the Charlie Hernández series

CECE RIOS

and the

DESERT OF SOULS

CECE RIOS

and the
DESERT OF SOULS

KAELA RIVERA

HARPER
An Imprint of HarperCollinsPublishers

Library of Congress Control Number: 2020937705
ISBN 978-0-06-294755-0
Typography by Catherine Lee
21 22 23 24 25 PC/LSCH   10 9 8 7 6 5 4 3 2 1

First Edition

*In honor of my abuelo, who shared with me
his precious memories and stories.*

*In defense of my mother, who has always had
a soul as strong as water.*

CECE RIOS
and the
DESERT OF SOULS

The Criatura of Progeny and Stars

I was seven years old when I met my first criatura.

I was wandering through the cerros—the hills of the desert beyond town—at night, barely avoiding low heads of cactus. In the dark, their spines looked more menacing than they did under the sun. But then, I was a child. Everything looked menacing in the dark.

I was lost. No matter where I turned, I couldn't see the light of town. The other children had left me hours ago. I should have gone home with them, but I'd wanted to watch the sunset by myself.

I should have known better. It was winter, and with winter came danger.

Not because of the cold. But because it was los meses de la criatura—the criatura months.

Since before I could remember, Mamá had taught me the legends of the criaturas. They were creatures unlike humans, children of the Desert goddess, who the Great

Namer created from dust and words. Mama taught me the difference between animal criaturas, who were made to fill the desert, and dark criaturas, who were made to attack the descendants of the Sun god—us. But her advice for dealing with both types was the same.

"You must steal their souls and command them to leave you," she'd always said. "For you cannot outrun a criatura once it sets its sights on you."

Her words seemed to wrap around my throat as I turned in the darkness, trying to find the distant outline of my town.

"Are you lost, human child?"

I gasped and whirled around, clutching my shirt. Out of the shadow cast by the hill, a creature slipped into view.

She walked forward on legs of flesh, just as smooth and brown as anyone's in town. Her skirt was bright with reds and greens and blues. Her headdress shimmered with sleek owl and quetzal feathers to match, and its ornate moon-stone beads swayed from side to side. But from the waist up, she was *bones*.

My voice froze in my throat. Her face was a skull, her jaw hanging just slightly open, as if ready to speak. Her eyes were empty black sockets, but I could feel them on me. I met their gaze, craning my head back in silent terror as she stopped in front of me.

It was Tzitzimitl. The Criatura of Stars and Devouring—a dark criatura.

Her lanky shadow fell over me in stripes, the gaps in her rib bones letting through beams of moonlight. Her jaw opened, and a voice came out of the motionless cavity: "You are far from where your people dwell in the once-great city of Tierra del Sol. Surely you are lost."

My heart hammered so loudly I was sure Tzitzimitl would hear it and try to bite it out of my chest. I crossed my arms over myself and stumbled back a few steps.

"Don't eat me!" I turned to run, but bony fingers wrapped around my shoulder before I got the chance.

Tzitzimitl's strength was irresistible. "You do not want to wander through Mother Desert's land alone, human child," she said. "Here, criaturas roam freely for two more months. And La Llorona is loose in your world right now—she will drown you, or snake criaturas will eat you."

I shook under her grasp. "P-please. I just want to go home."

She cocked her skull, and her headdress shifted so its metallic stars clattered. "I will take you home." She offered her bony hand. I stared at the fingers. "Don't you know you can trust me, human child? I am Tzitzimitl. The Great Namer made me the protector of human children."

Mamá had always said that criaturas would kill me. La

Llorona would drown children in rivers, and Golden Eagle would snatch us away in his talons. El Sombrerón would steal daughters from their families, and the Gray Wolf would feast on the lost.

But . . . wouldn't Tzitzimitl have hurt me by now if she were bad?

Slowly, I put my hand in hers. Her bones closed over my soft skin carefully, and she led me in a new direction.

"What is your name, human child?" she asked as we wandered between scrub and cacti.

I stared up at her. She wore a necklace that flashed in the moonlight. The simple stone on leather swung with every step we took. "Um . . . Cece. Cece Rios."

"Another Rios," she said. "I believe humans carry their names from one mother to another, correct? Your family has a history with criaturas, then. Do you know of Catrina Rios? In Devil's Alley, they call her Catrina, Cager of Souls."

Mamá had mentioned her once, but she hadn't been very happy about it. "Is she my mom's sister? My tía?"

"I do not know your mother." She pulled me sideways before I could step on a sleeping snake. "But you share a last name, and you have her eyes. Perhaps she is your tía. Though I think you do not share the same heart."

As we walked, my muscles slowly relaxed. Tzitzimitl didn't do any of the things Mamá said criaturas did. She didn't try to eat me. She didn't try to drown me or lure me into a volcano. And after ten minutes, the town lights appeared in the distance—so I knew she was helping me after all.

I jumped up and down, pointing out the distant buildings. "That's it! That's Tierra del Sol!"

Tzitzimitl smiled down at me, her soul necklace swinging with my movement. At least, I thought she was trying to smile. It was hard to tell since she didn't have lips.

"Tzitzimitl, can I ask you something?" I asked as we continued toward town.

"You may. Though I can't promise I will answer."

I pouted. "Mamá's books said you were the Devourer. I don't know exactly what that means, but it sounds bad. Why are you helping me?"

"Ah," she said, and then didn't speak for a long time.

After several unbearable moments, I shook her arm. "Well?" I asked.

The town lights grew brighter, each building like a lantern warming the edges of the desert. We crossed into the town's shady, abandoned outskirts—the Ruins, Mamá called the area, left over from an ancient battle with criaturas. Large, empty husks of adobe buildings lined us left and right as we walked. But I kept my eyes on the lights. They were bright beneath the shadows of the cone-shaped oil wells lying far, far on the other side of town.

I'd never been out in that direction, but Papá said the oil fields lay all the way outside the Ruins that ringed my town, toward the east. And when he got a job there, he'd make enough money to build us a real house out of adobe.

Tzitzimitl's fingers closed more tightly around mine. I looked up at her again.

"When the moon blacks out the sun, and Naked Man trembles in wonder at the heavens," she said, using the name our legends used for humankind, "I am called to be the Devourer. It's what I was named for. But I was also named the Protector of Progeny, the keeper of Naked Man's children."

I stared up at her as the worn, dirt road leading through the Ruins and into town appeared beneath our feet.

"I don't get it," I said. "How can you be both?"

"I wonder the same thing sometimes." She sighed and patted my head with her other hand. "But it was the name given to me, so it is what I am. Only the Great Namer knows why."

The Great Namer. I scrunched up my forehead as we reached the edge where the Ruins met my town. Warm yellow light fell over us as we crossed over. Mamá had definitely told me about the Great Namer before, hadn't she?

"You mean Coyote!" I exclaimed when I remembered his other name.

Tzitzimitl flinched. "Shh, child!" I pulled my shoulders

up to my ears. Her stance relaxed when she saw no one was around, and she nudged me to start walking again. I followed quietly.

"That is his name," she said in a hushed tone.

"He's my favorite," I whispered. "Out of all the legends, I like Coyote's the best." Then I straightened up. "Oh, but yours is nice too, Tzitzimitl. Well, not *nice* exactly . . ."

I paused and looked up at her. The Devourer, leading me safely home? I squinted as I thought about it. She couldn't be both. So she must be what I saw—the one who was nice enough to bring me home.

We entered the town square, and she glanced across the many avenues. "Where is your home, mija?" she asked.

I was about to point to the street when we heard a voice behind us.

"Miguel, she must be here somewhere. She knows better than to leave town—"

"Quiet. We will find her."

The voices piled up into noise. I turned around, and Tzitzimitl let my hand slip out of hers.

From one of the streets behind us, Mamá and Papá appeared at the head of a great party of people. They held torches high, and the square was soon flooded with orange firelight. I shouted, "Mamá!"

Their heads swung toward us. Tzitzimitl took a step back.

"Mamá, Papá!" I called, throwing my arms up in the air. Their mouths dropped open as they spotted me. I ran forward, laughing. I'd missed my familia so much—

"A criatura!" Mamá screeched.

She and Papá dove past me toward Tzitzimitl. I flinched as they and the party of torchbearers flooded by. Without hesitation, they mobbed my friend, pulling her under their mass of strength.

At first, she fought back. She delivered powerful blows with her bony arms. She tossed some to the side. She even grabbed the man nearest her and opened her jaw wide. Someone screamed as her teeth aimed for the man's shoulder. My stomach suddenly knotted up. She wasn't going to devour him, was she? She was good. She wouldn't.

Just before she bit down, her wide sockets stopped on me. I looked at her. And held my breath. And hoped.

Slowly, her bony fingers released the man. She stopped fighting. Immediately, the adults yanked her under a mass of torches and rope.

I dove into the crowd. "Don't hurt her!" I filled my lungs to the brim and let out a scream: "*Stop it!*"

I found Papá and dug my fingers into his belt. He looked down at me, over his shoulder. His dark eyebrows crushed downward as he shoved me away from the fight. "Stay back, Cece!"

At the center of mayhem, Mamá reached down, gripped

the necklace I'd noticed swinging from Tzitzimitl's neck bone earlier, and yanked. The leather snapped. Tzitzimitl let out a painful-sounding gasp.

"Call the head of police!" Papá cried out as Mamá gave him the stone. "We will kill her tonight, before she can lure any more of our children away."

"No!" I said, but the mob still dragged Tzitzimitl away.

Mamá crouched down beside me and turned my face to hers. "Cece, calm down, pepita. You're safe now."

I shook my head. "She's not bad, Mamá. You—can't—hurt her!"

Mamá's hands froze on my face. "Mija," she said, her voice like iron. "Criaturas are dangerous. If we do not destroy them when they come after us, they will overrun our people as they did in the days when the curanderas failed." She gripped my face. "You *must not cry*! You must not be *weak*." She gave my chest a hard pat. "You are a Rios, a descendant of the Sun god. You cannot let your tears make you more water than fire."

I didn't know what that meant, but I knew I didn't like it. So I pulled away and ran.

The crowd had finished tying Tzitzimitl to the criminal's post in the center of the town square, her wrist bones bound in a knotted wad of rope. Papá was speaking to the head of police, who was still in his pajamas. I ran up behind Papá and snatched Tzitzimitl's soul stone and a knife from his back pocket. Fortunately, he didn't notice.

I raced toward Tzitzimitl. Her chin lifted at my approach.

"Cece!" Mamá roared. "Cece, you stay away from that criatura!"

I skidded to a stop and cut her free.

Tzitzimitl stood on her muscular brown legs. The townspeople rounded on us.

"She let it free!" someone hollered.

Everyone surged forward. I offered her the soul stone. Where it rested in my palm, there was a tingly, warm sensation, the way I always felt when I looked up at the stars at night. Tzitzimitl took it from me in a clatter of stone and bone, already moving toward the outskirts of town.

But as she did, she looked at me.

"I am the Protector of Progeny, the Criatura of Stars and Devouring," she said, her voice booming over the noise of the mob. It was so powerful, the townspeople fell silent, and they halted suddenly a couple of feet behind me. "I was named to see into the souls of children. And this day, I tell you, Cece Rios, that you have been blessed with a soul like water. None shall have power to burn you or make you ash."

And then she fled.

Crisp, cool air settled on me after her words. My heart swelled. Then, as if breaking out of a trance, the crowd rushed past me after Tzitzimitl's rapid escape. Angry yells replaced the cool, peaceful feeling in the air. Someone's hand grabbed my face and shoved me into the ground.

In the dirt, I prayed to the Sun god that Tzitzimitl would not be taken. I prayed that Papá would not be angry. I prayed the townspeople would understand what I'd done.

The head of police marched over to Mamá, and the two screamed at each other. "I refuse to have another traitor like your sister in this town!" he spat. "You Rios women all end up the same. Go bury your daughter as a sacrifice to the Desert—"

Mamá straightened up furiously. "She will not be a bruja!"

"You heard the criatura's curse! It is only a matter of time until your daughter's weak heart betrays us."

"She will not!" she said. "I will save my hija from this curse, or Ocean take me."

The head of police went silent, stunned. No one in Tierra del Sol liked to speak of the Ocean goddess, with one exception—life-or-death oaths. In the face of that vow, the head of police had no choice but to believe Mamá and let me stay in town.

But no one would ever forgive me for the day I revealed myself to be the town's weakest link—the day I had mercy on our ancient enemy.

2

Noche de Muerte

My sister and I ran toward the fiesta, our dresses trailing us like nervous flames.

"Juana, wait for me!" I called, panting. She had lifted her skirts so only the back swept the flat dirt road between our town's adobe houses. "I still have to paint your threat marks! You can't dance without them!"

Juana skated to a stop. "Just hand me the nocheztli, I'll do it."

I clutched the paint jar and slowed. "Mamá said she wanted *me* to practice painting you. I'm not going to mess it up, okay? Just trust me."

Juana rolled her eyes and sighed. Ever since she'd turned fifteen and had finally become a woman, she'd been doing that a lot. I bit my lip to stop from saying anything. Tonight, her dream of being selected for the yearly Amenazante dance was finally coming true. She would be on full display as she defended our town from the dangers that would soon awaken in the desert. And I didn't want to ruin her night with—well, with me being me.

Juana saw my face and stalked over. "Fine, fine. I just wish you would worry more about yourself." She sighed as I dipped my fingers in the paint. "You didn't even put fire opal in your hair to protect yourself, you were so busy with my skirts. Everyone's going to think you're a fool for being so unprepared." Her mouth slanted sideways.

I flinched but tried to cover it up with a shrug. After all, the town already thought I was a fool.

I lifted my fingers to Juana's face. I was nearly as tall as she was already, even though I was almost three years younger. Her eyes grew harder, sharper, as I framed them in the red blood of the prickly pear—nocheztli, the dancer's war paint.

"Done?" she huffed.

I stepped back and smiled. Juana's black hair crowned her head in a voluptuous bun, ringed with beads of bright fire opal, and a silk red rose I'd made perched on its top left. It matched the full skirt that swayed like flames around Juana's ankles.

With nocheztli's red streaks finally cutting across her face and bare shoulders, she was living fire. She needed to be for the dance she was about to do—the Amenazante dance, where the fiercest women in our town gathered to frighten away the criaturas that would soon plague the desert.

I squeezed the paint jar in my hands. "You look amazing."

"Thanks." She smiled and patted the top of my loose hair. "You did a pretty good job helping me out this year. But try to pay attention to yourself too, okay? In a couple years, *you'll* be a woman, and if you impress the dancing committee enough, you could be invited to do the Amenazante dance too. Everyone would have to respect you then."

I hunched over and avoided her gaze. I was only twelve (going on thirteen!), but Juana kept bringing up my fifteenth birthday like it was tomorrow.

She tugged me back into a run. "Now come on, or we'll be late!"

We flew through the streets of town, Juana dragging me closer to the sound of voices. Merchants flooded past us, headed northward. Some rode burros, and a couple of rich ones even sped off in motorcars, but all of them were in a hurry.

Tonight was Noche de Muerte, after all. The night the secret door to Devil's Alley—the criaturas' world—opened into ours.

And its criaturas swarmed out.

Only a few people outside of Tierra del Sol did business with us, since we were so isolated from big cities, but the few who did would disappear during the criatura months. This was not their birthplace, after all. They had no desire to defend it.

A few women in brightly colored dresses joined us on the road as we came closer and closer to the western edge of the town proper—the place where the desert and the Ruins met our months of preparation.

My heart pounded faster as we merged with the crowd, and the outskirts of Tierra del Sol came into view. The sun had set. Night blackened the Ruins and desert beyond. Normally, people wouldn't come this close to the desert. But on Noche de Muerte, it seemed an appropriate place to face our ancient enemies.

The line dividing us from the dangerous landscape beyond was clearly marked. A Sun Priestess, Dominga del Sol, stood tying the red rope in place. Knotted clumps of basil bobbed along its length, nodding like living things.

Noche de Muerte was finally here.

"Juana! Cece!"

We turned as Mamá and Papá separated from the masses. Mamá grinned at us. Papá didn't.

"Juana, you look like you're made of fire!" Mamá enveloped her in her large brown arms. Juana laughed and looked to Papá. After a stony moment, he nodded. Juana beamed.

"We did a good job, huh? And look! Cece did my hem so well." Juana twirled, showcasing our hard work. My chest swelled as the multitiered, wide, crimson skirt moved with her. She'd cut out the patterns and shown me how to stitch the fabric together, just as Mamá had first taught her. I'd spent months on the hem so it would look just right.

Papá reached over and planted a heavy hand on my shoulder. "Juana is beautiful."

I stared up at his rough, oil-streaked face and tried to figure out if that was supposed to be a compliment.

"You did very well on Juana's dress, mija." Mamá came over and pulled my long hair into her hands. "But you didn't finish getting ready! Where is your fire opal?"

At the question, a few people in the crowd turned to look at me. A couple clucked their tongues disapprovingly. A few scoffed. Mamá glared at them, and they turned away. Papá rubbed his forehead like he was tired.

I smiled sheepishly. "You know fire opal doesn't work on me, Mamá."

For most people, fire opal was the best defense against criaturas. Legends said fire opal drew on the inner fire humans inherited from the Sun god—so while it wasn't lethal to criaturas who touched it, it could seriously burn them if the person's inner fire was strong enough.

But since that night when I was seven, it had stopped

working for me altogether. The stone didn't even glow at my touch like it did for most people.

Mamá knit her brow. "But mija, you must at least give the appearance to criaturas—and the townspeople—that your inner fire is something to contend with. Or else they will only see you as *weak*."

At times like this, I wondered if they'd ever forget—or forgive—what I'd done.

"Amenazante dancers!" The mayor's voice carried over our heads. We all turned to look where he stood, by the red cord. "The criaturas approach. Come show our enemies what they have to fear."

Chills ran over my body. Past the mayor, past the red cord, waiting in the darkness of the ruins, I spotted something. A flicker of red. Eyes catching the light of our torches. I let out a small gasp.

Fearlessly, Juana turned away from us and joined the other dancers at the front. They lined up against the rope that barred us from the coming dangers. Mamá took a deep breath as Juana, with the others, ducked under it.

"She will burn bright like the Sun," Mamá whispered.

Drums filled the air. Something began to approach the dancers from the depths of the Ruins, and eyes opened in the darkness—yellow ones, purple ones, black ones, blue ones. And they were moving closer. I gripped Mamá's hand and tried to calm my racing heart.

The dancers weren't afraid. Even as the darkness-cloaked criaturas moved toward them, they took their first rigid, military steps. And as I expected, my big sister was the most ferocious one at the fiesta.

> *"Go my opal, heart, and hands,*
> *filled with the fire of my land.*
> *I'll burn bright as child of Sol,*
> *cower now, fiends from below!"*

The dancers' chanted warnings stalled the approach of the glittering, animal gazes. With every turn and flourish of Juana's wide skirt in the torchlight, she appeared to catch fire. I clasped my hands together at the sidelines, in awe of her strength.

> *"Child of Desert, corre, corre!*
> *Flee or you'll be dead this day.*
> *Fuego souls will make you fall,*
> *avenge our own, and burn you all."*

The dancers pressed the war declarations deep into the darkness. The criaturas began to slip backward. Juana bared her teeth at the nearest one, where its clawed fingers were just visible in the light of the fire. It scuttled backward, swallowed by nighttime.

Suddenly, the dancers fell still. The oldest one stepped forward, face as dark as the desert beyond. "We will have no mercy if you provoke us, our ancient enemies!"

In unison, they let out a sharp cry. The last of the shadowy enemies scrambled away.

In the following silence, the townspeople held their breath. Hope filled the crowd—hope that the criaturas would stay afraid of us, and that for the next three months, they would not come near our homes. I stared into the darkness and listened for the sound of frightened criaturas running away. For some reason, it made me sad.

Once all signs of the criaturas had vanished, the dancers turned back to face us. Juana's chest lifted and fell like a warrior who'd won her first battle, and she looked at us with a confident grin.

The townspeople clapped. The cheers were so loud, they echoed through the street.

"Thank you, dancers. You may return to your familias." The mayor, standing at the center of the throng, waved his hands. "Everyone, follow the roped-off road back to the town square. And remember to stay close to your familias and away from the Ruins!"

Juana immediately spun toward where Mamá, Papá,

and I were waiting. She dove into Mamá's arms first.

"Oh mija, you were wonderful!" Mamá squeezed her.

Papá's dark mustache twitched upward. "You made our familia proud, mija."

Papá stroked her head, his face softer than usual. It nearly made me smile. But then he looked down at me, and his warm expression vanished. "Remember this, Cece. *This* is what you must do—aspire to be like your sister."

The words stung me, like the strike of a scorpion. Right. I bowed my head and wished the desert would swallow me up.

Juana pulled hard out of Mamá's arms and wrapped me in a hug. "That's right, Cece. You'll be just as bright as me one day!"

The words didn't bring any comfort. But I was grateful to hide my flushed, embarrassed face in her shoulder for a few moments.

Mamá patted Juana's back and offered her a small, fried tortilla dipped in cinnamon sugar—a buñuelo. My mouth watered just looking at it. "Here, the first of the batch for my firstborn. Go dance for fun now. Your Papá and I will handle the buñuelo stall."

Juana gasped excitedly and took it, still holding me in one arm. "Gracias, Mamá! Cece will stay with me, so you two don't have to worry." She rocked me back and forth in both arms again. My anxiety loosened its grip, and I giggled. "We'll come by for more buñuelos later."

Noche de Muerte wasn't exactly a celebratory festival, but there were a few game booths and plenty of sweets. The smell of cinnamon and fried tortillas already seeped through the crowd. Mmm, buñuelos were my favorite treat, and Mamá always made them with the best ratio of cinnamon to sugar.

Mamá and Papá disappeared among the partygoers. Juana finally let me go. She stared after them, and for just a moment, her mouth tightened and her gaze grew dark.

"Juana?" I asked quietly.

"Just wait, Cece. They'll be proud of you too. When you perform the Amenazante dance, they'll see your soul has as bright a fire as anyone's."

My insides fell quiet. For a second, I tried to hold on to her hope. Maybe she was right. But more likely, she wasn't.

She looked at me. "Don't you think?"

"Well . . . I can't imagine the dancing committee ever picking me," I said. They chose Amenazante dancers for the thing that Juana had always carried inside her, like weapons in her eyes. They chose them for their fierceness. For the fear they could inspire in the criaturas.

Juana frowned at first, but then lit up with a sparkling smile. "We'll just have to show them that you're the best choice! Here, Cece, we'll practice now. Stand like this."

She posed with the first move of the Amenazante dance—one foot forward, one firm and bent close—and lifted her skirt so I could see her feet.

I looked around nervously. There were still a few people nearby chatting with familia or friends. "You mean here? In front of everyone?"

"Sí! Come on, don't think about them. Just put your feet like this and crouch."

Easy for her to say. When people watched her, it was in admiration. But going unnoticed was better for someone like me. The best I could hope for was being a shadow cast from the light of other people's fires.

"Can't we just go have fun?" I rubbed my arm. "Think of the churros and buñuelos and tres leches—"

She waved Mamá's buñuelo in front of my nose. "You can eat this *after* you practice dancing with me. Okay?" She grabbed my arm with her free hand and tugged me into place beside her. A few people glanced our way. I swallowed hard but mimicked her step, if only so this could be over faster. "Great! Now, just scowl. Come on, you've got to look the part."

I tried to frown like she said. She rolled her eyes. "You look *scared*, not scary." She pursed her lips. "Never mind, we'll work on that later. Next you'll do this—"

She pinched her skirt hem with her free hand and pulled

it high in the air until it became a wide red flag. A couple
of people passed us, their eyes drinking in Juana's grace. I
tried out the same stance. The people's expressions turned
from awe to scorn instantly, and they shook their heads
dismissively as they left us behind.

Heat spread up my chest and neck.

"And then you turn in a circle." She turned her feet in a
complicated three-step pattern and stopped to face me. She
grinned. "Now you!"

"I don't even want to do the dance, Juana." I squeezed
out.

She frowned harder than the dance required. "Come
on, you can do this."

She didn't get it. The townspeople didn't want me to
be a part of their dance. I could accept that. Why couldn't
she? I hunched over and looked around, hoping for an
escape. Juana waved the buñuelo in my face until I looked
at her again.

"Cece!" The warmth in her face gave way to agitation.
"At this rate, you're never going to learn the dance, and
then how will you get picked?"

My shoulders slumped. "I'm—I'm not—"

"What? You're not what?" She leaned in, jaw set.

The embarrassed heat in my neck flushed upward into
something pricklier, something hurt. "I'm *not* going to get

picked, Juana!" I snatched the buñuelo out of her hand and shoved it in my pocket.

"Holy sunset!" She threw her hands up. "You're not even trying! I know everyone's mean to you, but they won't be if you just—just—"

"Just stop being me?" I spat. Juana dropped her arms to her sides. "You always act like you can make me into someone else, but being my big sister doesn't mean you can change reality!" A hiccup jogged my chest. "You don't understand. So just leave me alone."

I turned and stomped off in the opposite direction, heading for the area with the least number of people—the edge of the Ruins, where the red cord bobbed. A couple of footsteps followed me.

"Moon above, Cece, I'm trying to help!" Juana called. "What's wrong with you?"

I paused about five feet from the rope. The area was completely empty of townspeople now; there was just me and Juana and our argument. The answer to her question should have been obvious. Ever since the night I released Tzitzimitl back into the desert, my familia had become obsessed with the Amenazante dance. Because especially on this night, they wanted to believe I had somehow gotten better. That the fire in my soul was stronger than the water Tzitzimitl had cursed me with.

What would they say if I told them I wasn't sure it was a curse at all?

I moved forward again, toward the red rope, where I knew she wouldn't follow. I needed a break from her, just for a bit. Then maybe I wouldn't cry, and Juana wouldn't get twice as angry at me for exposing the water in my soul.

I hadn't gone five steps before Juana shouted after me again.

"Don't even pretend you're brave enough to go into the Ruins!" she called. "We both know you're not strong enough to fight off a criatura."

I hadn't been planning to go past the red rope. That would be dumb. I turned back to look at her and glared at her high-and-mighty lifted chin and flared nostrils.

But now being dumb felt worth it.

I grabbed the red cord. She put her hands on her hips. I jumped over it.

"Cecelia, get back here!"

I sprinted into the dark landscape of the Ruins.

3

El Sombrerón

Since I was seven, I'd never ventured this far from the safety of the town proper. I liked to, you know, be alive. But anger gave me temporary armor as I ventured between the abandoned, crumbling adobe buildings of the Ruins, sinking deeper and deeper into the desert's darkness.

It took about ten minutes before the anger gave way, and I started to realize what I'd just done—and that I was now in the outskirts. By myself. Possibly surrounded by criaturas hiding in the darkness.

I stopped, frozen between two abandoned adobe houses that were once homes. A chill crept up my back. I really was an idiota.

I took several deep breaths to calm down and glanced back the way I'd come. The lights were distant but visible. I started to shiver. Okay, time to go back before—

Something creaked nearby.

I turned, shoulders stiff, to look behind me. The front

entrance of the nearest adobe house was quiet and dark but for two glowing, golden eyes trained on me.

Holy sunset! I held my breath. A criatura had found me already.

The creature slunk forward into the almost-light. Its back was hunched over, calico fur standing on end. It was a coyote. I relaxed my shoulders and let out a sigh. Thank goodness. I'd thought it was a criatura for sure.

The animal's growl pierced the air, its top lip pulled back in a snarl.

Oh wait. A coyote was still pretty bad.

It cocked its head, golden stare tracing over me. It had eyes as hard as metal. I swallowed. Its fur was mottled, its white-tipped tail low to the ground. And despite the fur, I spotted the sharp outline of its ribs.

It was starving.

"Hey, you're hungry, huh?" I whispered.

It snarled, but slowly the growl softened until it was almost a purr. I slipped my hand inside my pocket, where I'd stored Juana's buñuelo.

"This is probably what you're smelling," I whispered and threw the morsel to it. The coyote's intelligent gaze didn't leave mine. I felt goose bumps erupt all over my back. I'd never seen a wild animal with eyes so focused and—warm.

"I was planning on eating it"—I pointed to the buñuelo between us—"but I think you need it more."

It eyed me for a second longer. Slowly, it ducked its head to chow down.

I let out a nervous sigh. "Yeah, good boy. You eat up—I'm going back before any actual criaturas find me."

It cocked its head at me, chomping through the fried dough. I waved goodbye to the animal and headed back toward the town's lights.

"Cece!" Juana's voice floated through the darkness. "Cece!"

She'd *followed* me? I started running, looking around, trying to spot her. Half of me was relieved that she'd come. If anyone could protect me out here and get us back safely, it was my big sister. But the other half of me knotted up with dread. What if she wasn't—

A scream tore through the air.

I kicked into a sprint. "Juana?" I cried.

"Stay away from me!" she shouted.

I skidded through the dusty landscape, tore around corner after corner of abandoned buildings and scrub. Stark panic flooded my veins the faster I ran. I followed her voice until I skated into an intersection framed with decrepit storefronts, my chest heaving.

"Stay back!" Juana cried again. Her voice shivered at

the end but her upright stance was bold. She stood with her back to me, facing a monster alone.

The criatura was a shadow, nearly eight and a half feet tall, standing just a few steps from her. He lifted a hand, made of crisp nighttime, and traced the brim of his wide black hat, a gleaming white smile carving out from the darkness beneath.

"You are most beautiful, Juana Rios," he said. My knees locked as his voice poured across the street, as sweet as honey and as sharp as cactus needles. "Brujas speak of your obsidian hair with words that shame the sun."

My heart stopped. I knew this criatura. The black hat, the praise, the way he blended into the shadows—Mamá had warned us about him especially.

It was El Sombrerón, the Bride Stealer.

He only stole the most beautiful of women, ones with big eyes and long, flowing hair. Like Juana's. The only way to save yourself was to plug your ears, block out the strumming of his guitar, and lock yourself inside so you wouldn't succumb to his siren song.

Only, Juana hadn't covered her ears. Her stance looked brave, but it trembled at the edges.

"I will steal your soul!" she cried. Her voice wavered more now. "I-If you come any closer, I will rip it from your throat and wear it myself. I will become your master."

It was what our mother had taught us to say to all criaturas. The prospect of being enslaved by a human was frightening to most of them. It made the weaker ones run away.

But El Sombrerón was a powerful dark criatura; he only chuckled.

The sound of his laughter merged with the shadows and ran over every surface in the old street. Everything felt muffled. His hand shifted in front of him, pulling a metal guitar into the light of the half moon. Silver strings lit up, glowing beneath his fingertips. My heart tripped over itself. Once he started playing, it would be nearly impossible to save Juana. I had to get to her before he played his song.

"Juana, run!" I threw myself forward.

Juana half-turned, her dark eyes wide and glistening and desperate. "Cece!" she said. Her bravado broke the moment she saw me. Her face crumpled; her hands shook. I'd never seen my sister this afraid.

But terrified as she was, she waved me away. "Run, Cece! He'll hurt you!" she said just as El Sombrerón strummed his first note.

The music poured through the alley, warm and brilliant. It moved over my skin like the distant smell of roses, an old memory of sweet and sticky cactus fruit. But it didn't drown me. My senses didn't fall away.

Because the song wasn't meant for me.

Juana's face clouded over in an instant. She turned her back to me, her tense muscles relaxing.

"Juana?" I called hesitantly.

She was closer to him than I was to her. As she reached out for him, El Sombrerón's head tilted, welcoming, watching.

I ran and tackled my sister to the dust.

She fought me. Her movements were jerky and limp, the way Papá moved when he came home late from the bar. Her eyes didn't see me. They turned upward, searching for the song, for El Sombrerón, for the Bride Stealer. I slapped my hands over her ears.

She blinked, stunned, as we fell to the ground, my hands tight to her head. Her eyes found mine, and they were clear again.

"Cece," she whispered. Her voice was twice as frightened as it had been moments ago.

"Juana, we have to—"

I didn't notice El Sombrerón's guitar until it slammed against the back of my head. I spiraled off Juana, rolling through the dirt. Metal strings twanged in the air. I squeezed my eyes shut, clasping my throbbing head through tangled hair. The impact shook through my entire body. I gasped through the pain.

"I'm not here for you." El Sombrerón's voice reverberated through the ground, almost more sensation than words.

Juana stumbled up from the ground. "Don't you dare hurt her!" She raised her fists. "I'll show you how the Rios women treat criaturas!"

El Sombrerón paused. His black hat tilted toward her, like he found her curious.

Juana shoved a hand into her hair and tore curls from her bun, gathering beads of the fire opal. She balled them into a fist. They glowed bright orange as she pulled her arm back to throw them at him—but just then, El Sombrerón flicked his fingers over his glowing, silver guitar strings.

Her arms went limp. The beads poured out across the ground and ceased to shine.

Panic thundered between my ears. El Sombrerón had knocked me clear to the opposite side of the street, so I lay at the foot of a crumbling adobe building. Juana was nearly fifteen feet away, facing El Sombrerón, just four or five steps from being in his grasp. I forced myself to stand. Impossible as it seemed, I had to do something, anything, to save her.

I glanced at his neck. In the shadows of his figure, the silver line of a necklace peeked out from beneath his collar.

His soul.

No matter how powerful a criatura may be, each wore

its soul around its neck. And all a human had to do was steal it to become their bruja or brujo—their witch master.

I couldn't hide Juana somewhere. I couldn't use fire opal to burn his shadowy skin. But I could steal his soul. I wouldn't keep it permanently like a real bruja, of course. Just long enough to save my sister.

I sprinted in between the two before he could grab her and leaped for his chest.

He jerked back as I slammed into him. He let out a grunt that shook the street like an earthquake. I latched onto his collar and reached for his necklace.

His hand caught me by the throat.

He lifted me into the air. I struggled to breathe. He looked so ethereal—more shadow than person, more painting than creature—but his grip was as solid as a rock. I scratched at what I thought should be skin on his hand, but only smoke rose from the wounds.

"You have heart, child," he said. "And that will be your undoing."

He slammed me into the ground beside him.

My air escaped in a rush. I lay there, bruised, back aching, muscles frozen. And incapacitated on the ground as I was, El Sombrerón had two hands free to wrangle my dazed sister onto his shoulder. He threw her over it like a limp sack. I watched helplessly as the last of the opals fell from her hair in a rain of fire. Through her obvious terror, her hand stretched for mine. Desperate. Shaking. Pleading.

"*Cece*!" Juana screamed.

It was ragged. The voice of a child wrenched out of a woman.

My vision swirled as I struggled to get up. Juana. I had to—had to save—I blinked desperately and finally found my feet. I stumbled forward to find nothing.

The world righted, and my vision cleared, but there was only nothing. El Sombrerón had disappeared.

And taken my sister with him.

4
The Burning Familia

The fires of the festival were still roaring bright when I made it to the town square, shoving my way through the crowd.

"Mamá!" I cried. "Papá!"

I was average height for my age, but still so many people loomed over me that I felt as if I were lost in a cluster of cacti. I stumbled into one of the señores. He pulled away from me.

"Ey, chiquita," he snapped. "Get ahold of yourself. What, did you see your own shadow?"

The man laughed and shoved me away. I barely found my footing, searching for my parents. "Please, I need to find my mamá and papá!" My side burned with the bruises left over from El Sombrerón, but I pushed through people and toward the stage where the band was performing. The sound of blaring trumpets, drums, singing, and clapping drowned me out—until I bumped into the wooden edge, and a microphone toppled toward me. "Please, El Sombrerón took my sister!"

My voice echoed through the town square.

The dancers stopped dancing. The musicians lowered their brass instruments. Everyone stopped clapping. The mayor and the head of police looked down at me from the stage.

A ripple moved toward me through the masses. Through dark heads of hair and colorful hats, I spotted Mamá's broad frame and Papá's leaner one pushing toward me.

"Mamá! Papá!"

Papá reached me first. His brown face was lined and hardened from the sun, and his thick black eyebrows weighed down his forehead, his frown framed with wrinkles.

"Cecelia," he said. "What did you say?" He cupped my cheeks, his touch surprisingly gentle. "Mija, where is Juana?"

Tears filled my eyes, but my words vanished. Mamá toppled out of the masses beside him. Her gaze swept over me, and in a moment, I knew she saw my hair in disarray, the bruises on my neck, the terror in my eyes. I pulled from Papá's grasp and rushed into her arms.

"Cece." She took my face in her hands. "Is it true—"

"He took her," I burst out. "Mamá, El Sombrerón stole her. I tried to do what you said, but he—he was taller than I thought, a-and—"

"You tried, mija." She swooped her arms around me

and buried her nose in my hair. I curled into her, trying to get smaller, safer, in her warm arms. Papá came closer and wrapped us in a tight hold. Together they cocooned me, but the news still sent shudders through them.

Footsteps rumbled across the stage behind us. "El Sombrerón has taken Juana Rios!" The head of police's voice grated with anger.

"Can we believe her?" Someone cried out. "She's cursed!"

"Yes, what if the Rios girl is leading us into a trap?"

"Quiet!" The head of police hollered. "El Sombrerón has not taken one of our girls in years. He was bound to come again. Quickly, send notice to the police posted at the edge of the Ruins! We may be able to find her before the criatura escapes." He turned to the police guarding the stage. "Tell the priestesses to return to the Sun Sanctuary. Ask them to light candles for our success."

Under his command, civilians, dancers, and police alike leaped into action and raced for the Ruins. Dust rose in their wake. It settled on my face and stuck there, to my tears, until I felt as much like mud as I did human.

The rescuers moved with determination, but we knew they would fail. No person had ever been quick enough to rescue the stolen brides of El Sombrerón. He was too fast. Too powerful.

Juana was never coming back.

★ ★ ★

"Go to bed, Cece," Papá said.

It was just him, Mamá, and me now, in the silent tomb of our home. The adobe walls felt barren, coated in darkness. No one had the heart to light a candle or the stove.

I stood at the edge of the living room, where it met our small kitchen. I leaned on the ladder that led up to the attic entrance above me, where Juana and I shared a bedroom. It would be so quiet in there without her.

Mamá stood a few feet away, facing the front window, looking out into the cold desert nighttime.

Before he died, Abuelo used to say Mamá was made of fire. Right now, trembling but with wide and silent shoulders, she looked just like a fire that had gone out. She was stiff coal abandoned in pieces, with just a hint of something too hot to touch beneath.

Papá stopped beside me. He was so close, I could feel his body heat.

His hand landed softly on my head. "You need to rest, Cece," he said. His voice was quiet, maybe even tender. "Straighten up and go upstairs. Go to bed."

Did he think I could sleep? Maybe he just wanted me out of his sight. Hidden up in the loft where my face wouldn't have to remind him of Juana, where he could pretend he wasn't stuck with the worst of his daughters.

I expected him to push me upward when I didn't stop

hunching over or move up the ladder. Usually he would make me stand tall and straight. I was an educated girl, he often reminded me. I must do my familia proud and act like it. He'd sacrificed so much to put me through school. But right now, there was no mention of his sacrifices or our familia's pride. There was no mention of how high my chin should be.

Maybe even my papá, beneath his hard face, felt the thing falling between us now: el vacío. The emptiness.

Slowly, he lowered his hand, placing it between my shoulder blades, and pushed, encouraging me to move. I gripped the ladder rungs tightly, despite my trembling hands.

"Cece," Papá whispered.

I paused.

"Where was she?" he asked. "When it . . . happened?"

I cried so much, I didn't think I had any more tears left. But my eyes stung, and my throat tightened. When it came to Juana, I would always, somehow, have more left.

"The Ruins," I whispered.

There was a tense pause.

"Why?" His voice was deep enough to drown in.

I pressed my forehead against the ladder. "I told her I'd be right back . . ."

Papá didn't say anything after that, but I sensed the anger

in his breath, and the unsaid words piled up inside of me until I could feel them in every follicle, every pore, every blink of my eyelids—*I had lost my sister. I was the reason she'd been stolen. I had destroyed my familia.*

The ladder rungs bit into my hands as I climbed up into the room above. It was terribly quiet. On the far right, Juana's unmade bed sat in the low moonlight. It was surrounded by opal beads and strips of red fabric from our preparation this morning. My hand shook as I reached out and stroked the dent her body had made in the mattress.

The moment my fingers grazed the empty space she left behind, a powerful thought forced its way inside me.

No. I wouldn't let Juana be the prisoner of El Sombrerón.

There had to be a way to fix this, and I had to be the one to do it. Somehow, I would find a way to bring my sister home.

The next morning, I woke up before the sun. The loft was cold and dark, and leftover nightmares still clouded my brain. *I have to save Juana,* I chanted over and over in my mind. *There has to be a way.*

As far as I knew, there wasn't one. Every year, El Sombrerón stole a bride from one town or another, and none of them had ever, ever come back.

Really, the only way to get her back was to find the place El Sombrerón had taken her—Devil's Alley, the criaturas' world. But the secret entrance moved each year, and legends said ordinary human beings couldn't pass through it and survive without permission from the rulers of Devil's Alley.

So that complicated any plan I tried to think up. But that didn't mean I should stop trying. There had to be some human being, somewhere in history, who had descended into Devil's Alley and returned.

I just had to figure out who'd already done it, and then I could do it too.

Juana was waiting for me.

"Cecelia!" Mamá called from below. "Come down!"

I knew that tone, and my heart immediately raced up into my throat. Without pausing, I stumbled out of bed and practically flew down the ladder rungs to the first floor.

Mamá was waiting in our small kitchen alcove. The downstairs was eerily quiet besides the sound of her rustling through a large trunk filled with papers and bound books.

I walked over to her. "Mamá? What are you doing?"

"We're going to the Sun Sanctuary," she said instead of answering me. She made an annoyed sound as she pushed papers around in the trunk. "Help me find the *Cantos de Curanderas*, mija. It was your abuela's book, and we need it for what we're going to do."

I went to the opposite side of the trunk. It was about three feet long, made of thick wood and intricately carved. I'd seen it only a couple of times before, since Mamá usually kept it hidden beneath her bed, but I knew its significance. It was filled with our family history, with stories older than our adobe home, and records winding far, far back into the history of Tierra del Sol, our town, and all of Isla del Antiguo Amanecer, our country.

It was, to put it mildly, extremely important to Mamá. She'd never even let me look inside before.

Besides the mess of papers, I noticed an image painted inside the lid. It pictured four women holding hands, walking through a sunset with a dark beast before them and Tierra del Sol behind them. I recognized this legend. Though people in my town didn't like to tell the story, unless it was to emphasize the women's failure.

It was a depiction of the two-hundred-year-old tale of the curanderas, powerful women who had once guarded Tierra del Sol against criaturas. Except, they'd apparently failed. And our town had nearly been wiped off the map, leaving the Ruins behind. That's why no one but Abuela had ever really cared to study them and their old magic. Nowadays, people said they had been weaklings at best, and traitors at worst.

I bit my bottom lip and tried to focus on finding the book Mamá had mentioned. I passed by several old papers and even my favorite book, *The Legends of Criaturas and Their Beginnings,* which Mamá had read to us growing up. After a few minutes, I spotted a book I'd never seen before: *Cantos de Curanderas.* I plucked it out of the pile, and another, smaller book fell out from between its pages. It landed at my feet, the cover bright red.

The sound made Mamá look up, but she only noticed

the book in my hands. "There! You found it, mija." She took the *Cantos de Curanderas* and went to place it in her bag by the door. "Now, go get dressed—we need to make it to the Sun Sanctuary before the priestesses wake up."

"Before they wake up?" I snatched up the red leather book from the floor and headed for the ladder. "How will we get in then?"

"Before *most* of them wake up," she said. "If anyone but Dominga del Sol talks to you, look away and say nothing. No one can know why we're there."

So *that's* why this felt familiar. The last time Mamá took me to the Sun Sanctuary and told me to hide from the Sun Priestesses, it was to perform a limpia. Memories flooded over me, and I shuddered. I didn't mind the ritual cleansing, but I didn't like all the sneaking around we had to do to perform it.

I scampered up the ladder and back into my room. After tugging on proper clothes, I scanned the red leather book I'd grabbed. Strange. It looked much newer than anything else in the trunk. I frowned and flipped the book open.

The first page was signed by Catrina Rios.

My heart nearly stopped. What?

After my run-in with Tzitzimitl when I was seven, I'd learned that Catrina, my tía, had left home to become a bruja—and disgraced our family in the process. Mamá couldn't even say her name without looking disgusted.

So why was her diary still in our family trunk?

"*Mija*," Mamá called from below.

I dropped the journal, and it landed on Juana's bed, in the dip she'd left behind. "Coming, Mamá!"

I gave the journal that shouldn't exist one last look before running after her.

Mamá pressed her hand against my back, guiding me through the still-dark streets toward the Sun Sanctuary.

"Almost there, mija," she said.

"Are we going through the back door again?" I asked quietly.

"Sí," she whispered. "Now hush until we're inside."

I frowned to myself. I loved how peaceful it was inside the Sun Sanctuary, but because I was me, I'd only been allowed to come a handful of times, and never through the front door.

We took a last turn, and suddenly the Sun Sanctuary rose above us, its golden dome and white-painted brick clean and welcoming. It wasn't a huge building—only about double the size of our small house—but it was taller than most with three floors of ascending stained glass windows. I tilted my head back to better take in the scenes they depicted. Some had people dancing under the Sun, others animals frolicking across the Desert, others showing people bowed under the Moon, and a chosen few depicted people swaying among Ocean's waves. I stared at those windows the longest. That was something I never understood about the Sun Sanctuary—why all the gods, Desert goddess, Moon goddess, and even Ocean goddess, were included in the Sun god's dedicated haven.

When I'd asked Mamá that before, she told me the Sun Sanctuary contained many mysteries. It was the oldest building in Tierra del Sol, nearly six hundred years old, and there were many ancient stories recorded in it that we didn't remember or need anymore.

That didn't sound right to me, but it was the only explanation I'd ever gotten.

"Come on, Cece, no daydreaming." Mamá tapped my head. I looked away from the windows to find us at the back entrance. A red-painted wood door waited up a couple of concrete steps for us. I climbed them first and knocked gently.

The door opened to reveal Dominga del Sol.

The old woman looked a little tired, but she smiled at us both. "Axochitl and little Cecelia! My, I must have done something good for the Sun god to bless me with the two of you before he's even risen this morning."

Mamá didn't look nearly as happy to see her. "Dominga del Sol, can we come in?"

Dominga del Sol stepped aside to let us in, and Mamá closed the door behind us.

"I'm sure you've heard what happened last night," Mamá said. Her voice was low and curt.

Dominga del Sol rested a hand to her heart. "Yes. I'm sorry about Juana—"

"Cece was there when El Sombrerón took her," Mamá said, and the sorrow rose in my chest like a geyser. "I need you to perform a limpia for her."

I wasn't sure whether it was the low light or the sternness in Mamá's voice, but Dominga del Sol's mouth hardened at the edges.

"I thought you didn't believe in the power of the curanderas," she said. "Isn't that why you refused to bring your mamá to me when she was hurt?"

Mamá straightened up, eyes harder, face sharper, than Dominga del Sol's could ever be. "I *don't* believe in it," she snapped.

"Then why are you here?"

I looked between the two women, a clash of firmness and fierceness.

"You know about Cece's curse," Mamá said softly. Somehow, the more quietly she spoke, the louder her voice felt. "Curandera magic failed our people. But my mamá believed in it." She met Dominga del Sol's unwavering gaze. "So, just in case, and for her sake, I'm asking you to try. It's better than nothing."

The beginning of morning slowly swept the nearest window with gray light. It caught in Mamá's eyes and made them glow. Dominga del Sol's mouth softened into sadness. But she nodded.

"All right," she said. "Help me prepare the herbs. Did you bring the book?"

Mamá passed Dominga del Sol the book we'd found earlier and pulled out ingredients as Dominga del Sol named them. Then, they instructed me to undress. I peeled off my dress and waited in the chilly laundry room in my underclothes, listening to the hiss of steaming water as Dominga del Sol filled a pot from the tap. She hefted it onto the counter afterward, stirring in some cooler, fresh water, and outstretched her hand. Mamá poured the ingredients into her palm as she asked for them.

"Rosemary to clear the eyes," Dominga del Sol whispered as she poured in the leaves. "Basil to protect the skin. Morning glories to bless the mind with truth—"

"And tobacco, to heal from the darkness," I finished the chant.

I was surprised I still remembered the words from the last limpia she had given me. For some reason, they'd come so easily. Dominga del Sol looked down at me, and her sad face seemed to gain some life back.

"Very good, mija," she said. "The curandera's words feel natural to you, hm?"

Mamá scowled. "Don't fill my hija's head with non-sense, Dominga del Sol."

"Sí, está bien. Here, mija. Come stand by the drain." Dominga del Sol pulled the pot off of the counter.

I planted my feet over the drain in the stone floor. I couldn't help feeling small and unwanted there, shivering in my underclothes, hidden away in the laundry room so that no one would know I was there.

"Axochitl, could you help me?" Dominga del Sol asked.

Mamá came and helped her heft the pot over my head. After the count of three, they tipped it over me.

Bright tingles of hot and cold rushed down my skin. The water rained down until all my worries, fears, and hurts were chased away. And then suddenly, it was done, and I was coughing and spluttering to get the residue out of my mouth.

Mamá grabbed my chin before I had time to rub my eyes. She smoothed my long hair out of my face and gazed at me.

"You are Cecelia Rios," she said, with a fervor I could feel through her thumbs on my cheeks. "You will be clean and safe, and no one will ever take you away. You will burn as bright as any descendant of the Sun god, and no curse will change that."

I stared at her. For a moment, I was seven years old again, watching her broken expression. But there was a new and darker depth to the cracks in Mamá's strength this time. Cracks that spelled out my big sister's name.

I nodded, trying not to cry.

"Bien." She dropped her hands and scooped up her bag from the counter. She passed by Dominga del Sol without looking at her. But Dominga del Sol didn't seem surprised.

It was like Mamá didn't want to acknowledge her. Like she was afraid that doing so would be admitting that my abuela had faith in the curanderas and their old magic, and that somewhere, deep down, she did too. But with the way the townspeople felt about curanderas—and me—it made a lot of sense. Even if it was pretty rude.

"I have to get to the fields now, mija," she said. "Dry yourself in the daylight, where the Sun god can claim you. But don't let anyone see you when you leave here!"

She shut the door behind her and disappeared into the gray of coming dawn. I stood there, dripping like a wet rat. I didn't have time to dry out in the sun. Every moment I wasn't looking for Juana was another moment our familia was broken.

Silent tears ran down my face and mingled with the basil. My chest shuddered, and I rubbed the limpia out of my weeping eyes. Turning from the door, I found Dom-inga del Sol waiting with an open towel.

She smiled over the brightly colored cloth. "It is okay to cry, Cece Rios." She wrapped it around me and rubbed my shoulders down. I looked up into her small black eyes, at the thick wrinkles framing her large smile. The jade beads in her hair rattled as she drew a second, smaller towel over my hair and squeezed the water out. "Familia is one of the worthiest things to mourn over. Your abuela was like a sister to me, you know. I wept for weeks after she died."

The sun's first rays broke through the nearest stained glass window. It touched the crown of Dominga del Sol's salt-and-pepper hair. "Your abuela always felt different, too. She loved the stories her familia left behind, about curanderas and their ancient powers."

"Mamá doesn't like to talk about the curanderas," I said. "Or about Abuela, either."

Her smile softened into something sadder. "A criatura killed your abuela," she said. "The Criatura of the Scor-pion, who came to take revenge against your tía, Catrina, the bruja. Your mamá probably doesn't like to remember it."

My mind flashed back to the red leather journal. "Did you know my tía too?"

"Yes. She used to like to come to the sanctuary, to light

candles to the Sun god." Her smile fell, just a little. "You have her eyes, you know. But I don't think you have her heart. If I were to make a guess, I'd say you have the heart of Etapalli, your abuela."

She said that like it wasn't a bad thing. Fragile hope filled my chest.

"Dominga del Sol," I said. "Can I tell you something?"

"Of course."

"Do you promise not to tell anyone? Not even my mamá or papá?"

Her face grew more serious. "What is it, mija?"

My heart beat faster. "I want to get my sister back. I—I'm *going* to get my sister back. I don't know how. But I'm going to find a way."

She stared at me for a long moment, and my guts churned. I wondered if she'd ever smile at me again after I said something so ridiculous. I was the weakest person in the village. How could I get my sister, the brightest soul in Tierra del Sol, back?

But to my surprise, she just smiled again. "Do you know what a limpia is for, Cecelia Rios?"

It felt like a trick question, but her eyes held no guile. "For cleansing," I said. "Mamá says it's supposed to help fight the power of the water curse Tzitzimitl put on me, to make sure my soul's fire isn't put out."

She folded the towel she'd used to dry me. "A water curse. That's an interesting choice of words." Her smile widened. "You see, a limpia is old magic left over from the curanderas, made of herbs, a chant, sunlight, and clean *water*. With those ingredients combined, curanderas asked the four gods to purify their souls in preparation for a great quest or battle." She placed the towel down on the nearest counter. "That means you are ready now, Cece, to take on whatever challenge is set before you."

I stared up at her, soaking in her words like they, too, were a limpia.

She patted my cheek. "If there is anyone in Tierra del Sol who can do this impossible thing, it is you."

6
The Path of Brujas

All the way home, I did my best to hold on to the warmth Dominga del Sol had given me. I could do this. There had to be a way for me to get Juana back.

When I arrived, I went up to my room first thing to grab something warm. I tugged on my old woolen serape cloak (it was a bit too small, but I loved its blue and green stripes), determined to set off for the library, the Sun Sanctuary again, or anywhere that might have the answers I needed. Just when I was about to head back downstairs, I noticed Tía Catrina's red leather diary.

I stared at it hesitantly. When someone in your familia became a bruja, you were supposed to burn all their old belongings and bury them in the desert cerros, to plead for forgiveness. Mother Desert hated brujas, Mamá said, because they enslaved her children, the criaturas.

Legend said the world had been peaceful before brujas came into the world. Coyote created animal criaturas—humanlike beings with strange-colored eyes and the ability to shape-shift into the animals they resembled—shortly after the Sun god made us. And for a while, criaturas and humans shared the desert peacefully.

But one day, an early group of humans stole a few animal criaturas' souls and enslaved them. These were the first brujas.

At first, this story confused me. Mamá had always counseled Juana and me to take a criatura's soul if we ever faced one, so we could command them to leave us. But the great difference between this action and a bruja's, Mamá emphasized, was that you always had to return the criatura soul to the desert after you were safe. If you didn't, and kept it instead, you would bring down Mother Desert's wrath.

It was after some of the first humans became brujas that dark criaturas appeared. They were monstrous and more powerful than their counterparts, and they came from the desert to take revenge on all humans because of the brujas' greed. We'd been enemies ever since.

And that's why we hated brujas, too. If brujas had left well enough alone, criaturas might not have become our enemies at all.

But I couldn't resist checking inside the journal—just out of curiosity. It fell open to a random page near the middle.

I hear them whispering all the time now, she'd written.

Everything around me has a voice. Axochitl—oh, that was my mamá—says that I'm messing with old magic I don't understand. But I've tried to ignore them, and the voices don't stop. The stones in the cerros speak of days long since past. Animals warn me danger is near. The plants whisper of weather to come.

Axochitl doesn't understand. She's afraid to. She ignores my voices, and she ignores the way Papá hurts Mamá, and she ignores how Mamá's mind is going because of it. She wants me to ignore it all too.

The desert's voices are not so passive. If something hurts them, they fight back. If a coyote stalks a rabbit, the rabbit runs. It doesn't lie down and accept being eaten. I don't want to either.

I say this all of course because Carlos asked Papá for my hand in marriage today. Papá doesn't care that I've refused. The wedding is set for after the criatura months are over. But he will find I am no rabbit—I will fight back. I don't care what it takes anymore.

My fingers trembled as I turned a bunch of pages, landing near the end of the book.

Papá will burn this journal if he finds it. He refuses to understand how my becoming an official bruja tonight is better than the life he wants for me. He would never listen if I tried to tell him about my criatura. My criatura is good. He values me. He protects me with the power I give him, and it is right that he does because I am powerful, and I will never let anyone take that power from me again.

I've made him so strong that we've won all three rounds of the Bruja Fights. No one has been able to stand against us. And once we win in the finals tonight, even the rulers of Devil's Alley will see and respect me.

Soon, I will enter Devil's Alley—and there, I will be a queen.

It ended there. That was the last entry.

I set the book down. Chills ran from the roots of my damp hair to my newly dried toes. The house felt extra quiet as realization hit me.

If all she said was true, my tía, a *human being*, went to Devil's Alley.

I snatched the book up again and flipped back through it, suddenly hungry for everything she'd written down. How hadn't I thought of it before? In school, they'd taught us how to spot brujas who'd lived in Devil's Alley by their glowing eyes or fangs, but each bruja or brujo was originally human. That meant if I became an official bruja by winning the Bruja Fights, I wouldn't even have to sneak into Devil's Alley. I'd be welcomed in. Where Juana was waiting.

This is what I had to do. It was the perfect plan.

Okay, maybe "perfect" was the wrong word. Everyone in town already hated me, and things would be a thousand times worse if they discovered that I was trying to become a bruja.

The first light of the sun slanted in through the window.

I lifted my head from Tía Catrina's journal. The light settled on the concrete sill, where a large red silk rose rested. Juana had made it yesterday while I'd prepared the one she'd worn.

"It's for when you're older," she'd said, when I'd looked confused. "I'll wear yours this year during the Amenazante dance. And when you dance, you'll wear mine."

My throat nearly closed up as I took in Juana's last gift. My fingers clutched Tía Catrina's journal. Yeah, this wasn't a perfect plan. It wasn't even a good plan.

But if this was the only way I could bring Juana home, then it was worth it.

A few hours later, I plodded through the Ruins outside of the town proper, winding closer and closer to the first stop on my mission.

My knees shook a little with each step. If the graffiti and strange signs painted on the abandoned adobe houses around me were any indication, I was definitely getting closer. I checked Tía Catrina's journal one last time to see if I was on the right path.

The woman called Grimmer Mother nurtures all apprentice brujas on their path to becoming true brujas. She told me I must meet her in Envidia to become powerful. She said I must meet her there, and then she could teach me how to be a bruja. I hope she's telling the truth.

Next to the writing was a small, scribbled map. I'd been following it out of town for the last thirty minutes, keeping an eye out for the signs depicted in the journal. Envidia was supposed to be out here somewhere, to the west of town. Partly broken adobe and abandoned ranchos dotted the surrounding landscape. It was hard to believe Tierra del Sol had once been as large as this, before the dark criatura attacks had reduced our numbers.

The illustration led me to the farthest section of ruins from town. I stopped as I spotted an outcropping of nine decrepit buildings, all clustered together strangely, unlike the other houses around them.

The two houses facing me were set so the space between them created an archway. Black charcoal markings had been scraped across their faces, warning people away from the makeshift entrance. A purple papel banner waved over the narrow street, the paper decorated with symbols I didn't recognize and didn't really want to. Beyond it lay a narrow path, but shadows hid whatever waited there.

I exhaled nervously and glanced at the warnings on the wall. "I'm going to get myself killed."

I tried not to think as I forced my feet to move forward. The air seemed to grow colder as I approached the archway. My footsteps reverberated in my ears, or was that just my heartbeat? I swallowed hard as I crossed the entrance-way, my hands shaking. The narrow alley closed in on me left and right. The shadows were cold. I was terrified, and it was obvious I didn't belong here.

But I had to try. If I did this right, I really might be able to get Juana back. Papá would be able to smile again. Mamá would embrace her and me, and she'd be proud of me then.

Or at the very least, she'd have Juana to be proud of again.

I came out the other side of the alley, and just a few steps into the center of Envidia, I realized I was even more out of my depth than I'd thought.

It was pretty obvious by the way the inhabitants looked at me. There weren't many, only about fifteen brujas and brujos in total. Some sat on the concrete back steps of the old houses while they sharpened their black knives; others leaned against the walls in the shade, stringing together jewelry made of bone. But all of them immediately turned to glare at me as I entered the small space. I froze there, holding my breath. A few looked me up and down. Most of them scowled or smirked. One flipped her knife up and down.

I gripped my elbows, forced myself to move forward, and looked around for Grimmer Mother, the woman Tía Catrina's journal spoke of.

I didn't get very far before someone bumped into me.

I stumbled back. Oh no, I'd hit a bruja! Wait, no. Tía

Catrina's journal said only those who'd been accepted into Devil's Alley and developed fangs and glowing eyes were really called brujas. This girl had to be an apprentice. She whirled around, eyes narrowed to slits. Half of her hair was shaved off, and a bullring piercing hung between her nostrils. She cocked a sharp black eyebrow as she turned to face me, her hand fingering the necklace strap at her throat.

She was only two inches taller than me, but held herself like she was six feet tall. "Do you mind, pollo?" she spat. Literally, I mean. Drops beaded my face.

I tried not to look hurt that she'd just called me a chicken. "Sorry. It was an accident—"

The moment I said "sorry," her gaze traveled the length of me, taking in my age and lack of a criatura's soul stone necklace, and met my gaze again with a sharp, predatory smile.

"Oh, you're an accident all right." She pressed toward me. I backed away. "What's a little kid like you doing in the heart of brujería?" She plucked at my serape cloak's tassels. "Did you get bored? Want to see what a *real* monster looks like?"

"N-no," I said. It came out smaller than I wanted, so I swallowed and tried again. "No, I've come here to *become* one."

She stared. And then laughed. "You're joking, right? You don't belong here—"

A hand struck the girl across the face.

My shoulders shot up to my ears as Bruja Bullring stumbled back, holding her cheek. An old woman stood between us now. Her hair was long and black and fell past her waist in a thick, luscious braid. Thin streams of gray ran through it, almost as metallic as her narrowed eyes.

"You fool," she said to the other girl. "Do you know who this is?"

Oh, my holy sunset. Did this woman recognize me? Bruja Bullring looked somewhere between angry and almost as confused as I was.

The old woman reached for me. I flinched back. Her fingers paused, so the black moths tattooed across her light brown–skinned hands hovered between us. The eyes on their wings moved to watch me. I gasped at the sight.

"You share blood with us," the woman said. Her mouth curled up on one side, and a thin white fang sliced into view. I bottled up the instinct to scream. Behind her, the girl scampered away. "Don't you, Cecelia Rios?"

I gripped Tía Catrina's journal to my chest. I knew who she was—but how did she know me?

"I am Ascalapha Odorata," she said. Her hand pulled one of mine from the journal and curled around it like a snake constricting. "But you may know me by a different name."

"Grimmer Mother," I whispered.

Later in her journal, Tía Catrina wrote about this woman with the tenderness of a student admiring a mentor, and her descriptions made one thing clear—Grimmer Mother was the teacher an apprentice bruja needed if she wanted to win the Bruja Fights and enter Devil's Alley.

The woman tugged me indoors. Immediately, a plume of charcoal and the smell of burning candles hit my nose. My eyes watered, but I tried to pretend it didn't bother me. I ended up coughing anyway.

She pushed me down into a cushion on the floor and moved around, shoving blankets, books, and random animal skulls off of the cushion opposite me. Smoke hung in the room like a bad dream.

"You are Catrina's blood," she whispered, leaning forward. She took my hands in hers. The moth eyes looked at me again.

Fear traipsed up my back like a cluster of spiders. I shivered. "So, you really are the one who taught Tía Catrina."

"Yes," she said, petting my hand. I resisted another shiver. "You have her eyes. And I see," she tapped the journal, "you have her words too. Now, do you want to travel her path?"

Not even a little bit. But I did want my sister back. So I said, "Yes."

She didn't look bothered by how quiet my voice was. "Ay, que bueno!"

She turned away, hunting around the room for something. I let out a shaky sigh. Her grip had been so hot, I could still feel it in my palms.

"You're cutting it close," Grimmer Mother said. "The Bruja Fights start in just two days." She opened a hulking chest and burrowed through it. "You have much to work on. Do you have a criatura yet?"

"Um—no." I was suddenly very itchy.

She made an annoyed sound. "Just like your tía. A procrastinator."

Probably shouldn't bring up the fact that I'd just decided to become a bruja this morning then.

She turned around. Something shone in her moth's grip. I stiffened as she walked over to me.

"Here," she said and offered the object. I took it hesitantly. It was a knife, its obsidian blade sharp as winter wind and black as the shadows of a well. "This is the knife I made your aunt use to shave her head. Each apprentice bruja selects a portion of her hair to cut off. It is how you first step into your new life. Your tía cut away the bottom half of her hair." She eyed me. "Your hair makes your face kind. For you, I suggest removing it all."

I gawked at her. "*All* of it?" I'd never cut my hair before, and it was long enough for me to sit on. Papá called it my one great beauty. What would I be without my hair?

"All of it," she said, with satisfaction this time. "Then you will seem more predator than prey. You can grow it back after you win the Bruja Fights and become a true bruja. Then no one will question you, regardless of your soft eyes."

But—my ears were going to be so *cold*. I closed my hands around the knife and tried desperately to keep my expression even. Like I wasn't dreading the idea.

"You have much gentleness inside you, Cecelia Rios," she said, and I really wished I knew how she'd found out my name. "You will need more stone inside you to get a criatura's soul to bow to your control."

That was going to be a problem since I didn't have *any* stone inside me. I almost sighed. No matter where I went, my soul didn't seem to have what people wanted. Not enough fire for my familia. Not enough stone for brujas. Was water welcome anywhere?

She leaned forward. "Your tía had softness in her as well. But it shriveled quickly once she no longer fed it. You will no doubt be the same." She smiled, but there was no warmth in it. "Go to the old dried-up silver mine to the south, and travel through what hides beneath. There, you will find the criaturas lurking, and there you will test yourself. Make sure to catch a criatura before Friday night, when the first round of Bruja Fights begins."

She stood and moved to leave. I jumped up.

"Wait!" I said. "What if I'm not strong enough to control a criatura's soul once I find one?"

She paused in her doorway, and her mouth split in a grin. "Then the criatura's teeth will prove you are not worthy to enter Devil's Alley." She turned away. "If you survive, return to me. I will teach you how to bend your criatura's will, body, and soul to your own."

She left me alone in her house, surrounded by eye-watering smoke. I frowned, stooped, and put out one of her candles. There. Take that, you not-at-all-comforting bruja mother.

"I saw that," she called.

I hurried to light the candle again.

7

The Makings of a Bruja

A few hours later, secluded in the narrow outhouse behind our home, I dropped Grimmer Mother's knife in the steel basin.

My hands shook as I lifted them to my head. The thick strands of heavy hair were gone. My neck was cold and free. I ran both palms over my skull, and a wave of coarse prickles scratched my fingers.

Tears filled my eyes as I looked in the old mirror balanced across the sink.

I pumped my breath in and out. "You're fine. This is fine."

I shook my head and swallowed most of the tears down. Even if my head looked like a cactus, this new haircut was exactly what I needed. I looked like I could be a bruja now. That was the first step to actually becoming one.

But a haircut alone wouldn't make me look like a bruja. I scrambled out of my frilly white dress and serape and tossed them to the side, yanking on my old, roughest, wool shirt instead. Next, I pulled on Papá's old red buckskin pants. They weren't exactly flattering, but they were rich in color and attitude, two things I needed. To top it all off, I tugged on Papá's worn green jacket and played with the holes that riddled its hem. He'd asked Mamá to turn it into cleaning rags last week. Luckily for me, she hadn't gotten around to it yet. Now I got to enjoy its raw petroleum smell and roomy extra-large size.

The outfit didn't help me make the same strong impression as the brujas I'd seen in Envidia, but it was close enough.

Except for my face.

I pouted at it in the mirror. I'd always thought my eyes were average, but with no hair to distract from them, they were a large, soft brown, ringed with black eyelashes.

They looked like the eyes of a scared child. Just like Juana had said. Yesterday, she'd teased me about it. Today, she was gone.

I closed my eyes and thought of my hermana. She needed me, so I had to try to look frightening. I pictured her face as El Sombrerón dragged her into the darkness. Listened to her screaming. Calling my name.

I opened my eyes.

With no hair to soften it, my angry face was as welcoming as a skillet. My mouth sharpened into a tough line.

My eyes squeezed into menacing, charcoal slashes beneath thick, cutting eyebrows. I'd never seen myself like this.

A knock at the door jarred the expression from my face. "Cece! Is that you in there? I need the bathroom."

Holy sunset, Mamá was home from the fields. "Just a minute!" I scrambled around, hiding the knife Grimmer Mother gave me in my jacket pocket before sweeping up my cut hair. I gathered the long locks in a thick, massive black ball and hid it in the darkest corner.

"Cece!" Another knock. "I've been holding it in for hours!"

I whipped Papá's jacket off, knife still in the pocket, and shoved it in my small bag. While Mamá continued to knock, I yanked my white dress back on, where it hid the embarrassing buckskins.

"Okay!" I unlocked the door.

She stumbled back as the door swung out. "What were you doing—"

Her mouth fell open. I was about to change the subject when I realized that my hair was shaved off, my dress was rumpled, and all in all I looked like a madwoman.

"Your hair, mija!" she wailed. Her hands leaped to my head, tracing the prickles. "Your beauty! My daughter is a cactus!"

"I'm sorry," I said. "It was just so heavy, and hot, and—"

"Moon above!" she swore in exasperation. "What is

happening inside that empty head of yours? Why your hair?"

My mind raced in panic. "I—I didn't want El Sombre-rón to take me too."

There was a beat of silence, and Mamá's face softened. "Oh, mija . . ." She stroked my cheek and pressed her lips together. "Pepita, I see. But you have to remember that brujas sometimes shave their heads. The police may get suspicious if they see you like this." She shook her head. "Everyone already worries about you. And now you do this? So soon after—" Her mouth opened, but she couldn't say her name. "After—"

"Juana," I said.

Tears filled Mamá's eyes until they almost overflowed. Her chin dimpled. I stared. She had never cried during the criatura months. It invited weakness, she always said. And weakness invited death.

Slowly, she shook her head until the tears receded. She pointed back at the house. "Get inside now. You're grounded. No dinner tonight."

I straightened up. I'd been looking forward to having her atole—a hot, creamy drink thickened with cornmeal and flavored with sugar and cinnamon. It was warm and comforting, two things I could do with before going cri-atura hunting.

"But Mamá—" I started.

"You have to think about the consequences of your

actions, mija," she said. "Even if you're afraid of El Sombrerón, you must think about the message you are sending others. Now is the time for strength." Her eyes moistened again. "Go to your room."

I stared at her a moment longer, my mouth hanging open. But I bowed my head and, quietly, stepped outside with my bag, knife, and jacket in tow. Mamá entered the outhouse and closed the door behind her. I trudged across our small backyard and up the steps back inside.

I lifted my head. Wait a second—this was perfect! I grinned and hurried up the ladder to my room. I needed to sneak out to go criatura hunting anyway. This way, Mamá wouldn't question why I was holed up in my room when I usually preferred to stay by the fireplace in the evenings.

The moment I closed the loft hatch behind me, I pulled off my dress again and put on Papá's jacket. Next, I opened my small bag and filled it with everything I thought I'd need to catch a criatura—matches, a torch I'd made with old rags and some rancid cooking oil, the knife Grimmer Mother had given me, and Tía Catrina's journal. Finally ready, I headed to the window.

I waited there for a while, listening for sounds of Mamá returning from the outhouse. A telltale slam of the back-door and then clanking from the kitchen below told me it was time to escape.

The loft wasn't far from the ground, but it would still

make for a hard fall if I jumped. The house's exterior wall was nothing but flat adobe. The nearest spot to get my footing was the first-floor kitchen window, where the oven's smoke pipe trailed out. I might be able to step onto it if I dangled off my sill, but Mamá would see me.

I scowled and scanned the scruffy ground beneath me. There was nothing but tufts of dry grass to cushion my fall. I sighed and leaned back against the wall. There was no easy way out.

A frown deepened between my eyebrows. What, had I thought getting my sister back was going to be easy?

I took a sharp breath and turned to face outside again.

My bag hung heavy on my back. I closed my eyes, gripping the outer edge of the window, and sucked shaking breaths in through my nose. I could do this. For Juana.

I launched myself out of the room, even as my heart twisted up into my mouth.

I hit the ground the way a bird first takes flight—quickly, unexpectedly, and with a scrambling, raw instinct that makes up for lack of experience. I rolled, legs tucked in, and finally hit the fence. I sat up, hand pressed against the unstable wooden posts. For a moment, I could only stare at the window I'd just leaped out of.

Had I really just done that?

My legs shook, but I crouched and ventured ahead

anyway. I followed the wall of my house until I came beneath the kitchen window, where I paused, listening. The smell of cinnamon and the sound of a spoon's steady stirring made it clear Mamá was preparing the atole. My stomach cramped a bit. I crept a little farther before breaking into an all-out run.

My bag thumped against my back as I raced down the street. I still had no idea what catching a criatura entailed, but for the first time in my life, I hoped Mamá was wrong about me—and that Dominga del Sol was right.

It took about half an hour for me to reach the south side of town. I ducked under signs and the old, tattered rope warning that I was about to enter the Ruins and exit the town proper.

Tía Catrina had drawn several maps in her journal. The one that I was following right now led to the old silver mine, where she'd apparently found her criatura.

I kept myself on track, heading toward where x marked the spot. I knew I was nearing the mine when I passed Criatura's Well. It was a crooked stack of stones surrounded with signs warning people not to drink from its poisoned water. Stories said a criatura had fallen in it before I was born, and the townspeople had boarded it up to keep it from escaping. Some even said the criatura's cries could still be heard all the way in the town proper in winter, when the world was quiet.

But I noticed that the boards were broken now. And the exposed hole, decorated with clawmarks in the surrounding stone, was deafeningly silent. I shuddered a little before moving into the mine's treacherous landscape.

Craggy rock surrounded me, seeming to fill the area, and tunnels punctured horizontally through the ground on each step down. The nearest tunnel opened up on my right, set into the top layer of the mine. The opening was intimidating, dark—exactly the kind of place criaturas might hide. As I ventured toward it, I tugged the stinky torch I'd prepared out of my bag. After a couple of nervous strikes of a match, I got the torch to catch fire.

I stopped in front of the opening, and red light bloomed into the stone tunnel. My heart pounded. Above me and the mine, the sun lowered on the horizon, like a tired man returning home. If I wasn't careful, I wouldn't be so lucky.

I entered the tunnel. The ground sloped downward almost immediately. My feet grew heavier with every step I took deeper into the earth, and after about ten minutes of trekking into the darkness, I heard scuffling and hissing sounds. I held my breath. Criaturas.

I pulled the torch as close as I could without burning myself and took Grimmer Mother's knife out of my bag.

I held it out with my free hand, the way I would to cut onions with Mamá.

I took a trembling breath. "You can do this, Cece."

The ground finally evened out. It was colder down here than I expected. I gripped my light source as the tunnel walls widened. I came up on a turn and held my breath. The hissing sound came from beyond it.

Something was in here with me. I just had to hope it was a criatura I was capable of capturing.

Ever since I was seven years old, the idea of capturing a criatura's soul had reminded me of Tzitzimitl's pained gasp. But I couldn't let that stop me. I held on to Mamá's advice and tried to drown out Tzitzimitl's memory. As I took the next turn, a deep, grating snarl filled the shadows beyond my light.

"Pesky, pesky, human," a voice came from the darkness.

I jumped backward as the slithering sound grew louder and closer. Just out of reach of my torch's light, two large yellow eyes opened. The pupils were pin-thin slits.

My mouth went dry.

"The human is quiet," the hiss continued. A snake criatura? I hated snakes! "Does it want to fill Cantil Snake's stomach?"

No, I did *not*.

The eyes moved closer, their narrow glint so monstrous

I felt as if I were falling backward into a nightmare. The figure paused in the light. He looked mostly human, but like all criaturas, the animalistic features were a dead giveaway. It was easy to tell what he was by his scaled face, flat nose, and snake eyes.

His gaze fell to my black knife, and his sharp teeth came into view. "A *bruja*?" There was more venom in that word than in his fangs. "You will never take Cantil Snake's soul!" he cried.

His body coiled up. With a hard pop, his shoulders came out of their sockets, his spine stretching apart so he loomed over me. His jaw unhinged, his mouth widening and poised directly over my head, ready to swallow me whole.

My mind finally jolted back to life. *Plant your feet*, I remembered Mamá's words. *Keep your stance. Let them come to you. When it is near victory, a criatura is its most vulnerable.*

He lunged down at me. I gripped the knife, locked my knees, and braced myself to take his soul.

"Stop!" someone cried out behind me.

A dark figure rushed up behind me and seized Cantil Snake by his open jaw. Cantil Snake screamed as the stranger yanked him down to the ground, and the two started thrashing across the floor. Pebbles shook free of the ceiling. The ground rumbled. My torch fire gave off a wicked spark. I stood rooted to the spot, just trying to keep track of the wild fight, until they slammed against the far stone wall.

Now that they'd stopped moving, I could get a glimpse of the new person. White and black hair. No, red hair. No, brown hair—maybe gray? From what I could tell, it was nearly every color, and his body was lean, tall, and strong.

Especially the forearm he had at Cantil Snake's neck, pinning him to the stone.

Cantil Snake's nostrils flared. "They always said you were a human-lover." He glared at the boy whose face remained just out of reach of the light.

This looked like a pretty ugly fight, and the argument was something I didn't understand. Maybe I should just . . . go?

I tiptoed back a couple of steps until I noticed the rock in Cantil Snake's hand. The boy had him pinned pretty securely, but if Cantil Snake popped his shoulder out again, he could easily smash the boy's head in with the large piece of granite.

"Watch out!" I cried.

Cantil Snake's arm burst out from the stranger's hold, and he swung the stone toward the boy's temple. I launched forward and body-slammed the boy to the ground. Cantil Snake's stone grazed the top of my head as we fell, missing the boy. My torch and knife tumbled out of my grip as we hit the floor.

I barely had time to grab my tools and turn around before Cantil Snake was on me. His wide, fanged mouth opened in my face and hissed. I squeezed my eyes shut, angled my knife, and smashed my torch into the side of Cantil Snake's face.

He went sprawling to the ground between me and the stranger, covering his face. Holy sunset. Did I just actually take out a criatura?

Cantil Snake reared up again. "I'm going to kill you for that!"

Okay, no. Not yet.

He lunged toward me. I squealed as he got near enough for me to see the snake carved into his soul stone. I aimed for it with my knife. With a flick of my blade, the strap snapped. His soul necklace unraveled.

"*No!*" he roared.

I kicked his stone far down the tunnel, away from where I'd come. He whirled around on his knees and scampered after it. The stone echoed until it, Cantil Snake, and his scream faded into the darkness.

I dropped the knife and torch. Slowly, the adrenaline faded. Wow. I had just survived a criatura attack. I started to smile. Wait—I'd just survived a criatura attack and *hadn't gotten his soul.* I slapped my hands to my face. No! I needed a criatura! He'd been that close, and I'd kicked his soul away instinctually. What was wrong with me?

Footsteps came from behind me. I turned and found the boy who'd attacked Cantil Snake standing in the light of the torch. He shook out his multicolored hair, disguising his face. His breath steamed in the cold darkness.

Finally, his eyes flashed to mine. They were like gold coins, bright as fire with none of the warmth. Oh. He wasn't just a boy.

He was a criatura.

"I *knew* it was you," he said, like he knew me.

I froze beneath the intense stare. He'd tried to take down Cantil Snake just moments before. Did that mean he was going to let me go? Or that I was next?

8
The Soul Debt

Now that the young criatura stood in the light, I could see he was around my age. He had the jaw and shoulders of a thirteen-year-old at least, though he was taller than most of the boys I knew. He wore a worn red shirt that looked like it'd been stolen from someone bigger and a pair of tight tan charro pants, with holes interrupting the twisting patterns that lined the sides.

It was almost easy to think he was just a human boy—until his burning gold eyes and sharp white canines caught the light. I froze and held my breath. Maybe if I didn't move, he wouldn't attack.

He looked me up and down. "I didn't expect you to save yourself."

"Um," I tried not to wheeze. "Please don't hurt me."

His white eyebrow lifted, the black one resting low. "Hurt you? Wait—you don't recognize me?"

I stared. He stared. There was an awkward silence.

I squinted. "I don't talk to criaturas often, so I feel like

I'd remember meeting you . . . But it's, uh, nice to meet you *now*. I'm Cece. Thanks for—um, what were you doing back there exactly?"

He folded his arms. "*Saving* you. Or I would have if you hadn't shoved me."

"So, you weren't trying to kill me? Que bueno." I tried to smile. He looked alarmed, so it must not have come across right.

"Are you okay?" He took a step forward.

I stumbled back. "Hey! Keep your distance."

He dropped his hand and his concerned expression at the same time. "I'm not going to hurt you."

"Wow, that changes my mind completely!" I frowned. "I'm no idiota. My parents taught me not to talk to criaturas." He didn't need to know how bad I was at listening.

The left side of his mouth curled up. "But you *are* talking to me."

Agh! Moon above! He was right. "So, you admit you're a criatura!"

"Naturally." He grinned mischievously, and a pair of sharp canines poked out from between his lips. "This is the perfect vacation spot for criaturas who've escaped Devil's Alley; there haven't been humans here since the silver dried up." He picked up the torch where I'd dropped it, and the humor in his face dissolved as he held it out to me. "Except for you, I guess. The one human I owe a debt to."

I blinked. He owed me a what?

He saw my face and sighed. "Coyote. I'm the Criatura of the Coyote. The coyote you fed on the night Devil's Alley opened?"

The name brought images into my mind, from the cover of our familia's legend book to the scraggly coyote I'd found in the alley during Noche de Muerte. I held my breath. My favorite legend had appeared right before my eyes? It was almost too much to believe. "Wait—the legendary Coyote, the Great Namer? You were the coyote I fed a buñuelo to?"

"Keep up, Cece." He frowned and held out the torch. "Anyway, I was starving, and you fed me. So, I'm in your debt."

I took the offering. Beyond the flame, he looked away.

"I'm guessing you don't like to be in people's debts," I said.

He frowned even harder. "Especially Naked Man's."

I may have only just met him, but he didn't exactly live up to the legend of the Great Namer I'd always admired. I guess it didn't help that I'd always imagined him as a giant man with a coyote's head, not as a scruffy teenager.

"Wait." A flare of hope shot up inside me. "Does that mean you have to pay me back?"

He slouched. "You couldn't have just let me save your life. No, you had to save your own life *and* mine." He shook his head. "I don't appreciate that."

I gaped. "He was going to hurt you!"

"The point is," he snapped, "now I owe you not only for the buñuelo, but also for stopping Cantil Snake." He slouched. "This is turning into a really bad week for me."

He thought *his* week had been bad? I'd lost my sister, my hair, and obviously any good sense I'd had before all this started.

"I'll tell you what," I said. "I'll give you an easy way to pay me back. I need a criatura to enter the Bruja Fights."

He lifted his white eyebrow again. "So that's why you are here."

"I need a criatura to enter," I rushed ahead. "I have to win so I can get into Devil's Alley—"

He turned his back. "Forget it. Whether you saved my life or not, I'm not helping a wannabe bruja."

I lurched forward and grabbed his wrist. He tugged, and even that small movement sent me stumbling over myself. Holy sunset, he was strong! I dropped the torch and locked my arms around his elbow.

"Please, I have to save my sister!" I said.

He stopped. "What does that have to do with the Bruja Fights?"

I peeked up at him. He stared down at me, chin rigid. But he waited. Listening.

My heart shivered with hope. "I have to win the Bruja

Fights so I can rescue my sister from Devil's Alley. Unless you're kidnapped by one of the leaders of Devil's Alley, winning the Bruja Fights and being admitted as a bruja is the only way for a human to enter, right? Well, El Sombrerón stole my sister, and it's my fault because"—my breath hitched—"I ran off and she came to get me. It's my fault."

Deep orange torchlight flickered across his unmoving expression. His free hand suddenly reached for my head. I winced, but it landed softly, balancing on my prickly hair.

"You shaved your head," he said.

That's right. I'd almost forgotten he'd seen me before, when my hair was long. It was eerie realizing this wasn't our first meeting, however much it felt like it.

"I have to look like a bruja to enter the fights," I explained. "But I—I don't want to *be* a bruja. I just have to pretend so I can get into Devil's Alley with the yearly bruja winners, and then get my sister back."

He tilted his head, considering. The mannerism was so much like the curious, watchful coyote in the alley, I could finally see how they were one and the same. He didn't say anything for a long time. I tried to hold back the tears filling my vision, but one leaked down my face. I didn't brush it away, not daring to let go of Coyote's arm.

His eyes grew cold and low. "If you're the kind of person who'd cry over your familia, you won't last in the Bruja Fights, let alone in Devil's Alley."

Heat rose in my cheeks, and I finally let go of his arm. I stood as straight as I could and lifted my head to meet his gaze.

"I know," I said, and my voice wavered. "But I'm going to try. Whether you say yes or no, I have to *try*."

He sighed. "Do you understand what you're asking?"

I clutched my bag's strap, trying desperately to keep more tears from falling. They slipped down my cheeks anyway.

"Your life will never be normal again," he said. Flickering torchlight haunted his gold eyes. "Those who rule Devil's Alley will test you in the Bruja Fights. And if we make it inside Devil's Alley, El Sombrerón will never let your sister go without a fight to the death. And even if you managed to defeat him, defying El Sombrerón means defying El Cucuy, the king of Devil's Alley."

My breath froze between my lips.

"El Cucuy will not let you steal back what his second-in-command, El Sombrerón, has taken without punishing you." He uncrossed his arms. "Can you risk your life, Cece?"

That was a big question. Could I provoke the most powerful criaturas in existence? I couldn't even dance the Amenazante dance. I couldn't even stand up to my father or explain myself to my mother.

But despite all that, I knew two things: Juana was my sister—and she needed me.

Coyote started to pull away. "Naked Man never changes."

I caught his hand. "I'll do it!"

My voice echoed through the stone tunnel. Coyote looked down at where my hand touched his. His mismatched eyebrows tugged together. My blood raced, and the hard, steady beat of my heart helped solidify my resolve.

"I will," I said again, still clasping Coyote's hand. "I will do anything I have to do to save her from El Sombrerón, or Ocean take me."

His eyes widened. Thank the Sun god—he must know how important that oath was to my people. I trembled, looking up at him as tears filled my eyes again.

"You're crying," he said. "But you mean it. Don't you?"

I nodded. "Sí."

He turned his head away. "Maybe . . . I can put things right this time," he said quietly.

I wasn't sure whether he was answering me or talking to himself. To be safe, I said nothing and held on to him so he wouldn't run away.

"Well," he said, louder now. "You did save my life."

I resurrected a smile. "So you'll help me?"

"Ugh." His shoulders slumped. "I'm going to regret this."

He stooped down and picked up the fallen torch, handing it to me. As I palmed it again, he grabbed a leather strap hiding beneath his red shirt and tugged it out. A stone pendant caught the torchlight as he whipped off the necklace and held it out to me.

His soul.

My mouth opened in wonder.

"To own a criatura," he said, "you must carry their soul. From now on, your pain is my pain; your will, my will." His nose wrinkled slightly. "Take it. And whatever you do, don't lose it."

The soul spun in the air. With a reverent breath, I cupped my hand beneath it. Coyote let it fall into my palm.

It was warm and, for a moment, a vibration fluttered through it almost like a nervous heartbeat. I pulled it close to my chest and angled it in the light. It was a simple reddish-brown stone, not even large enough to fill my palm. It was smooth but for one deep, large scratch running horizontally across its back, and the jagged, carved lines of a coyote howling at an invisible moon on the front. I could almost hear the lonesome sound.

So this was the soul of the legendary Coyote.

"Congratulations," Coyote said. "You're an apprentice bruja now. Happy?"

I squeezed his soul briefly and slung the necklace around my neck. It sat below my collarbone, heavy and warm and full of all my hopes. The moment it touched my skin, a rosy fire pressed down into my bones. I took an unsteady breath as the sensation rolled through me.

His soul was tangible—more than just a smooth rock against my skin. It was the sensation of who he was. It was an awkward, new presence seated beside my heart, deep in my chest.

"Thank you," I said.

Because I was one step closer to winning the Bruja Fights, one step closer to Devil's Alley, and one step closer to rescuing my big sister.

Coyote's nose wrinkled a second time. "You're crying again. I don't know what to do—stop."

I wiped my eyes and laughed. The joyful sound echoed in the tunnel. I imagined it reaching Juana, on the other side of Devil's Alley's hidden entrance, telling her not to give up hope.

I was coming for her.

9

The First Fire

By the time Coyote and I climbed out of the mine, the moon hung high in the sky. The desert air was chilly now, just a bit too icy to bear. I rubbed the cold tips of my ears and shivered. Coyote pouted at me like human frailty was annoying.

He strolled forward. "So where are we going, bruja?"

"Cece," I said and started after him. "I know you know my name. If you're going to be my criatura, you might as well use it."

He gave me a cold, sideways glance. The moon caught his hair and lit the white parts with a ghostly glow, leaving the gray and brown patches dark.

"Is that a no?" I asked.

"You can force me to say yes, if it will make you feel better." His black eyebrow lifted in a taunt.

"I don't even know how to do that." I glanced around the landscape, trying to get my bearings. Tierra del Sol was to the north, where small lights roamed the town. Oh, that's right. During the criatura months, the police enacted a curfew and nighttime patrols to keep everyone safe. "Do you think you can get us back inside my house without my parents noticing?"

He pouted at me.

"Please? I really don't want to spend the night in the desert."

He grinned. "What? You afraid of the big, wide, scary, dark desert?" He wiggled his clawed fingers at me.

I leaned away from him. "Mother Desert doesn't exactly like humans the way she does criaturas, you know." I frowned and finished dusting sand off my jacket. "Can you get me home or not?"

He sighed, crouched, and motioned for me to climb up his back. I hesitated. He gestured more impatiently. With a sigh, I came over and wrapped my arms around his shoulders. He straightened up.

"So, to Tierra del Sol?" he asked as he pulled me into a piggyback ride.

"Yeah. My house is northwest, around—"

"It's fine. I'll be able to smell it."

And suddenly, he took off, and the dust fell far behind us. We practically flew through the landscape, streaking past Criatura's Well, weaving through the Ruins, and jumping onto roofs once we hit the town proper. I dug my fingers into his shoulders. He was so fast, I was sure my stomach had blown out of my body about a mile ago.

He slowed a bit. "You okay?" he asked.

I peeked an eye open. Had he noticed I was scared?

"Yeah," I said.

He leaped more carefully, and ever so quietly, from one roof to another. Now that we weren't going so fast, I could see the streets below. Police held torches above their heads, scanning each dirt path between houses. They did these kinds of patrols every year during the criatura months, but there were more police around than usual. Probably because of Juana.

Coyote skated to a nearly soundless stop on the roof of my house. He glanced down at the adobe beneath his feet. "This is your place, right? It smells like you."

"Yeah, this is it—wait, what do I smell like?"

He tilted his head. "Kind of like . . . salt. And water."

"I smell like *sweat*?" I gawked at him. "I'm not even that hot right now."

"No—more like ocean spray, or brine, or um . . ." He suddenly looked nervous. "It's not a *bad* smell."

"Never mind, I don't want to talk about this anymore." If it wasn't sweat he was whiffing, why would I smell like water? Unless—it was my water curse. Had it somehow changed my scent? Embarrassing. "Is there any chance you can sneak me in through my window?" I pointed to the right side of the house.

Coyote walked us over to the edge and looked down. "No problem."

He leaped down and crouched in my windowsill. Coyote leaned inside slowly, carefully, to avoid notice. But a light filled the alley behind me. I glanced back. A member of the police, holding his light aloft, was headed past my house.

I lunged our weight forward, and Coyote and I tumbled onto my bed. He rolled off and hit the floor. I winced.

Coyote scowled and looked up from the floor. "What in Desert's voices was that for?"

"I don't want the police to see us," I hissed. "They execute brujas and criaturas, you know."

He looked like he was going to snap back, but he paused and looked at the floor. "Are those your parents?"

"Did they wake up?"

He pointed to the hatch. "Yes."

The hatch started to open. I scrambled forward and threw myself in front of it, to block Coyote from view. He caught on and moved to the other side of the hatch flap, crouching in the darkness.

"Cece?" Mamá's sleepy face surfaced. "Why are you

making so much noise? You know I have to get up early—"

"Just a nightmare, Mamá," I whispered. I made a low sniff for good measure.

She sighed and peered at me blearily. "Cece, don't cry."

My heart sank a little. I grabbed the hatch and started closing it. "Sí, Mamá. Lo siento. I didn't mean to wake you up. You can go to sleep."

Mamá let me lower the hatch, but stopped it halfway down. "Do you need me to hold you?" she whispered.

Her voice was tender now. I gripped the hatch's edge. I'd wanted her to ask that question so many times. But I couldn't indulge it right now.

I swallowed and shook my head. "No, Mamá," I said. "I'll just go back to sleep."

Her dark eyes caught the police's torchlight from my window. "Cece—I'm sorry about earlier," she whispered. "You know I just want to protect you, mija."

My throat tightened. I nodded. She watched me for a moment longer before descending the ladder into our living space. I eased the hatch lid down and stepped back. Coyote watched me from the darkness.

I wrapped my arms around myself and turned away from the question in his eyes. I wish he hadn't heard my conversation with Mamá. He was probably going to think I was weak too, if he didn't already.

"It's freezing in here," I whispered, like that would distract from what had just happened, and tunneled into my bedcovers. I wrapped them around me as closely as possible, but the desert's cold felt like it had sunk into my bones. "Good night, Coyote." I shivered beneath my covers, staring across my bedside cabinet, hoping that I'd feel better in the morning.

Coyote slowly crossed into view. I stiffened as he stopped in front of my bedside cabinet, eyeing my candle stub.

"What?" I asked him, careful to keep my voice low.

He pulled out a match from my matchbox and lit the candle. I furrowed my eyebrows. He shifted awkwardly under my stare. "Are you still cold?"

"Well—" I looked down at myself wrapped like a brightly striped burrito. "Yeah. But it'll be fine."

The moment I said yeah, Coyote brought both his calloused hands around the flame. I sat up in my blankets. "Hey, careful. You may be a legendary criatura, but you could still burn yourself."

His top lip twitched upward, but otherwise he ignored me. He closed his eyes, hummed quietly, and started tapping a small, steady beat on the candle's wax. Suddenly, the flame crackled and roared with life, now four times its previous size. My mouth dropped open as the heat pulsed out from the wick and rolled over me.

Coyote pulled back without a single burn and looked at me. "Better?"

"Yeah. Thank you." I looked from him to the fire. "But—how did you control it like that?" I asked.

The most famous legend about Coyote was, of course, his role as the Great Namer. But in his earliest tales, he was called the Bringer of Fire. Legend said that after the Sun god sacrificed himself so humans could be born, Naked Man was happy and well—until the first winter began. Then, we started to die off as the cold reached its peak. Thankfully, Coyote descended from his cerros and gave fire to Naked Man to save them from freezing. It was one of my favorite stories.

But nowhere did the legends say he could control the fire he brought.

Coyote sat back in my chair. "I didn't always know how." He lifted his thumb and traced down the white side of his hair. "This is where the first fire burned me."

"You mean when you gifted it to Naked Man?" I hunched forward, grinning.

"*Gifted* it?" He looked at me in surprise. "I didn't give fire to Naked Man. You all made it." He looked back to the candle. "It was the first humans who taught me how to avoid its burning and inspire its flame."

My eyes widened, and I scooted to the edge of my bed.

"What? But the legends I know said *you* gave us fire."

He shook his head, still staring into the candle. "When I came down from the cerros, I brought Naked Man *music*." He closed his eyes for a second and hummed. The fire crackled, just a little, on the wick. "They were so cold, huddled up on the ground, freezing away. So I taught them to get up. I taught them to use drums, to sing. I showed them how to dance so they could stay warm." He opened his eyes, and they lit up as he looked at me. "And when Naked Man danced, they were *beautiful*. They danced so ferociously, their feet kicked up sparks. And from their twirling, they made the first, magnificent fire." He'd nearly started grinning but suddenly caught himself and coughed. "Anyway. The flames burned my hair and all the way down my back, to the tip of my tail." He fingered the white bits of his hair again. "Naked Man rushed to put it out. Before long, they mastered both fire and my music and dance. Soon they were the ones teaching me, so I could make the fire breathe in return."

Oh, wow. The true story of fire was even better than the way our legends recorded it.

Before I could wipe the eager look off my face—I was still such a sucker for Coyote stories—his mouth softened in return. He smiled tentatively, and I grinned back. For a moment, his gaze was less metallic. I was less afraid.

For a moment, we were equals discussing the most successful trade in history.

I wiggled excitedly. "That's so cool! I can't believe we have fire because you cared enough to come share your music and dance with us. It's amazing." Coyote let out a single, awkward chuckle. I settled back in my bed and looked him over. "Can I ask you something?"

The softness in his mouth disappeared again. "You own my soul now. I suppose you can make me answer if you want."

I huffed. "No, I mean—*if* I ask you something, will you answer it? Please?"

After a moment's hesitation, he nodded.

"*Why* did you do it?" I asked. "Why did you help us?"

His smile dropped slowly. "I . . . don't really know."

The candle's flame whirled and twirled beside us, steady and strong.

"Maybe it's the same reason I'm entering the Bruja Fights," I said.

He rolled his eyes. "Please don't say the power of love. Humans are always going on about that. As if you've ever understood what love is."

Well, that sounded like a sore spot. "Of *course* that. But I was thinking of something else."

"What?" he asked.

I smiled at him over my blankets. "Hope."

What he'd been hoping for when he revealed his secrets to save a strange people, I didn't know. I wondered if he ever regretted it now, considering we'd become enemies. And that we used his gift of dance to ward off criaturas every year. But when he'd told the story, Coyote's eyes had lit up, like the embers of hope were still inside him somewhere.

Coyote's silence made me think I was right.

After a moment, he gestured at my bed. "You should sleep. Those Bruja Fights are soon, right? You'll want to be well rested."

"Oh, and so will you." I stood, gathered a spare blanket and couple of pillows, and spread them on the floor at the foot of my bed. "I guess you can stay here tonight."

He lifted an eyebrow and pointed at the other side of the room. "What about that bed?"

I looked at Juana's mattress. I hadn't changed a thing about it since yesterday. The dent, the trimmed pieces of fabric scattered about it, the quilt laying half on and half off—it was all just as she'd left it.

"That's . . . my sister's," I whispered.

Coyote looked from Juana's bed to the floor. Quietly, he took the crocheted blanket from my hand. "Buenas noches, bruja."

He settled down on the floor, wrapping the colorful blanket around himself. I stepped back up onto my bed and stared down at him. For a criatura, he seemed strangely . . . reasonable. I squinted. Unless he was trying to trick me?

"You're not going to kill me in my sleep or anything, right?" I whispered.

"Not if you let me go to bed already." He yawned. "Now shh."

It shouldn't have, but the comment made me smile. I blew out the large candle flame. The heat remained in the air for a few moments after, and I curled up in my covers.

The first battle of the Bruja Fights was in two days. I had the bruja look. I had the legendary Coyote by my side. I had Grimmer Mother and Tía Catrina's guidance. I had everything I needed to do this.

I'm coming, Juana, I mouthed into the night.

And like Coyote when he brought music to Naked Man, I clung to the hope that I wasn't wrong.

10
The Moth and the Coyote

The next night, Envidia was just as unwelcoming as it had been the day before—except for one big difference.

Everyone stared in awe.

Their gazes weren't on me, of course. The huddles of brujas and brujos watched Coyote, who lingered a couple of steps behind me as we moved through the narrow streets.

I'd spent nearly an hour convincing him to come with me. Grimmer Mother had promised to teach me how to win the Bruja Fights, I told him. I needed to return, and I needed him with me. He'd finally agreed. But the new feeling in my chest, the echo of his soul, hadn't felt happy about it.

Grimmer Mother waited for me in front of her house. Smoke trailed out of the door behind her. Her smile sliced upward as I approached.

I bit my bottom lip when I stopped in front of her.

Coyote's bare feet disturbed the dust behind me. His presence was like wearing a pair of new, stiff gloves, both attached to me and not.

Grimmer Mother didn't greet me right away. Her focus was on Coyote. "Great Namer," she whispered. Then slowly, like she was coming back to life, her grin spread. "You conquered the Great Namer, Cecelia Rios."

"Uh-huh." I nodded awkwardly. "Sure did."

I felt Coyote's eyes bore into my back.

"He's younger than I imagined." She considered the necklace around my throat and beckoned me with her tattooed fingers. Hesitantly, I pulled the stone out of my shirt. Coyote bristled as she leaned in for a closer look at the wide, horizontal scar carved through the back of the stone.

Her mouth spread wide. "He's *died*. You have good timing, Cecelia Rios. He might have been too powerful in his last life, but in his second, you can be his master."

"What do you mean?" I whispered.

"Catrina really should have come back to teach you more about bruja life." She straightened up, and I tucked the necklace back into my shirt. "There are many secrets to criatura souls. The most important one is knowing how close to the forever-last death a criatura is."

My eyebrows pulled together. "Forever-last death? But criaturas are always reborn—"

She waved her hand and headed up the steps. "Criaturas may be reborn from their soul stone, but with each life they come back weaker. If killed nine times, a soul stone grows so weak that it turns to sand. It is called the forever-last death." She paused on her steps and turned back to tap my collarbone. "That scratch in the stone is a sign that Coyote has died. It is one scratch, so you know he has died once. You must keep this in mind. A good bruja must not kill her criatura or get it killed too often, or she will lose a valuable tool. Understand, mija?"

I had to force myself not to look back at Coyote. Nowhere in the legends did it say criaturas could die forever. The fact that they could be reborn and come back for revenge was one of the reasons they were such a torment to Naked Man.

"So, wait. Have any criaturas *really* died permanently?" I tried not to look horrified.

"Oh, yes. Have you heard of the Desert Grizzly Bear?"

"No."

"Exactly." She returned to her doorway. "Now come, I have much to teach you." She pulled me inside the house and into a side room I hadn't noticed before. Coyote trailed us, frowning. "We must work quickly to get you ready for tomorrow's first round. If you are anything like your tía, you won't need much time to master your criatura."

She moved around the room—a small, simple square with no windows—and headed to the far end, where a great brass cage sat beneath a ratty cloth. She pulled it off but blocked whatever hid inside it from view.

"Before you can master a criatura, you must see a criatura's master in action," she said, and the sound of hinges screeched. "Let me show you how much power the heart of a true bruja can wield over a criatura."

Grimmer Mother turned around, and a criatura tumbled out of the brass bars.

I immediately recoiled. It was La Chupacabra—the legendary dark criatura.

Like most dark criaturas, there were warning murals of her painted all across the edge of the Ruins. I'd been brought up seeing her balding, scrawny body and large teeth illustrated in books and reading about how she preyed on farmers' livestock. She'd always looked and sounded monstrous, ravenous—like all dark criaturas.

Now, curled up on the concrete floor, she was small and vulnerable.

Her shape was mainly human, but her legs bent backward like a dog's and her fingers ended in long claws. She shivered against the stone, and when she snapped her head up to look over her shoulder, her eyes were clouded like a mist had settled over the pupils.

My heart lurched. I coughed and placed a hand to my chest, struggling to breathe. Something hard and gray swelled up in my chest, seeking exit through my throat. Wait—no, that wasn't me. It was the alien warmth that had started in my chest the moment I placed Coyote's soul against my skin.

I glanced up at Coyote. His mismatched eyebrows pulled together, like he might be slightly uncomfortable.

But his soul felt like it was withering.

"Meet the goat sucker. My criatura." Grimmer Mother kicked La Chupacabra forward.

The dark criatura fell on the ground in front of us, and her few spindly strands of black hair fell over her cloudy eyes. She hissed then, showing rows of sharp, spit-covered teeth.

"She is young in this lifetime," Grimmer Mother said. "I owned her in her last one as well, but she died during a training accident. A shame, but she has at least two lives left. I'm glad she's finally regrown enough to help me train you." She stopped beside me and slipped off her soul stone necklace. Seven deep gouges interrupted the flat limestone. The sight made me flinch.

"She looks so skinny," I said, averting my eyes.

Grimmer Mother clucked her tongue. "It takes a long time for criaturas to die of starvation, so there's no point in feeding them more than once every couple weeks." She snapped her fingers, and La Chupacabra winced. "In a fight, you must be ready to force your criatura to dodge, lunge, or strike at a moment's notice. Let me show you how to gain control over your criatura." She finally spared Coyote a glance. Her smile widened. "How you make it *beg* permission for every breath."

I didn't like the sound of that. Coyote's gaze narrowed, and the gray inside my chest shifted into a darker shade. Grimmer Mother closed her hand back over the criatura's soul stone.

La Chupacabra's eyes went even duller than before. Both her arms launched into the air. They waved back and forth. Then, she crouched, slashing at nothing. A low, whining howl crawled out of her throat—and then she froze mid-step toward us.

Everything about her movements looked unnatural, more like a puppet's movements than a living criatura's. A shiver climbed my spine. Grimmer Mother released the soul stone, and La Chupacabra gasped, finally placing both feet on the ground.

Grimmer Mother turned to me and tapped my chest, near the leather lines of Coyote's necklace. "Now you," she said.

I gawked at her. "Now me what?"

"You won't be able to make Coyote's body move the way I just made La Chupacabra move, not right away. That takes practice. But pain is the easiest thing to make a criatura feel," she said. "Start by making your pain his, and make his body cower with it."

I nearly shouted "No!" but wadded it up in my mouth. If I didn't do it, she'd know I wasn't really like Tía Catrina at all. Plus, she was trying to help me win the Bruja Fights— is this really what I had to do to succeed?

My hand wrapped around Coyote's soul. The stone was so warm, the temperature gentle.

Grimmer Mother's eyebrows tugged together when I didn't say anything. "What is it, mija? Is his soul hard to tame?" She reached for the stone. "Let me—"

"No!" I lurched back, clasping his stone to my chest. "No, I—uh—I just don't understand how to press that feeling into him. Do I need to push into the weird warm feeling in my chest?"

She waved her hands. "No, no, no. That feeling is his emotional feedback. Ignore it. Once you crush his soul and make it submit to your will, you won't even notice it."

Well, that explained how she could puppet La Chupacabra so easily.

"You press *your* will into their stone. The criatura's feelings are just a symptom that will fade." She looked at Coyote. He scowled.

But his soul was still so warm. Even in my chest, gray battled with something small and fluttering. It seemed to have a lighter color—something closer to pink, maybe?

I tucked Coyote's soul back into my shirt, like that would somehow protect it. "Do I have to try pain? What about something happier? Can I practice with happiness?"

Coyote's eyes cut to me, studying my face, as Grimmer Mother scoffed.

"Estúpida," she said. "You'll never need to make your criatura *happy*. That won't win you the Fights." Grimmer Mother stepped toward me. "I see the softness is still sleeping in your heart. You remember what I said about that, don't you?"

She backed me up to the nearest wall. I froze against it, hand flat over Coyote's soul. Coyote studied me over the woman's shoulder. La Chupacabra crawled quietly toward him and reached out to touch his ankle with her pale, hairless hands. His face stayed stoic, guarded, but gray filled his stone. She tilted her head, like she was worried about him. He gave her a small nod.

Grimmer Mother noticed the direction of my stare and rounded on them. "How many times have I told you not to distract other criaturas while I'm training?" She grabbed La Chupacabra by the arm and dragged her to the doorway. Coyote flinched as La Chupacabra thrashed. Grimmer Mother nodded to me. "Just a minute, mija. I'll deal with her, and we'll get back to your lesson."

I gave a weak thumbs-up.

She slammed the door behind them. I held myself together for all of ten seconds before hyperventilating.

"I can't do this," I blurted. Coyote came up beside me. "Why did I think I could do this? She just made that criatura into an . . . empty doll! I can't do that. I don't *want* to do that."

"Well, panicking's not going to fix anything. If she sees you like this, she'll definitely know you're a fake bruja." Coyote crossed his arms.

He was right. I should focus—Grimmer Mother would be back any second. I nodded shakily. "Okay," I said. "But I don't want to hurt you or turn you into a puppet. Ugh, what am I going to do?" My throat tightened.

Coyote sighed a little. "Just focus on calming down. I'll think of something."

"This is my sister," I said. "This is my life. I have to be the one to do something about it."

He stared into my face, and after finding something there, unwound his crossed arms. "Okay," he said. "Okay, *we* will handle this. Any ideas, bruja?"

The sound of footsteps grew closer on the other side of the door. I whispered hurriedly, "Maybe we just make it *look* like I'm hurting you. How are your acting skills?"

He gave me a mischievous smile just as Grimmer Mother reentered the room. I buttoned my mouth. La Chupacabra was no longer with her.

Grimmer Mother dusted off her hands. "Where were we?"

I gave Coyote the briefest glance I could. His head moved a fraction. The tiniest nod. I hoped that meant what I thought it did.

"Oh that's right." Grimmer Mother gestured at me. "Practicing. Go on, bundle your pain tight in your heart and press it into Coyote's stone."

I turned to him, wide-eyed. His soul was warm as my hand embraced it. He gave me another tiny nod. So I screwed up my face, mimicking what I thought pain should look like, and narrowed my eyes on him.

Coyote cried out and dropped to the ground.

It was so startling I nearly let go of his stone. But I squeezed it at the last second and watched, face frozen, as he writhed in the dust, crying out occasionally, his face twisted with pain.

Grimmer Mother smiled. "Muy bien."

She watched Coyote scratch through the dust, clearly hungry for the sight of the Great Namer cowering on the ground. Soon, I didn't have to pretend my scowl. But my gaze rested on Grimmer Mother as I did.

After a few moments of Coyote's pretended pain, Grimmer Mother flicked her hand. "You can stop now. You don't want him too tired to continue."

I let go of his soul. Coyote caught sight of the movement just a few seconds late and stopped. He breathed heavily on the ground. I bit my lip at his shaking limbs. He *was* pretending, right?

"As I thought. You're a natural, just like Catrina." Grimmer Mother didn't spare Coyote a glance as she nodded at me. "Now, let's try something a bit more advanced, mija. Let's try making him stand." She circled Coyote where he still lay on the ground. He did a good job of looking tired, but his eyes still followed her every move.

"All right," I said, loudly, to give Coyote the hint. "So just—make him stand up, right?"

Coyote held my gaze and lumbered upright. He swayed for a moment there, like his movements weren't quite his own, but he flashed me a conspiratorial smile.

I tried not to smile back.

Grimmer Mother clapped her hands together. "Muy bien! Now, make him crouch."

I nodded to him. "Right. Okay, so crouching—"

His knees bent, and he got into an animalistic squat. The corner of his mouth tweaked, like he was suppressing a smile.

Grimmer Mother's grin cut like a razor across her face.

"Mija, this is the fastest I've ever seen a bruja master her criatura." She came over and clasped my arm and gave it an almost-too-hard squeeze. I tried to look grateful, but all I wanted to do was pull away.

"Now." She let go and headed for the door. "Make sure you keep practicing before the Bruja Fights. At this rate, you'll have him completely under your control by tomorrow." She paused in the doorway. "No doubt you will make your tía proud."

She disappeared from the room.

The moment she was out of sight, I rushed to Coyote. "Are you okay?"

His smiled playfully up at me from his crouch. "Of course." Coyote tapped his soul as it dangled from my throat. The single scar rotated in and out of view. "Nice acting, bruja." His gazed flicked up to mine. "I mean— Cece."

I couldn't help but smile back. "You nearly scared me to death with that first one. You shriek like an owl!"

He snorted. "I bet you've never even heard La Lechuza."

"I'm guessing you have." He opened his mouth, and I rushed on, "And *no*, I don't want to hear the story right now. We need to leave this crazy woman's house already."

His smile broadened into a grin. I offered my hand, and for the first time, he took it.

11
The Bruja Fights

I stood next to Coyote in the vastness of the desert beyond
the Ruins, staring up at the crooked silhouette of the abandoned silver processing plant. It had gone out of business
when the silver in the mine had run out, around four years
ago. That's when Papá had gotten his new job in the oil
refinery.

The building perfectly matched the description Grimmer Mother had given me before I left Envidia yesterday.
Large, dark, and foreboding. I squeezed Tía Catrina's journal in my hands, holding it open to the entry about her
first night of Bruja Fights. Below the rough sketch of four
criaturas fighting in a ring, she'd written a short note to
herself: *From now on, no one stands in my and my criatura's
way. He is good, and he serves me loyally. Together, we will con-
quer today.*

It was strange to know I was following in her footsteps
so closely. But my path led to Juana, not to whatever power
Tía Catrina had wanted so badly.

Brujas and spectators strode past Coyote and me, either filing into the concrete factory or gathering around a smaller building off to its side. Here, so far from town, the brujas and brujos hadn't bothered to disguise themselves. Shaved hair, piercings, dark tattoos, and thread-wrapped necklaces with criatura souls were on full display.

They looked strong, that was for sure. I hunched a little.

"The small shed's where we register," I said breathlessly. "That's what Grimmer Mother said."

"Lead the way." Coyote scanned the crowd.

I slouched even more. "You're bigger, could you go first?"

Coyote covered his mouth, like he was trying to hide a smile, and started ahead. "You're a bruja. Try not to phrase it like a question next time."

Right, no questions, just be a jerk. Brujas were supposed to treat their criaturas like slaves. I nodded and lowered my head, so I glared upward as we headed near. We stopped at the end of the registration line and waited as someone called the brujas and brujos over one by one.

"Can you hear what the person checking us all in is asking?" I whispered to Coyote. I didn't want to be taken off guard.

"I'm a coyote. I hear more than I should." He scanned the line. Then, he leaned down slightly to whisper. "It's just the basics—name, criatura name. They record the participants every year so El Cucuy and his two advisers, together known as the Three Dark Saints, know who's participating and who they'll eventually welcome to Devil's Alley." I nodded, a little shaky, as we neared the front. He frowned a little. "Try to look like you're here on purpose."

I steeled myself. I'd changed my entire life in just a few days to be here; I *was* here on purpose.

The bruja and criatura ahead of us stepped up to speak with a man cloaked in shadows. Sweat suddenly gathered down the line of my spine. They spoke in hushed tones before the girl and her criatura departed.

Then it was just me and the cloaked man, only a few feet apart. He lounged cross-legged on a tipped-over machine surrounded by large hunks of broken, untreated stone left over from mining. He looked creepily similar to El Sombrerón, with his face completely hidden in the shadows cast by his large black hat. But he was shorter, probably an inch or so shorter than me, with a high-standing collar and cloak that poured down the length of his body. His hands were pale and bony, and he clutched the strap of a bag slung over his shoulder and a small pad of paper in the other hand. White rods peeked out from his bag.

He waved me forward with two long fingers. I stepped up.

"Name?" he asked.

I went to answer him, but then the white sticks in his knapsack came into focus, and I realized they were bones. Ribs, femurs, and forearms all crowned with a broken jaw.

He tilted his head when I didn't speak, but no matter which way he moved, his face was as dark as the bottom of a well. "Name?" he asked again.

I tried to keep my fingers from shaking. A bag of bones? He could only be one criatura—El Silbón, the Father Killer. A dark criatura.

"C," I forced out.

"C? That's your *name*?"

I wasn't going to tell him my real name. He was the Father Killer! "Yeah, C. You know, C, C from the alphabet."

"Oh, Cece. Okay, that's an actual name. Now, who's your criatura?"

Well, so much for that. "Coyote," I said, with a huff. "Criatura of the Coyote."

He straightened up a little, and the bones in his bag clinked. "Coyote? As in, the Great Namer?"

"Is there another Criatura of the Coyote?" I asked, but for a second, I was actually terrified there was, and I'd gotten the wrong one.

The dark criatura slouched again. "Well, you definitely

have the attitude of a bruja, anyway. But it'll take more than that to get you into Devil's Alley." He tapped the pad of paper against his knee. "Coyote, huh. I haven't seen him in nearly a thousand years." He chuckled and tilted his head so he could get a better look at Coyote standing behind me. "I guess it's your turn to be under a bruja's thumb. How's it feel to have finally gotten what's coming to you, Great Namer?"

Coyote didn't respond, his gold eyes flat and unbothered. But a distant twist of gray snaked through my chest. He was obviously uncomfortable. I glared back at El Silbón. What did he mean about Coyote getting what was coming to him?

"So, can we go?" I asked.

He sighed. "Humans are so impatient. Fine, fine. You're registered. Go on inside and wait until I call you up." He scribbled on the pad of paper. "Today we're holding four-body elimination rounds. You'll be in the first one. If you survive that, you'll automatically be entered in tomorrow's two one-on-one battles. And if you win those"—he glanced up and down at me like he thought it was doubtful—"you'll have one semifinal round before the Finals. Got it? Good. Now, get going."

I opened my mouth to ask more questions—a four-body elimination round sounded kind of terrifying—but he shooed me away. Reluctantly, I left the line and headed for the factory.

"What was that about?" I asked Coyote. "El Silbón was kind of mean to you."

He looked away. "He's a dark criatura. Of course he's mean."

I was going to press for more, but just then we entered the building, and the noise of drums, chatter, and excited roars crushed down on us.

Music thumped and pounded and just generally sounded like a toddler having a tantrum. The brujas and brujos were obvious in the crowd with shaved hair like mine, or dyes meant for blankets and clothes staining the ends of their hair or even their scalps. A surprising number of regular townspeople were also present. I didn't recognize any of them, but more importantly, I hoped none of them would recognize me. Though it was unlikely they'd report me— they'd be in just as much trouble for being here as I was.

Coyote nudged me. "Look over there."

He gestured across the floor, at three brujas and their criaturas all eyeing each other like meals. One in partic- ular caught my eye, with hair shaved on either side of her head. She stood beside a ferocious-looking young man with sharp green eyes.

"Those are our three opponents," Coyote said. "Most

of their criaturas aren't too much to worry about, but we'll have to watch out for the green-eyed one, Scorpion. He's known for being bloodthirsty."

A knot formed in my throat. "You've got to be kidding me."

"Hey, don't make that face." Coyote frowned at me. "You look scared."

I pulled into myself. "That criatura killed my abuela."

Coyote paused. I avoided his eyes and set my jaw. He reached out to me but dropped his hand before he touched my shoulder. "Cece," he said, leaning down. I stiffened at his closeness, but the noise and chants and smells bled away as he looked at me. "You went into the criatura quarries alone. You fought off Cantil Snake. You saved my life. You even tricked Grimmer Mother."

I stared at him. His stone soul grew warm inside my shirt.

His eyes brightened in the dim lighting. "You can do this and still keep your soft heart." He squeezed my arm gently. "You *can*. Okay?"

I opened my mouth but didn't know what to say. The way he looked at me—it was like he needed to believe I could do this as much as I did. I looked at him and, despite everything my people were supposed to believe about criaturas, trusted him.

"Okay," I whispered and hesitantly gripped the back of Coyote's shirt. "Can you help me push toward the ring?" If we were the first fighters, I'd rather get into position now.

Coyote nodded. My heart beat faster and faster as he pushed us through the crowd. Brujas scowled at my hunched pose. They could see it; practically anyone could tell I didn't belong in a place like this, doing things like this. What would they do with me if they realized I wasn't cut from the same cruel cloth as them? Being Tía Catrina's niece wouldn't save me. Would they feed me to their criaturas? Or worse—turn me over to the criatura authorities like El Cucuy before I had time to save Juana?

No, I couldn't think like that. Slowly, I forced my back to straighten. I lifted my chin, even though I was shaking. The fighting ring came into sight. I had never been able to convince my town that I wasn't their weakest link, but for Juana, I *would* pretend to be a bruja.

Like she'd always told me—I had to at least *try*.

"Welcome everyone to this year's Bruja Fights!" El Silbón, cloaked in his long, light-eating jacket, stood at the center of the room. He climbed up a pile of old crates that must've once been used to ship silver. At the top, he threw his head back and let out a high-pitched, energetic grito—an undulating howl, signaling the beginning of something great. The spectators cheered. "We're disgusted and impressed to see how many brujas and brujos have shown up this year. At the end of this tournament, El Cucuy will be pleased to welcome up to five of the fiercest among you into his castle in Devil's Alley. Who's ready to join the most powerful regime in all the world?"

The brujas howled and chanted and hollered their dedication. I pumped my fist awkwardly.

"So here's a reminder of the rules for all you fresh, squirming apprentices!" El Silbón shouted. "One, brujas and brujos aren't allowed inside the chalk circle during the battle. And two, they must make their criaturas fight until their opponents are no longer capable of fighting back. Whoever's left wins. Got it?"

Someone banged a pair of drums. My chest felt tight and icy as Coyote and I stopped just short of the battlefield.

It was just a large circle on the dusty concrete floor. It had been marked with chalk, and already some of the circle had been smudged by feet and hands. On the other side of the circle, the bruja I'd noticed and her Criatura of the Scorpion stepped up. I stiffened as the other two Coyote had pointed out also took positions along the circle. Each of them checked the others out, but all their sharp gazes inevitably landed on Coyote and me.

"Our four brujas are in position for the first round. We have Bruja Cece with—get this—the famous Criatura of

the Coyote!" Whispers and awed sounds echoed as confused spectators scrambled to get a look at him. He didn't
react. "And going clockwise, we have Bruja Adriana with
the Criatura of the Grisón; Bruja Manina with the power-
house, Criatura of the Scorpion; and Bruja Ximena with
the Criatura of the Pygmy Skunk! Is everyone ready to see
who deserves a place in Devil's Alley?"

The spectators screamed and stomped their feet until
their passion drowned out the sounds of the drums. There
were a large number of apprentices who, from their clothing, must have come from regions across the western cerros
and the south. As the birthplace of Naked Man, Tierra del
Sol was as important to brujas as it was to my people, so the
Bruja Fights were always held here. Some said the power of
the sun still lingered in the sand, and that being born here
made a soul's inner fire—inner power—stronger. I wasn't
sure about that. But the bruja community must have been,
since they continued meeting, training, and holding Bruja
Fights here, even with the police always after them.

"All four will enter, but only one bruja makes it into
tomorrow's second round." El Silbón turned to look at us.
"Now—begin!"

Coyote, Grisón, Scorpion, and Pygmy Skunk stepped
into the ring at the same moment. And then lunged at each
other.

Coyote moved with the ease of a dancer and punched

Grisón unconscious. The criatura went limp, and after a moment, the concrete broke open and let her body sink into the desert. Then the thin stone stitched back together into a smooth block. Grisón's bruja wailed with rage. I gaped. Holy sunset, that was fast. Across the circle, Pygmy Skunk dove on Scorpion, and the two struggled against each other. But Scorpion was faster. And his tail swiped across the smaller criatura's neck in near seconds. Pygmy Skunk dropped to the ground. The ground swallowed him next, his bruja's scream sending him off. My stomach felt queasy.

It was just Coyote and Scorpion now, eyeing each other. Bruja Manina smirked at me from across the circle.

Coyote made the first move. Scorpion tried to dodge the incoming attack, but Coyote's claws scraped the criatura's face, leaving marks. Scorpion dodged left and landed a punch in Coyote's stomach. I winced. Holy sunset, that had to hurt. Was that what he'd done to my abuela?

Coyote slammed relentless fists into Scorpion's jaw, until the shorter criatura had to stumble back. I winced again. No, I shouldn't care—this should be payback for my abuela. I'd never known her, but I knew the story so well, I could almost imagine Abuela cowering beneath Scorpion.

The thought made me sick, and every flash of Scorpion's shining green eyes sent chills down my spine.

Coyote was about to punch again, but he grimaced suddenly. Scorpion's black tail scraped down Coyote's arm. A deep red line appeared on his skin.

"Coyote!" I screamed.

The crowd started to laugh at me. "Can you believe how the legends described Coyote?"

"Look at him now, he's pathetic."

"He'll die with his tail between his legs."

I grabbed the stone hanging around my neck. He could do this, right? "Leave the fighting to me," Coyote had promised last night. He didn't need me controlling him to win.

But cold coiled up in my chest as Coyote lunged backward and sideways, barely dodging Scorpion's venom-tipped tail. He was faster than Scorpion. But the longer this went on, the more his knees seemed to tremble. Flickers of fear appeared in his eyes between each strike.

I gritted my teeth so I wouldn't scream again. But thoughts of Mamá crying over Abuela shook my bones. My throat tried to close up. What if Scorpion killed Coyote like he'd killed my abuela?

"Cece!" Coyote just barely managed to slice open Scorpion's shoulder. "Stop!"

Stop what? The audience hollered and cheered as Scorpion pulled his tail back and struck Coyote full in the stomach. Coyote flew across the ring. His limp body skidded to a stop just on the inside of the circle at my end. I gasped. He didn't move.

No, no, no. My heart squeezed. If he didn't win, I'd never see Juana again. Coyote would die and it would be my fault, and I would have to live without my sister for the rest of my life.

"Coyote!" I cried.

The crowd whooped and stomped its feet. Jeers and taunts rained over me. But I couldn't react.

I was busy watching my hopes and dreams pass out on the floor.

12
The Fighting Ring

Coyote lay with his face in the dirt, motionless on the ground.

I came down on my knees, just outside of the ring, beside Coyote. "Coyote!" I hissed. His face was shielded by his hair. "Coyote, are you okay? I'm sorry—what do I do?"

He didn't react. I bit my lip. Was he unconscious or—dead? Across the ring, Scorpion nursed the bleeding wound on his shoulder. His bruja just laughed. The announcer, El Silbón, leaned forward and watched. Everyone was waiting to see if he was a goner and would sink into the desert.

Suddenly, Coyote's finger twitched. He barely managed to lift his head and pin me with tired golden eyes. "Stop being so afraid."

I balled my hands into fists. "You're dying out there! I think I have a right to be *scared half to death*."

He planted his hands firmly in the dust. "Your fear is what's killing me."

El Silbón lifted both arms from his perch. "And he's moving! The Great Namer's not out yet, damas y caballeros!"

"Ha!" On the other side of the circle, Bruja Manina grinned. "I've heard so many legends about the great Coyote, but it looks like you've been tamed by a weakling. Don't worry, this time Scorpion will send you back to Devil's Alley."

Scorpion rolled his shoulders and readied himself to strike. "No!" I cried, but before he could leap forward, he winced and stumbled, holding his wound again. Bruja Manina scowled as she waited for him to recover.

Coyote leaned toward me. "Listen to me," he said. "You carry my soul, Cece. Even if you choose not to control me, your pain is my pain, your will is my will. I draw on *your* power, your emotions. Do you understand?"

The crowd hissed at me. Over Coyote's shoulder, Scorpion started advancing toward him again, but slower than before.

"I'm only as powerful as you let me be." Coyote pushed off the ground and managed to sit up. "Right now, I don't need you to be scared. I need you to be angry."

Across the ring, Bruja Manina paced, her bare feet kicking up dust. "Hurry up, Scorpion!"

Coyote's words burned through the insults from the crowd as Scorpion limped up behind him: "I need you *furious.*"

Furious?

Maybe I couldn't do fierce. But I could try furious.

I leaped up. Air stung my throat as I sucked in a breath—and let out an animalistic scream.

I screamed at my abuela's death. At the pain in my mamá's face when she told the story, at the confusion I felt over Tía Catrina causing abuela's death and yet being so similar to me. I screamed as hard as I'd wanted to when I realized my sister was stolen. Even harder, because it was my fault.

Coyote got to his feet just before Scorpion reached him. "That's it, Cece."

Everything inside me boiled over. The fear—so real before—hid beneath the blinding rage. Everyone here thought I was a weakling? Well, I was going to show them exactly how strong a weakling could be.

"Go, Coyote!" I called out.

He turned and leaped on Scorpion before I could finish, before Scorpion could prepare. Bruja Manina jolted to attention and stretched out her arms, ready to command Scorpion to block, but it was already too late—

Coyote slammed him to the floor.

The impact reverberated through my feet. Scorpion went limp. His bruja stumbled back, gaping. I forced back a shiver as the factory fell silent. He didn't move.

Everyone's eyes were on the fallen criatura. Was he

dead? Or just biding his time, like Coyote had earlier? The answer came as the concrete beneath him crumbled, and Scorpion's body sank into Mother Desert, its original home. His bruja gaped. She still had his soul, so Scorpion would regrow from it eventually. It was an unnatural thing, Mamá always said. When a criatura died, their soul should always be returned to the desert, so they could return to Devil's Alley and regrow back in their true home.

For now, he was gone. And Bruja Manina had definitely, officially, lost the match.

Everyone erupted in cheers. Coyote stood up in the ring as the concrete and sand stitched back together into solid ground. He whipped his head back and forth, shaking the dust from his hair, before turning to eye me across the distance.

I had to lock my knees to keep from backing away when he stalked over to me. He stopped in front of me and smiled. His canines were streaked with blood, and I wasn't sure whether it was his or Scorpion's.

I tried not to throw up.

"Now that," he said, "was the strength I needed."

El Silbón leaped into the ring, under the lights. "What a stunning turn of events! Bruja Cece and her criatura are our winners! We look forward to seeing more from them tomorrow. Moving on to the next fight, we have our next four competitors . . ." I tuned him out. Coyote and I pushed through the crowd, focused on the exit.

"Are you okay?" Coyote whispered.

I glanced up, fully expecting Coyote to be glaring at anyone between us and the door, but he stared at me, face soft and curious. For a second, there was no predator in his gaze. Just soft concern. A pup worried for its caretaker.

I leaned away, frowning. "Of course, why?"

"You're nervous . . ." He squinted, like I was a bigger puzzle than he was used to. "And . . . sad?"

Sad was an understatement. Even thinking about it, a knot climbed into my throat. I locked my jaw, and I found my eyes filling with water. I squeezed them shut and struggled to keep my breathing even as we pressed for the exit. Come on, Cece. We just defeated three random criaturas. Including the one who killed my abuela. It wasn't like hurting real people, right? I shouldn't feel bad.

Why did I feel so bad?

As Coyote and I made our way through the doorway, someone on the way in bumped my shoulder. I wiped my eyes and started to apologize—habit, I guess—but the person turned around and studied me.

He was much older, probably in his early thirties, and the hint of a necklace lined his collarbone before disappearing into a dark shirt. Probably an apprentice brujo, then. And just when I thought I was going to get some sign of displeasure for bumping into him, he smiled.

The smile was warm and intense, completely intended for me. The knot I felt in my throat eased up, and my heart fluttered for a moment. Strangers almost never smiled at me. It was a weird feeling, to be so welcomed.

"You did well today, Cece," he said. His smile twisted wider.

"Thank you," I whispered. And then tried not to slap my forehead. Brujas didn't *whisper*.

But the man just chuckled. "So polite for a bruja. But no less talented." He patted the top of my head and started to turn back to the next match. "I'll be excited to watch you next round! Keep up the great work, chica!"

I watched him make his way into the factory longer than I should have. He'd complimented me about three times in the thirty seconds we'd spoken. My lips climbed a bit. It was pretty nice to get a compliment. I guess not all brujas and brujos were unkind.

I turned and exited the building with Coyote. We'd just made it outside when he stumbled sideways into the exterior wall.

"Coyote!" I went to steady him.

He'd caught himself with his left hand, but it was obvious he'd nearly fallen. His face crumpled. His other hand cupped his stomach, pressing against it.

I rushed forward. "Are you still injured?" I fussed around him, not sure what to do. He swatted my hand away, and I caught sight of blood dotting his shirt. He quickly covered the wound again. "I thought my anger made you better! You took Scorpion down like this?"

"Sí." He pushed off the wall. I wrapped an arm around his waist and helped him down the street. "Your fury can't heal me. It just helped dull the pain."

I stood up as straight as possible, so he could lean on me. The desert was dark on either side.

"I'm sorry," I whispered.

"It was still impressive for your first fight," he said. "We'll do better next time."

I shook my head. "Not just for that. I mean—we're partners. I should have asked how to fight alongside you instead of making you do it alone. That was dangerous for both of us."

He looked down at me, sweaty and a bit unsure. "Partners," he said.

I nodded. "Yeah. If we're going to do this, we have to do it together."

"Like we did with Grimmer Mother," he said.

I nodded.

A spark came back into his eyes, and he nodded back.

"Okay. Well, first thing you should know is that the leaders of Devil's Alley invented the Bruja Fights to measure a bruja's inner power—her ability to *control* a criatura in battle—rather than the strength of the criatura. But it doesn't have to be that way." His black and white brows drew down together. "Grimmer Mother was right about one thing—you can push your feelings into me. After a bit of practice, you'll learn how to pick one emotion to feed into my soul instead of every flash that passes through your heart. That way, you won't take control of me, and you won't weaken me like you did earlier. You'll power me. Make sense?"

Power him, eh? That sounded similar to what Tía Catrina had said about her feelings making her criatura powerful. A chilly breeze swept down the dusty alleyway. I shivered. I was brushing a little too close to Tía Catrina's life for comfort.

"You really don't like any of this bruja stuff," Coyote said. "Do you?"

I didn't look up at him. If I admitted how much all this disturbed me, I'd probably just get a lecture on how I needed to be stronger, or more fearsome, or less—me.

"What can I do to help you heal?" I asked instead.

The Bruja Fights were every night for the next three days. He had to be ready.

Coyote's hand shook against his stomach. "Find me a place to rest. Bandage the wound. Feed me. Make sure no one else finds me. I should be all right by Sunday."

I whipped my head up to look at him. "In two days?"

His eyes narrowed. "You're lucky I wasn't hurt worse. Criaturas may heal more quickly than humans, but if it's bad enough and we don't get the rest and energy we need to recover, we can die."

Fear climbed up my insides. I clasped his side harder, lending more support, as sweat dripped from his hair.

"Don't worry, I have a plan for tomorrow night." He took a hard breath.

"It can wait, let's just get you home." I tugged him forward and bore as much of his weight as I could. Which wasn't as much as I would have liked. "Hey, why don't you transform into a coyote? Then I can carry you."

He squinted at me. I raised my eyebrows, making my eyes as big and pleading as possible.

"You won't make fun of me?" he asked.

I tried not to laugh at the unexpected insecurity. "What? Why would I? I've already seen you as a coyote."

He blushed and looked away. "Fine. But be careful, okay?"

I nodded. In a moment, his body morphed. It was soundless, faster, and less dramatic than I'd expected. He was an illustration, with his lines changing in soft movements, like the flick of a pencil nib. And then he was a young coyote, scraggly and with a long white-tipped tail, hanging in my arms.

"Oompf." I let out a surprised breath as his weight settled on me. He was heavier than I'd expected.

He glared up at me as I grunted.

"I'm not making fun of you," I said and tugged off my jacket with one arm. I laid it across his shivering body and bundled it around him. He closed his eyes. A little coil of worry started inside me again. He really did look so tired. "Just hang on, okay? I'll get you back safely. I promise."

I took off into the Ruins, a cold fear in my bones. I glanced down at Coyote as I weaved through crumbling buildings. His eyes were still closed, his ears wilted and limp. He looked quiet, trusting. Trusting me to take care of him.

I shook my head and ran faster. This plan of mine was getting complicated.

13
The Life Favor

The next morning, Coyote sat propped up on pillows at the end of my bed, his middle bandaged, drawing in my school notebook.

"I know a guy," he said, holding the pencil awkwardly. "Well, a criatura. Lives out in the desert. He's strong and owes me a favor." He glanced up at me and offered the notebook back. "Use this map to find him, and you can have him compete tonight while I'm healing."

I took the offering but couldn't focus on what Coyote was saying. He looked so *tired*.

We'd made it home safely last night, thank the Sun god. I'd taken a roundabout way, the one Tía Catrina had drawn out in her journal. I'd memorized the path out of nervousness the night before, and I was glad it had paid off. We had to wait a long time in alleys or by trash cans as police went by, but as if Juana were blessing us from afar, we'd made it without them catching us.

The moment we got back to my room, I'd bandaged his wounds and snuck him something to eat. He'd said he'd be okay, but he looked just as tired now as he had last night.

Coyote quirked an eyebrow at me when I didn't say anything. "This is the part where you thank me because I'm so helpful."

"Oh! Of course, yeah, thank you." I looked down at the notebook. "So what does this criatura owe you?"

His eyes closed. "A lot."

Okay, Mr. Dodging the Question. But he was hurt, so I'd ignore that for now. "What criatura is he? He's not a snake, right?"

"No." He rested his head back and smiled. "He goes by Little Lion. He's the Criatura of the Black Lion."

I went still. Black lions used to be a species native to our desert. In some towns, people even celebrated them on a special feast day. The way coyotes symbolized mischief and creation, black lions had once symbolized raw and indominable power.

But most of them had died out from overhunting years before I was even born. I thought they'd gone extinct.

I gripped the notebook between my nervous hands. I might've never seen one, but I knew one thing about the legendary black lions. They were powerful. Big. Strong.

"You think I can stand up to a black lion?" I asked.

"If it's to save your sister, I think you can handle any criatura standing between you and her." Coyote peeked an eye open. I smiled. Was that a compliment? He cleared his throat. "But there is a downside. He *may* try to kill you when you find him."

I jerked my head up. "He'll what?"

"He'll probably try to kill you." He shrugged casually. "Most criaturas don't like being a bruja's pet, but he's especially defensive. Just show him my soul stone and he'll listen. Probably."

That wasn't nearly as comforting as he seemed to think it was.

He pointed at the map again. "You should leave now. It's a long journey."

It took me a few moments of squinting and turning my head before I could orient myself on his rough depiction. He'd drawn me as a bald, smiling stick figure in my house—the starting place. A winding dotted line tracked my figure's way through the Ruins, past the cactus plains and silver mine, and into the rocky cerros. He was right. This trip was probably going to take hours.

I closed the notebook with a sigh. I was tired, and my legs and arms were sore from carrying Coyote home. And now I had to trek hours out into the desert? I wasn't sure if I'd make it.

My mind tiptoed back to what Dominga del Sol had said after she gave me the limpia. *" . . . you are ready now, Cece, to take on whatever challenge is set before you."*

I straightened up. That's right. I could do this.

I stuffed the notebook into my bag and slung it over my shoulder. "Is there anything you need before I leave?"

"No, the jerky is enough." Coyote pulled the bag of dried meat I'd fetched for him this morning a foot closer and then curled up around his pillows. Doing that, he looked like a puppy, even though he was in human form.

I frowned a little. He was a criatura, not a puppy. I had to remember that.

Coyote side-eyed me from his nest. "You smell confused."

"I just don't know why you want to help me," I blurted.

He looked at the floor. "You saved my life, remember?"

"I know. But that's never been a reason for criaturas to help humans before."

He shrugged. "You said it was your fault your sister was captured, right?"

Almost immediately, I felt my ribs constrict. I swallowed hard. "Yeah . . ."

"Well, it wasn't," he said. "It was El Sombrerón's fault. So one criatura should help fix what another one did, right?"

"But—that's still not . . ." My palms started to sweat.

Sure, that sounded like reason enough, but El Sombrerón had stolen so many brides over the years. And other criaturas had never helped get them back just because. It didn't make sense.

Coyote was a criatura, so he was supposed to be bad, but he'd only been kind and good to me. He was just like Tzitzimitl in that way. Just like Tía Catrina's descriptions of her criatura "being good." Thoughts of Coyote, my tía's journal, and memories of Tzitzimitl jumbled up in my head.

"It's—it's like when you gave music and dance to Naked Man," I said. "It didn't benefit you, but you still helped them. I feel like I should be worried about why you did."

He went still. "But you're not."

"Not as much as I should be," I whispered.

That had always been my problem. To everyone else in Tierra del Sol, the fact that he was a criatura was more than enough reason to hate him. Why wasn't it for me? Was Tzitzimitl's blessing—I mean, curse—making me weak like Papá and Mamá thought?

I had a sister to save. I couldn't afford to ruin things again.

I slipped on my shoes and pulled open the loft hatch. "Whatever you do, don't go downstairs while I'm gone. Mamá is working in the maize fields and Papá is in the oil refinery, but they could stop in at any time, got it?"

When I glanced back at him, Coyote was already asleep. Or pretending to be so he didn't have to answer. I frowned and started to climb down.

"Cece," Coyote said.

I paused on the ladder. He'd turned away, so I couldn't see his expression. But a tingling sensation built in my chest. Strong waves of anxiety and guilt wormed around my belly, and it took me a bit to realize they weren't my own. Strange. The longer I wore his soul, the more powerfully his feelings seemed to come through.

"He *will* try to kill you," Coyote spoke up. "I can't go with you, so be extra careful."

I rapped my fingers against the floor. "Don't worry, I will."

He made no further comment, but the gray emotions grew bigger. The feelings wrestled with each other, blurring until I didn't even know which feelings were mine and which were his. I wrapped myself in a hug and tried not to drown.

"Is that you?" I asked. My voice shook.

The feelings suddenly disappeared. I shivered as my chest grew light again, and I could appreciate all the beautiful colors in my room. But I concentrated on Coyote's back. It was still, calm. As calm as the feelings had been chaotic.

He didn't answer me. Maybe he really was asleep this time.

I closed the hatch door behind me. I still didn't understand what Coyote was getting out of this, or what battle was going on inside his soul, but I did appreciate him.

It was strange, really. I didn't think criaturas were supposed to be this—human.

I managed to follow Coyote's map into the cerros. It took about three hours of stumbling over rocks, weaving around elephant trees, and bypassing prickly cacti. I paused at the top of a hill, staring across the dry scrub and rising cerros folding over themselves into the horizon. I'd never come out this far before.

I expected to be tired, but there was something about the land out here that gave me new energy. I breathed in the smell. The sharp earth, the bristly strength of the cerros. It was different from the taste of dust in town. It wasn't concrete or adobe like the houses. Or stale and dry like the faces. It was lighter than the weight of stares at the schoolhouse. Here, there was space to be human.

Ironic, since I was on the lookout for a criatura.

I opened my notebook to check Coyote's map again. The wiggly dotted line and the X that marked the spot indicated I was in about the right place. Now all I needed was to find a cave.

I followed rocks and boulders all the way to the base of a mountain. The rocks, red and warm from the sun, rose far above my head. I dug my shoes into the pebbly grit and started to climb. Foot after foot, I scaled its craggy face and eventually stopped before a large cave.

Holy sunset. I tugged my torch out of my bag. It was a new one but still smelled of rancid cooking oil. I held the torch at arm's length, struck a match, and lit it. The light stretched into the dark crevice. Slowly, with the fire to guide me, I took a single, hesitant step inside the cave.

"Little Lion?" I called out.

There was no response. I didn't exactly expect him to dance into sight and offer his soul to me, considering Coyote's warning, but I hoped he wouldn't hide either. With a quavering breath, I held my torch higher. The stone around me transformed from dark gray to warm, pale limestone. I stepped forward, heading farther into the cave.

"Leave."

The voice was deep, rumbling, with a threatening growl near the end.

My heart quickened. "Little Lion?"

Two red eyes lit up. I stretched my torch out to catch a better glimpse, but the figure receded into the shadow. Only the edge of his eyes caught my light.

So he didn't want to show himself. That was okay. He hadn't tried to kill me yet, so I figured I was already doing pretty good.

"Little Lion, I've come to bargain," I said. "I need a criatura—"

"I said *leave!*"

His voice roared through the stone until even the pebbles by my feet quaked. I fell silent. Slowly, carefully, I dipped my hand inside my rough sweater and pulled out Coyote's soul. It dangled from my fingers.

"I'm a bruja," I said. "Coyo—"

A dark blur lunged toward me. I screamed as he tackled me to the ground. The torch spiraled out of my hand and landed with a clatter next to us. Strong hands pinned my arms above my head.

Little Lion's red gaze flashed above me. The fallen torch lit the side of his face, orange light glinting across his bared teeth and deep brown skin.

"Stop!" I barked. "Coyote! Coyote sent me!"

Little Lion paused. He looked about thirteen years old, with a young face, hard eyes, and black hair that stuck up across his head in spiky waves. His straight black eyebrows lowered on his small forehead.

One of his hands suddenly yanked away from mine, and he grabbed both my wrists in his other hand—the way Juana used to when we'd wrestle. With his free hand, he lifted the stone from my neck.

"Coyote's soul," he said. "You stole it?"

I shook my head wildly. "No, no. He *gave* it to me—"

"I owe him a favor," he spat. "I'll repay it now."

He tugged on the necklace, and I knew he was going to take Coyote's soul from me.

The world slowed to molasses. Little Lion's fist tightened as he began to wrench the necklace away. The warmth of Coyote's soul pulled further and further out of reach, and it felt as if someone were ripping the comforting sound of my heartbeat out of my pulse.

"No!" I cried.

Before he could snap the leather strap securing Coyote's soul, I slipped my sweaty hand from his grip and grabbed the quartz stone dangling from his neck.

His face froze like someone had stabbed him.

Just like Grimmer Mother and Coyote had taught me, I *pushed*. I pushed all my fear, all my panic, all the desperate, nervous need to get my sister back into his soul. I piled it on, higher and higher, until I couldn't even breathe for the panic we shared.

Little Lion's face twisted. He threw Coyote's soul back down on my chest.

"*Stop!*" he shouted.

I gritted my teeth and ripped his necklace from him. The snap of the leather echoed through the cave. Little Lion stumbled off me with a painful sounding gasp.

Quickly, I tied the strap around my neck. A feeling like a captured storm settled between my ribs.

"I'm your bruja now!" I sputtered. "You can't kill me!"

Little Lion had fallen to the ground beside me. His head hung low. "Desert's voices, *not again*."

"Coyote's calling in his debt now!" I scrambled to sit up. "He wants you to be my criatura! That's his deal. Then you're even."

For a moment, there was just the cool brush of wind from the cave's entrance, and the flickering tongue of the torch fire. Little Lion didn't move. I held my breath. Slowly, he lifted his head.

"Then we're even, huh?" he mumbled.

"Yeah." I let out a slow breath. "So you won't hurt me, right?"

He pushed off the ground with a scowl. He had broad shoulders for a teen, and they twitched with anger. "Not like I could, now that you have my soul stone." He stood and backed away, looking me up and down. "Coyote really gave you his?"

I sat up, rubbing my wrists. "Yeah. He said it was in return for saving his life."

Little Lion folded his arms. "You saved him?"

"He was trying to rescue me, but it didn't work out. It's complicated." I stood and tried to catch my breath.

"Anyway, I need another criatura to fight in the tournament tonight, and he said you were strong and owed him a favor."

Little Lion's nose wrinkled. "I am. And I do."

I smiled. "Perfect! Because I could use your help." I glanced down at his stone, and my excitement waned. Four cracks ran through the jagged quartz crystal. He'd died four times already. The thought weighed on me as I tucked his soul into my shirt. Unlike Coyote's soul, which was always pleasantly warm, Little Lion's was just a little too hot.

When I looked back up, he threw my torch back at me. I scrambled to catch it without scorching myself.

"Listen carefully, *human*," he said, with so much fire in his voice that I was suddenly more worried about him burning me than the torch. "I hate you soul-sucking brujas. So as soon as I've repaid my debt, I'm *gone*. You understand?"

I paused. "I think you're saying that you'll help me. Right?"

"For Coyote." He pointed a clawed finger in my direction. "And no other reason."

Wow, okay, he *was* mad. Whatever he owed Coyote must've been pretty important for him to agree to help me. But now probably wasn't the time to ask. We still had a long journey home.

"Well, I appreciate it anyway." I gestured to the cave mouth. "We'll talk more about my, uh, fighting style at my place. I have to be home before the sun sets or my parents will think I've skipped curfew." I started walking out. "Once night falls, we can sneak out for the Bruja Fights."

His footsteps followed behind me. "You care what your familia thinks?"

I glared at him. "Yeah, so? That's pretty normal."

"Not for brujas." He sneered.

"You'll find out soon," I said as we emerged from the cave. "I'm not like most brujas."

14
The Lion

"Okay, the window on the east side, the second floor, that's the one you need to sneak through," I said. "I'll meet you up there once I've had dinner. Okay?"

Even in the warm light of evening, Little Lion's face was no more merciful than it had been in the cave.

"Is that a command?" he asked.

I sighed. "It's a request. Please try to be reasonable. If my parents see you, they'll call the police, and then you and I will be captured together."

We stood outside my house, in the backyard. As I spoke, I tucked both necklaces in my shirt, so my dress collar hid the two leather straps and their stones. Little Lion watched the whole thing.

"What?" I snapped.

He raised a single eyebrow. "You're a bruja who can carry *two* criatura souls, and you're afraid of the police."

"Yes," I hissed. "Because if they realize I have two

criaturas, they'll imprison me and kill you and Coyote. Got it?"

He inclined his chin and said nothing. Well, he wasn't going to be very good company. Still, I should be grateful I'd gotten him here at all, considering I could have been dead in a cave instead.

"Por favor, just go up to the room. I'll be there soon."

He turned away, and then crouched and sprang into the air. He left behind a shiver of dust, disappearing from sight without so much as a sound.

I took a brave breath and marched to the front of the house, ready to face my familia and pretend like I hadn't just been hunting for a criatura all afternoon.

"I'm home, Mamá!" I called as I closed the front door firmly behind me.

Mamá peeked out from the kitchen but didn't say anything. I smiled and met her in the small cooking alcove. "What're we having for dinner? Is Papá home yet?"

She turned back to the tortillas on the comal. At the mention of Papá, her eyebrows tugged together.

"No, mija, he's *out*."

I'm not sure why I even bothered to ask. Papá rarely came home before sunset, and when he did, he was a stumbling, sweaty mess. For some reason, I'd thought that would change after Juana was taken. I didn't understand why he'd want to stay away now that our familia was even smaller.

Mamá pulled the tortillas off the stove and slapped them onto the table next to a single plate of beans and rice. Then, she rolled up her sleeves and stomped off toward the front door.

"Mamá?" I asked as she tugged on her worn coat.

She turned to me and smiled sadly. "I cooked your dinner, mija, but I have to go. The police are looking for volunteers to help them track down the Bruja Fights tonight."

I slipped my hands into my pockets before they could shake. "Oh yeah?"

Her mouth tightened. "Your Papá is too *busy* to help track down the criaturas who stole away his own daughter, but I am not." Her eyes flashed with something hot and brassy. My chest tightened. "Stay here and stay safe, mija. Lock all the doors. I'll be back sometime after midnight."

"But Mamá, it's dangerous," I said. "You haven't let *me* out at night—it's not safe for you either."

She opened the front door. "I have experience with criaturas, mija. *I* am not afraid, and *I* am not weak."

My toes curled at the implication. "But Mamá, it's one thing to take on a criatura when they come to attack you. But running into a den of brujas? That's—you shouldn't—"

"Do you remember your tía?"

My shoulders slumped. I should have known this talk was coming. Mamá had found a way to give Juana and me this lecture every year during the criatura months since I was little.

"Mamá, please," I whispered.

"Tell me what happened to her."

"She went too often into the desert," I whispered, reciting what she'd taught me. "And because she was vulnerable and trusting, she was seduced by the power of criaturas and fell to the greed of brujas."

I scanned Mamá's expression. She always looked like this when we spoke of Tía Catrina—her eyes granite, her hands balled into fists and ready to face a criatura even now. Only this criatura lived in her memory, and I wasn't sure she'd ever defeated it.

I bowed my head. "And once she became a bruja and left for Devil's Alley . . . criaturas seeking revenge came back to our home and killed Abuela."

Her eyes filled with burning, glistening tears. Mine filled with tears to match the ones she didn't let fall, because the air filled with her memories, and I wished I had gotten to meet Abuela before she passed away. Besides Dominga del Sol, almost no one spoke of her. But my heart always reached for her when they did.

"And you remember who defended our familia when the criaturas came?" Mamá asked.

"You," I said, voice even smaller. Abuelo used to talk about it all the time before he died. Every year on Noche de Muerte, he'd recount the way she'd stood by him to defend their home.

"I have fought against criaturas since I was your age," she said. "They took my sister thirteen years ago, they took my mamá soon after, and now they have taken my daughter. I will not let this go on. Someone has to stand up to these monsters called brujas and show them that the Sun god did not make us to be even worse than criaturas."

She slammed the door behind her before I could get out another word.

I stood alone, facing the front door, feeling lost and small and queasy. Mamá hated Tía Catrina. How would she feel if she knew I was following so closely in her footsteps?

A groan came from upstairs. "Cece, you're making me sick."

Coyote! I snatched my dinner from the table and scampered up the ladder to my loft.

Little Lion sat cross-legged on the floor, glaring as I closed the loft hatch behind me.

"*Try* to hold back your manipulative little emotions, bruja," he said.

I frowned. "Sorry."

Little Lion pushed off the ground and strutted over to Coyote's curled up body. He kicked his foot. "Hey. Wake up."

Coyote jerked his head up. He must have been only half awake when he complained through the floorboards, because he still looked a bit dazed. Once he spotted Little Lion, though, his face transformed almost instantly from sleepy pup to carnivorous animal.

"Little Lion," he said. "You're younger than when I last saw you."

A crease formed between Little Lion's eyebrows, and for a moment, a flash of something less steaming moved through his stone. But before I could figure out what it was, the quartz heated back up, and he looked as perturbed as usual.

Little Lion frowned. "So are you." His mouth flattened. "After this favor, we're even. You got that, Legend Brother?"

"Perfectly."

Little Lion stalked to the end of my bed, kicking aside worn clothes and sending spare books spiraling, and plopped down, expression dry.

I scowled. "Can you try not to ruin my stuff?"

His red eyes leveled on me. Then, he kicked my nearest

notebook and sent it flying onto Juana's bed. It slipped off quickly but dragged the quilt down with it.

I turned on him. "Were you *Named* a jerk, or do you just enjoy being one as a special pastime?"

Little Lion glared. "Funny hearing that from a bruja."

"The name is *Cece*." I rushed forward, fists clenched. "And please, keep it down. You have no idea what trouble we'll be in if my papá comes home and finds you here."

Little Lion threw a hand in the air. "What? You don't want me to kill anyone who gets in your way?"

"No, I do *not* want you to kill my familia." I threw my hands up in the air. "Or anyone, for that matter!"

Little Lion just smirked. "Oh yeah, because as a bruja, you're known for your selfless love for all living things." He batted his eyelashes to emphasize the sarcasm.

My cheeks flushed. "I—I'm not—"

"Not what? A stammering idiota?"

Coyote kicked Little Lion's foot. "Hey! Don't tease her, burro."

Little Lion scowled at him. "You've always been too soft on humans. When are you going to learn they're not worth your time?" He glared at me. Coyote stiffened. "This one isn't any different. She's just overly sensitive about her familia."

I was tempted, for a hot, blistering second, to grab his

soul and send waves of anger and sadness through him, but I fought back the urge. I had to pretend to be a bruja, but I didn't want to act like one.

"Yes," I settled on saying. "I *am* sensitive about my familia." I put my hands on my hips. "Familia is life. Without it, there is nothing, and I am nothing. Which is why you're both here. Now scoot over, I'm sitting there."

Little Lion didn't move. I huffed and took the only spot left, perched precariously on the corner of my bed, and offered my dinner to Coyote. He lifted his mismatched eyebrows.

"You haven't eaten anything but jerky all day," I said. "Here. And you can have some too, Little Lion."

Little Lion folded his arms, like he was too good for rice and beans. Coyote took the plate from me cautiously. A bit at a time, he scooped the dinner up in pieces of tortilla until at least a quarter of the plate was gone.

"Better?" I asked.

He nodded. I started to pull the plate back, but he grabbed my hand. I froze.

"Thank you," he said, with a tone of surprise, like he hadn't known he was going to speak.

Warmth filled my chest, either from his own soul or mine, I wasn't sure. But I smiled. I straightened up and started stuffing my face full of the rest of my meal. "Now

Little Lion, it's time to get ready," I said between mouthfuls. "The sun sets in thirty minutes."

He hunched forward. "Okay, *bruja*." he said. "Let's see if you have what it takes to force me to do battle."

"My name is *Cece*," I said. "And that's not the way I do things. Let's talk tactics."

15

The Lion Tamer

When we reached the abandoned factory, it was noisier than ever.

Even though the four-body elimination round should have eliminated three-quarters of the brujas and brujos in the tournament, there were somehow even more people in the crowd bouncing and hollering, roaring and dancing in the dust. Some of them looked like participants-turned-spectators who'd probably lost the first round but wanted to see who won tonight. Others were thrill seekers from Tierra del Sol and nearby haciendas.

Little Lion and I stood near the ring, waiting for our turn to be called, as the first round waged on. I tried not to look at the fight. Little Lion just glared into the crowd, arms folded. I nearly sighed. I wished Coyote were here, but he still needed rest.

"Their fight's almost over." Little Lion glanced sideways at me. "Remember, just give me your rage, bruja."

I pursed my lips. Why did all criaturas run on anger? Coyote needed my fury, and now Little Lion wanted my rage. He'd told me to keep all other emotion out of it. Just the blind, burning fire of anger.

Everyone wanted fire from me, but my soul was cursed with water. I tried not to worry about what that meant.

El Silbón crowed the winner's name as the losing criatura was swallowed into the crumbling floor. I cringed at the sight. Little Lion put a hand to my back and shoved me forward. I stumbled to a stop at the edge of the chalk circle.

"And our second fight begins with two more hopefuls, Bruja Alejan with her dark criatura, La Llorona, and Bruja Cece with"—El Silbón's lips twisted in a wry smile—"surprise, surprise, a new criatura, Criatura of the Black Lion."

The crowd rustled a little as Little Lion stopped beside me, all eyes turning to him. Most seemed surprised, a few glared with suspicion. I glanced around, wondering what everyone knew about my criatura that I didn't.

"They're not looking at me," Little Lion muttered, like he knew what I was thinking. "They're wondering how you can carry two criatura souls at once."

I straightened up. He'd mentioned that earlier too. Was that unusual?

Little Lion elbowed me. "Just focus and do your job, *bruja*."

I frowned a little. He stepped across the chalk and into the fighting ring. Everyone quieted for just a moment. Then my opponent's criatura stepped forward, and my stomach dropped.

Her skin was pale white, her lips red, her hands curled around her long nails. I swallowed hard and had to lock my knees so I wouldn't retreat. "Be careful of La Llorona," Papá used to say. "Stay in your bed at night or La Llorona will crawl out of the town well to drown you, just as she drowned her own children."

Papá had been adamant about keeping me away from water as I grew up. When rare rainstorms came in the summer, he'd usher me inside. When I volunteered to go draw well water (before we got a spigot of our own), he'd refuse and send Juana. Probably because he thought it would worsen Tzitzimitl's curse. And to make sure I'd listen to his warnings, he told me stories about La Llorona, who haunted bodies of water at night. Because of that, she'd been the dark criatura I'd feared most growing up.

And tonight, I had to defeat her.

"Little Lion, what a pity to see you stuck in another bruja's web." La Llorona's black hair stuck to her face as she circled Little Lion, her white, spindly hands twitching back and forth like a dying spider's legs.

The sight nearly made me sick. Even so, I couldn't help but notice she'd mentioned "another" bruja. So Little Lion *had* been in the Bruja Fights before.

Little Lion's emotional feedback spiraled into me. His pebble grew boiling hot. I snatched his necklace out of my sweater, holding it out by the leather strap, before the quartz could burn my skin. I was supposed to push rage into him, but his soul was burning. I didn't even want to get near it.

"Bruja!" Lion threw his head back and roared.

I jumped, struggling to summon anger into my body. El Sombrerón's face nearly did the trick, but just as the feeling rose—

"Calling for a bruja to save you again?" La Llorona laughed. "You must *like* servitude. You little pet."

Little Lion prowled around La Llorona, but he didn't attack, his muscles trembling with uncontrolled anger. His feelings, filled with shades of red and painful orange, exploded back into me.

I pulled back from them and gasped. No way. His soul was a raw, aching place, and the fire, the anger, was so strong I could barely think when I'd touched it. How could he want my rage when he already had so much of his own?

Then I realized—that's why he wasn't attacking. La Llorona was taunting him on purpose, keeping him so wildly angry that he couldn't think enough to make a move. And it was working. Because when Little Lion stopped to glare at me for not doing what he said, La Llorona took the opportunity to pounce.

She landed on him with her claw-like nails. I winced as she got one, two, three swipes in. She pinned him on the floor, her nails at his neck. He snapped his jaws but couldn't get a bite in to defend himself.

"Little Lion!" I ran forward but stopped myself at the chalk circle.

Little Lion's soul raged with heat. Laughter filled the horde, voices taunting me and him. They'd cheered for me last night, but I guess all they wanted was a good fight. They didn't care who the winner was.

I set my face into its hardest, chilliest lines. Here, there were no second chances. Here, I couldn't be scared.

Here, I had to be a bruja.

I lifted Little Lion's soul—safe in my closed hand—to my lips. On the floor, Lion kicked and thrashed, but La Llorona's hand was stealing his air. I'd expect nothing less from the criatura who drowned children.

I closed my eyes and let all the terror flood out of me with an exhale. Little Lion didn't need my fear. And he didn't need my rage, either. Gathering everything I had, I pushed cool waves of calm into him.

It was a struggle. Like Coyote had said, working with Little Lion wasn't easy. It was like wrestling a goat into its pen, only if you were on fire, and the goat was on fire, and actually everything was on fire.

But I reached into Little Lion's soul and parted the flames. In the small space left behind, I forced in every memory of cold I could think of: the desert at night, a hailstorm, the shiver of cold water down my throat—and on top of that, I sent him the cold of loneliness, the cold of calmness, and the cold of perfect, isolated, internal peace.

His soul stopped burning.

When I opened my eyes, Little Lion looked back at me from beneath La Llorona's straggly black hair. His red gaze was, for once, not aflame. Just clear and sharp.

He gave me a subtle nod. I took his soul in both my hands and let more memories of cold flow into him.

The rage in his soul vanished completely. And with it, Little Lion fell limp in the dust. La Llorona grinned. Her bruja screamed for her to finish him. But I could see he had a plan now that he could think clearly.

"Now," I whispered.

He thrust his knee into her ribs.

La Llorona choked on the surprise attack and lost her grip. While she winced in pain, Little Lion wrenched up both hands, grabbed her by the shoulders, and threw her off him.

She landed on her back and I heard a loud snap. Little

Lion leaped on her without hesitation, his teeth flashing. I let go of his soul stone and covered my eyes.

The mob chanted my name, almost drowning out the sound of the floor giving way to swallow up La Llorona's body. By the time I lowered my hands, she was gone.

I expected Little Lion's quartz to heat again with victory as he stood alone in the ring.

It didn't.

"In another shocking upset, the winner is Bruja Cece and her second criatura, Little Lion!" El Silbón roared. "Keep an eye on this one, comadres and compadres. If the fact that she can carry two criaturas wasn't enough to make her a contender, her battle moves sure are."

Little Lion started making his way back toward me. I looked away and tried not to think about how he must have taken out La Llorona.

The cheers shifted around me, and suddenly, I realized someone was standing in front of me. I straightened up when I recognized him. It was the brujo with the satin smile I'd bumped into yesterday. He grinned widely at me, as he had before. The ache in my heart started to ease away.

But there was something different in his eyes today. For a second, I thought something was moving inside his irises. Something dark and almost—purple.

"Well done," he said.

I smiled back hesitantly. "Thank you."

"You're getting better with every match, Cece. And now you can even carry two souls."

Everyone was bringing that up. "Practice makes perfect, I guess?"

"Perfection." He glanced over my shoulder, toward the ring. "Not everyone is capable of that. But I have high hopes you will be."

This was starting to make me uncomfortable, but I couldn't pinpoint why. I rubbed the back of my neck. "I'm not so sure about that."

His gaze lingered on me. The purple-something seemed to sharpen. He reached out and placed a heavy hand on my shoulder.

"Cece." His warm expression disappeared. I froze in his grip. "What *are* you sure of?" His eyes narrowed. "Are you sure that you want to be here? That you want to be a bruja?"

My heart rate picked up. I looked into his face as the purple in his irises grew brighter. I hadn't done anything suspicious, so why was he asking me this?

"Yes," I said. "Yes, it's exactly what I want."

"Why?" he asked.

I stared at him, not sure what to say.

His hold tightened and stung. "Why do you want to be a bruja, Cecelia Rios?"

How did he know my full name?

The scratch of footsteps stopped just behind me. I tugged out of the brujo's hold and whirled around, my knees shaking, to face Little Lion.

He was covered in dirt and scrapes, but that wasn't what I noticed first. I was shocked because, for a moment, his soul was just *warm*. So warm it nearly washed away the fear that had curled tightly in my chest. And the look in his red gaze was almost—though I hadn't thought he was capable of it—soft.

Then he sneered, and the feeling vanished. "What's with that scaredy-cat look?" He bumped my shoulder with his own. "Follow me."

Little Lion pushed out a path for me through the crowd. I scanned the entire room, but the brujo had disappeared. I rubbed my shoulder; it was sore where he'd touched me.

I shivered. I really hoped I didn't have to run into him again.

I followed Little Lion out of the factory, my stomach still in knots, and stumbled into the open desert air. I breathed it in and hugged myself for comfort.

"By the way, Lion, I'm sorry," I said.

He cocked an eyebrow. "For what?"

I smiled awkwardly. Most of my smiles were awkward, but this one felt worse than usual. Probably because I was still trying to get the brujo's question out of my head.

"About, uh, not listening to you. It just seemed like you needed . . . less rage?"

He wiped sweat out of his eyelashes. "Well, it worked, I guess. So we'll stick to that from now on." He pointed at me. "But don't get used to ignoring me, got it?"

I nodded. Screams and roars from the next match filtered out the door, and I hunched over. I'd never get used to those sounds. I didn't want to.

Little Lion noticed my discomfort. "You don't like the Bruja Fights."

There was very little question in it, but he looked like he expected an answer. I shook my head against the urge. No one here could know the person I was inside. "What I want is to get into Devil's Alley." I shot him a look. His cold expression didn't change, so I assumed he got the message not to press further. "How long do you think until our next match?"

He turned his head to listen for something. "Fifteen minutes," he said. A gurgling cry rang out. "Ten, if they all end that fast." He scowled at the doorway.

"Oh." I tried not to look queasy. "So, uh, I was wondering—what do you owe Coyote?" I asked.

His gaze cut to me. "What?"

"Well, it had to be a pretty big debt for you to agree to be my criatura." I bit my lip. "What—what did your last bruja do to you?"

His eyes flashed crimson. "What do you think a bruja is? A carefree magical girl that parades around with her criatura *friends*?"

I hugged myself. "No. Brujas are people who have given up their humanity to become a kind of criatura."

"They're *worse*. They're the kind of monsters who get their power from enslaving *real* criaturas." His soul flared with heat. "We're not friends, bruja. Just because you don't torture me doesn't mean we're going to swap life stories. I'll find out what you're plotting, you snake-daughter. Just you wait."

I stiffened. He thought my not torturing him was part of some scheme?

"I'm not planning to hurt you," I said, because I couldn't say I wasn't plotting something in general.

He lifted his chin. "Yeah, right. And an anaconda just wants a hug."

I stuck out my bottom lip. "Just remember, Coyote *gave* me his soul, so I can't be that terrible, can I?"

"Coyote is a human-loving glob of dulce de leche," Little Lion drawled. "He's been fooled before."

So even other criaturas didn't understand his penchant for humans. Did anyone? Just then, a scream rose from inside. I winced and covered my ears.

"You're particularly ill-equipped for this goal of yours," Little Lion snarled.

"Yeah? Well, that's what you do for familia," I spat. "You sacrifice yourself even when it's hard. It's called love." I hunched over. "But I guess you wouldn't know anything about that, would you? You've never loved anything in your whole life."

Heat filled my cheeks. I hadn't meant to say all of that.

Little Lion didn't respond, and I wasn't sure if it was because I'd struck a nerve or because he still didn't care.

"Criaturas can love," Little Lion spoke up quietly.

I glanced over at him, an apology already waiting in my mouth.

"We're not taught to, I'll say that." He stared off to the south, into the night sky. "We live in Devil's Alley under the rule of El Cucuy and his Dark Saints. There's no time for love when you're trying to survive." He whipped around. "But remember this, bruja. The criaturas who flood into your human desert during the criatura months are those *escaping* Devil's Alley, while brujas like you fight in tournaments to get into a place we're desperate to leave behind. So, it seems to me, we're both criaturas."

I placed a hand over the two souls hanging from my neck. "I'm sorry. I—I didn't know criaturas didn't like Devil's Alley. Isn't it your home?"

"More like a prison," he corrected. "When Coyote Named Devil's Alley thousands of years ago, it was supposed to be a safe haven from brujas. But once El Cucuy took charge, he set up the Bruja Fights and let the winners into our city. They're loyal to him because he bribes them with what they want most—power. And then he gets all the servants he desires."

I tried not to let the shock show on my face. "Wait— *Coyote* created Devil's Alley?"

"Coyote Named all criaturas. Of course he made our home." He looked at me as if I were stupid. "What, has Naked Man forgotten the legends?"

"No—well. I don't know. Maybe some of them." I looked out into the desert. "Or—maybe we rewrote them."

"Wouldn't surprise me." He folded his arms.

I stared at his profile. From the way Lion talked about him, it sounded like El Cucuy was just as feared among criaturas as he was among humans. So by enlisting Coyote and Little Lion in my plan, was I asking them to return to their prison?

". . . and up next we have Bruja Cece and her criatura, Little Lion, in the ring again!" A vicious cheer rose inside, and Little Lion and I went back into the building. El Silbón raised his pale, bony hands in our direction. "And here she is in her last battle of the second round, to face off with Brujo Gonzalo and his Criatura of the Bat. Whoever wins this one goes on to the semifinals tomorrow night!"

The semifinals. We were so close. I steeled myself as Little Lion and I stepped up to the ring.

16
The Reluctant Allies

Brujo Gonzales stood on the opposite side of the ring. He cocked his chin up, his wide nostrils flaring. "You're dead, chiquita—"

A giant slam echoed through the walls.

Everyone froze. I checked over my shoulder. The crowd had turned to face the closed entrance. Sweat gathered on the back of my neck and on my forehead.

Another bang reverberated through the steel doors. Everyone winced in unison like a wounded muscle. Then, a muffled call came from the other side of the door.

"We will show you no mercy!"

I stiffened. Those were the last words of the Amenazante dance. It's what the people of my town were taught to say whenever they confronted either a criatura or bruja.

"Little Lion," I whispered. "I think—"

Another slam caved in the door's hinges. "Criaturas, we come for you!"

Brujas, brujos, and spectators alike sent frantic looks toward El Silbón. He got up from his shadowed, lounging position on a pile of scrap metal and stood, watching to see if the door would hold.

Another smash. Moonlight slanted in from one of the door's busted corners.

"Run!" he yelled.

I whirled around to face the nearly forgotten fight. Criatura of the Bat reared away from Little Lion, stumbling back toward his frozen brujo. Lion and I locked eyes.

Then the doors broke in.

A mass of people flooded in like the wind of the cerros. Brujas who'd fought viciously just moments before suddenly scampered like rats trying to escape. Police uniforms flashed in the strands of moonlight pouring in through the door. Civilians—some I recognized, some I didn't—followed the officers' signals, their hands filled with glowing fire opal. They were a blur of roars and gritted teeth. Every one of the people of my town looked as ferocious as Little Lion or Bat or La Llorona.

A hand clamped down on my wrist. I whirled around, already guarding the precious soul stones, to see Little Lion glaring at me.

"What is this?" he demanded, like I was somehow behind it.

"I-It's the volunteer forces. My mamá said they were going to try to find the Bruja Fights . . ."

I stopped. Lion's anger was palpable, but for the moment my attention was elsewhere.

With my mother.

She was across the factory. Nowhere near me, probably hadn't even seen me yet, but I caught sight of her in flashes, between running bodies. Her hair glowed with strings of fire opal. Her cheeks and hands were smeared with red as bright as a rosebud. It was nocheztli, the dancers' war paint, tracing her high cheekbones and outlining her iron eyes.

Her hands were weapons in the darkness. She captured a bruja in her arms. The bruja struggled, yelled out for her criatura. But before a dark streak could reach the squalling woman, my mamá ripped off the soul stone necklace.

A shiver bent my spine. I turned away, but no matter where I looked, chaos mobbed the abandoned factory. The metal interior clanged and rang with the sounds of the brawl. I was the only quiet thing left in a war of criaturas and humans, laws and secrets. Dark fear swallowed me.

Little Lion suddenly shook my arm. "Don't you dare get cowardly on me," he spat.

The world revved back up inside me. Right. This wasn't the time to be afraid. I grabbed his arms in return. He looked surprised.

"We've got to get out of here!" I yelled.

He scowled and glanced behind him. Bat and his brujo were still there, on the other side of the ring, like they were too stunned to run. A frustrated orange squirm moved through Little Lion's soul. He wanted to fight them, end the battle here. But we needed to get away. I held his arms and hoped that the emotions holding us hostage to one another would convince him.

He let out a hard breath. "Fine. I'll get you home."

My heart swelled with hope seconds before someone wrenched me around by the shoulder.

Criatura of the Bat stood there, clawed fingers digging into my shoulder. How had he gotten behind me? On his other side, his brujo stood shaking.

"You can't fight tomorrow if I beat you now!" Brujo Gonzales said.

Was he serious? I had way more important things to worry about!

Bat's other hand slashed at my face. I threw my arms up over my head and braced my knees. Before the blow could land, Little Lion punched Bat straight in the gut and sent him skating through the dust. I gaped.

I hadn't even tried to reach out to Little Lion's soul. But he'd protected me anyway.

He turned to me. "Let's get out of here."

But Bat didn't stay down long. The moment Little Lion

had turned his back to speak to me, Bat leaped for him.

"Little Lion, look out!" I pushed him out of the way. Bat's claw sliced through my forearm before I could dodge. I screamed. Tears filled my eyes.

Little Lion roared. His soul stone burned blisteringly hot as he grabbed Bat and yanked him off of me. He swung him around and sent him flying into his brujo. The two bodies slammed into the wall. The police were on them in seconds.

I cradled my arm. Through the tear in Papá's jacket, I caught the shine of blood. Before the pain could fully register, Little Lion wrapped me up in his arms and raced out of the building.

Lion was *fast*. I mean, Coyote was certainly fast too, but Little Lion outstripped him. The scenery around us blurred, and I gripped Little Lion's back to keep from flying off him.

He ran and ran until even the stars couldn't keep up.

Sooner than I'd expected, we reached the rooftops of Tierra del Sol. We streaked from roof to concrete roof, eventually landing in a cloud of dust in my backyard.

The moment we landed, Little Lion shoved me off his shoulder. I stumbled until I caught my footing, ready to yell at him, when I spotted his expression. His red eyes shone with moisture, his hand covering his mouth, eyebrows low. He paced the ground in quick, hard steps. I raised my eyebrows. Someone was having a meltdown.

"What?" I asked.

"Why did you do that?" he snapped, like he'd been waiting to ask. "You could have gotten yourself killed diving in front of Bat's blow, and then how would you win the Bruja Fights? If it's so important to you, why risk that?"

I stammered for a second. "W-Well, I didn't want you to get hurt."

"Don't lie to me!" He closed in on me. "You have Coyote. You didn't need to save me."

We stood practically nose-to-nose. Hot confusion radiated out of his soul, and it was clear he was mad at me. For saving him.

"I'm sorry you hate me so much," I whispered. A deep ache bubbled up inside me. "But it doesn't work that way in my head! I may have Coyote, but you're a person too, and you still matter—"

"I'm a *criatura*," he hissed. "Not a person."

I bristled. The bubbling inside me grew, and my voice rose with it. "Who said criaturas aren't people? You have a soul. You live, and you die, and like you said, you even love. Who says you don't matter? Because I'm never going to pretend you're expendable because you're a criatura." I jabbed a finger in his chest. "So get *used* to it."

Our gazes met in a hard, silent clash. Slowly, Little Lion pulled back. I relaxed and all the tension that had built up in my shoulders finally eased away. His soul's heat still radiated into my jacket, but it no longer felt like a threat.

"If you really believe that . . . then why are you in these Bruja Fights?" His voice was a bit weaker, and his eyebrows upturned.

"I told you, it's for my familia," I said. With his eyes drilling into me, I didn't exactly feel up to sharing. So I kept it at that.

The vulnerable look disappeared, replaced by a smirk. "You think your family will benefit from the riches of Devil's Alley?" He stepped back, so the cold night air filled the space between us. "Then you are just as much of an idiota as I thought."

His figure blurred, and the next thing I knew, he was soaring over my head and landing on the roof. His dark figure disappeared beyond the adobe lip.

Well, I guess I knew where he'd be sleeping.

I shook my head. I hadn't thought Little Lion was going to become my best friend anytime soon, but Moon above, I didn't think he'd yell at me for trying to save him. Was it stupid? Probably. Did I regret it? Only a little. And only because my arm was throbbing with pain now that the adrenaline had worn off.

I needed to patch up the wound soon. I turned to the back door. It was locked.

Right. Mamá would have locked it and the front door before she left for the volunteer raids. I hadn't thought about it because Lion and I left out my bedroom window earlier. My stomach tightened as I thought about her fierce expression from earlier. What would have happened if she'd seen me? How would I face her tomorrow, knowing we'd both been in the factory, but on opposite sides?

Beneath my hand, the door handle jiggled. The air in my lungs turned to concrete. Papá. Of course, Papá would be home by now. Holy sunset, he would be so mad to find me outside the house, and in my bruja outfit no less. How could I explain myself so he wouldn't punish me?

The door opened, and I froze.

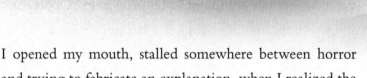

17
The Cerros of the Past

I opened my mouth, stalled somewhere between horror and trying to fabricate an explanation, when I realized the figure in the doorway wasn't my papá.

"Coyote!" I whispered. "What are you doing down here? Your wound—"

"Shh." He placed a finger over his lips. "Your father is asleep."

I buttoned my mouth. He gestured me inside, and I moved as silently as I knew how. If I listened closely, I could hear Papá's light snoring from beyond the curtain separating his and Mamá's bed from the rest of the main floor. I sighed. He only snored when he'd been drinking.

Coyote and I made our way silently up the ladder to my loft. The candles were already lit, so I was able to bask in the comfort of the light.

"You smell like blood," Coyote said once I'd shut the loft hatch. He stared at my wound through the tear in my jacket sleeve. "How bad is it?"

"It hurts," I admitted and settled on the floor. "But it's not too deep. Hopefully it'll heal fast."

Coyote sat down beside me and slipped both hands under my wounded forearm.

Heat filled my ears. Wow, he was really close. "Coyote?" I asked.

"I can heal it," he said.

I started. "What?"

"I can heal it," he murmured.

"I don't remember that power in the legends."

"I'm the Great Namer," he said. "Before Mother Desert and the other three creation gods sacrificed themselves so the world could begin, she gave me her voice. With it comes the power to create and to destroy." A crease appeared in his forehead. "That means I should be able to Name your arm healed."

I tried to meet his eyes, but he was focused solely on my wound. A trickle of gray filled his soul.

" . . . You don't remember how, do you?" I asked.

His eyebrows fell lower. "No."

I smiled and slipped my aching arm out of his hold. "It's okay. Most people don't get to heal their wounds with magical powers. I'll be fine once I bandage it."

Coyote watched me pull away. Inside his soul, colors tumbled around, trying to decide something. His throat jogged. "Cece, if I were—if I weren't the Coyote from legend you grew up hearing about—if I weren't the hero you've always admired . . ."

He stopped there. The gray stretched out of his soul until my ribs went cold. I placed my good hand over the freezing stone.

"I already know you're not the same Coyote from legend," I said.

His wide, gold eyes shot up to mine, catching the candlelight.

"You're only thirteen this lifetime. It's okay if you don't have everything figured out yet. I sure don't, and I'm *almost* thirteen."

He smiled a little. "That means you're still twelve."

"Ugh! So? You can't know that much more just because you were born a couple of months earlier."

"Well, at least I know how to handle Little Lion better than you do. I heard you two in the backyard." Coyote sat back, and his face lit up with a wide grin. "Sounds like you *just* missed getting on his good side out there."

I huffed. "Tell me about it. Why does he hate me?"

Coyote lay back on the floor, so his head rested at the end of my bed. "Because you treat him like a person."

I threw up my good hand. "That makes no sense! Why would that make him mad?" I stalked over to my bed and flopped down face-first. "Coyote?"

The bed creaked as he sat down beside me. "Yeah?"

"I don't want to be a bruja," I whispered.

Something tugged on my arm. I looked up and found Coyote rolling up the jacket sleeve on my bad arm— carefully, so it didn't touch my wound. Then, he wrapped the bandage roll I'd used on him around my cut. After winding it around a few times, he cut it and tied it off.

He pulled on the knot to secure it. "That okay?"

"Yeah," I whispered. "Thank you."

He sat back down on the floor. I turned over, onto my back, and held the injured arm to my chest. The knot Coyote had made was just loose enough that it didn't squeeze and just tight enough that it wouldn't unravel.

The stone ceiling above me glowed yellow in the candlelight. "Coyote?"

"Hm?" he said.

"I don't want to hurt any criaturas," I whispered. I wished I could make Little Lion understand that. But I also saw why he didn't. Brujas misused criaturas. And my town protected itself by treating criaturas with the same animosity it held for brujas. And criaturas responded with similar cruelty to keep *themselves* safe.

It was a painful cycle. I wished, somehow, that it would stop. If that bad blood didn't exist in the first place, Juana would never have been taken.

Coyote gave a single, quiet hum of laughter. "When you first said stuff like that, I didn't think I could believe you. But you're not pretending. You really mean it."

I grabbed a pillow and squeezed it against my chest. "Well, I want to hurt El Sombrerón. I'm going to destroy him. Probably." I squeezed the edges of my pillow.

Something shifted at my feet. I craned my neck to glance down at Coyote. His profile was set toward the window, candlelight flickering across the bridge of his nose. For a while, he just stared off.

"In his last life, Little Lion was in love with his bruja," Coyote suddenly whispered.

The moment he said it, a gray twang moved through his soul. It reverberated from the stone and reflected in my chest. I nearly winced. But not in pain, exactly. More like—guilt.

"I didn't know it was possible for a bruja and a criatura to fall in love," I said. But then again, there was something in the way that Tía Catrina wrote about her good, loyal criatura that made me think she'd had feelings for hers.

Coyote laughed quietly. "That's the worst part. She acted like she was in love with him, but in the end, she betrayed his trust." His voice caught on the last word.

Silence bloomed in the room. Coyote's soul carried a growing gray coldness that fought with a layer of warmth.

I'd felt that grayness from him before, but not with the same intensity as I did now. If only I knew what it meant.

"What happened?" I asked.

"They won the Bruja Fights," he said. "She was one of the chosen five that El Cucuy welcomes into Devil's Alley each year. She was apparently excited to climb the ranks in El Cucuy's royal court, but Little Lion didn't want to go back there."

Something dark entered his tone, the kind of darkness I'd seen only when he'd fought Scorpion.

I sat up, holding my pillow. "Little Lion mentioned that the criaturas who enter our world are trying to get away from El Cucuy and Devil's Alley."

Coyote's gaze strayed away from me. "You can't blame them for not wanting to go back there. It's an awful place. No criatura . . . should have to live there." He shook his head. "You have to understand that Little Lion had originally agreed to be her criatura because she promised to set him free after they won the Bruja Fights. He believed she cared about him. He thought she'd keep her word." He smirked humorlessly, shaking his head. "Safe to say, he was wrong."

I scooted a little closer. "How do you know all this?"

He scratched the back of his neck. "It was thirteen years ago. Little Lion was about seventeen in that lifetime, his bruja just a bit younger. They were fighting in the desert, on the way to meet the other four bruja winners and enter Devil's Alley. They passed the cave where I was staying at the time." He glanced back at me.

"He said that he'd miss her, but he couldn't face Devil's Alley again." His face hardened. "Most criaturas haven't been as lucky as me. I was created before the world became itself, so I've never had to endure Devil's Alley the way Little Lion has." He sighed. "When I saw him arguing with her, I was already thousands of years old, but it was the first time I'd seen a criatura talk back to his bruja." He scratched at the edge of his mouth. "I knew what was coming. But I couldn't stand it all the same."

I held my breath.

"She tried to kill him." Coyote dropped his hand. "I'd seen it happen to disobedient criaturas before. It was just so much worse, somehow, to see it happen to a criatura who didn't expect it." His throat jogged. "I couldn't help it. I dove on her and wrestled his soul away."

I pushed off the bed and sat down beside him. "You can do that?"

"It's not *easy*, Cece. It's probably the hardest thing for a criatura to do—to wrestle a soul away from a bruja. Because the moment you're close enough," he mimicked the grabbing motion I'd used to snatch Little Lion's soul, "they've got you. I managed to snap Little Lion's soul off and throw it to him, but she'd grabbed mine by then. I told him to run, and then she killed me."

A chill ran down my spine. I rubbed my arms. "She did?"

"My first time dying." Coyote smiled, like it was somehow funny. "Thousands of years of life, and I knew I'd be starting all over again. Just before everything faded, she held my soul up in front of me and promised to bury me in a well."

My chest squeezed. Criatura's Well. The one boarded up on the other side of town—the screaming criatura had been Coyote all along?

"She didn't," I whispered.

My town hated criaturas, of course, but we knew better than to stop one's soul from returning to Devil's Alley. Even when the town executed a criatura, there was a solemn ceremony where the head of police took its soul out of town and left it in the cerros. Almost instantly, the ground would separate around the stone and swallow it whole—returning it to Devil's Alley, where the criatura would eventually regrow. A lot like how the bodies of the losers had been reclaimed in the Bruja Fights.

Criaturas could be terrifying, but they still belonged to Mother Desert, not to us.

Coyote stared at the ground between his feet. "By throwing me in a well, she denied my soul its return to Devil's Alley." His lips twitched. "I don't think she recognized me, or she would have probably kept my soul. She was blinded by anger, and to her, regrowing in Devil's Alley must've seemed like too lenient a punishment for someone who'd stolen her criatura. In reality, she spared me from ever having to live there."

Something twisted in my chest, and I wasn't sure if it was Coyote's emotion or mine. He really sounded like he hated Devil's Alley. So—why had he made it, then?

"Did it hurt?" I asked. "The well?"

"Yeah." He shrugged, but his smile faded slightly. "Drowning doesn't kill a criatura, but it's not fun." He sighed. "It took about six months before I had grown enough to escape." At my horrified expression, he explained. "When criaturas are reborn, they're in their animal form. And we age quickly until we take human form." He stretched his arms. "I'm the equivalent of a thirteen-year-old human this lifetime. And I'll age like a regular human from now on."

I caught myself clutching his soul and forced my hands to drop into my lap.

"What I'm trying to say," Coyote said, rousing himself, "is that Little Lion has trust issues that have carried over from his last lifetime. He's mean because your kindness reminds him of his last bruja, and he's waiting for you to turn on him too."

I bowed my head. "I wouldn't do that to him."

"Even if it meant you couldn't save your sister?"

His eyes narrowed, flecks of gold haunting my room.

Slowly, I shook my head. "If he refused to go to Devil's Alley, I wouldn't make him." I placed my hand over the second pebble around my neck. Little Lion's soul. "I'd go save my sister by myself."

"You could die by yourself—no, you *would* die by yourself in Devil's Alley." Coyote sat up straighter, like he was afraid I was about to go off on my own right now.

I plucked the hem of my jacket. "You're probably right. But I still couldn't *force* him."

He watched me with the eyes of someone who'd spent six months drowning in a well.

"Would you force me to go?" he asked.

"No," I said, before I'd even thought about it. "I'd never do that to you, Coyote."

He'd helped me so much. And yes, I had to help Juana, no matter what, but I wouldn't make anyone else die for her. That was my job.

Coyote's eyebrows shot up. "You're crying."

I blinked and blushed when I realized he was right. The room dissolved in color.

"I just really miss her." I tried to laugh, but it came out

as a sob. "And it's my fault that she's trapped in a place that even criaturas want to escape from." My throat felt like a wrung-out dishcloth. I coughed.

Warmth pressed against my side. I wiped my tears away and glanced up, just slightly. Coyote's left arm wrapped around my shoulder. He didn't look at me, but he held me. He was warm—almost as warm as his soul felt against my skin.

"I would never force you to go to Devil's Alley," I said. "But I really, really hope you'll come anyway. Because I could use the Great Namer on my side. And so could my sister."

Even though I had his soul, it wasn't right not to give him a choice in the matter. It was an unfair thing to ask of him, but it was the most I could offer.

He gave a short, hard laugh. "I can't believe you're asking me that."

I hunched over. "I know. I'm sorry."

"No, idiota." He pulled back and nudged my shoulder. "I mean, I can't believe you're actually giving me a choice."

"I don't want to be a real bruja," was all I could say.

He sighed out his nose and faced the wall again. He still sat close enough for his side to warm mine. "You know, I agreed to this to pay you back. I'm *choosing* to help you save your sister." His mouth curved upward. "So if you could dry those tears and let me do my job, I'd appreciate it."

"Hey." I wiped my eyes. "I thought I was the one giving the commands around here." A hiccup caught in my laugh.

He chuckled and gave me a light push toward bed. "Get to sleep, Cece. We've got the semifinals tomorrow."

"In a minute." I shed my jacket and stumbled toward the loft hatch. "I'm just going to clean my cut first. But you go ahead and sleep—I'm glad you're feeling better. I was worried about you."

He rubbed the back of his neck and tried to pout. "Yeah. Thanks." He lay down and curled up in the blanket. "Buenas noches, Cece."

I smiled and descended the ladder to the sounds of Papá's snoring. The house was calm and dark, with only the moonlight from the kitchen window to see by. I pumped the tap in the kitchen alcove, and went to test the temperature with my free hand.

The moment my hand touched the water, a strange blue light caught in the clear stream. I jerked my hand back. The light vanished.

I squinted at it. Was I seeing things? I stuck my head out the window. No, the moon was behind clouds now, so it wasn't that. I turned back to the water faucet. Slowly, I reached for it again. The water spilled down my palm, racing down my arm—and the turquoise shimmer returned.

Where was that light coming from? I leaned in. It wasn't strong, but a tingle resonated through my skin wherever the water touched. Kind of the way the limpia felt when Dominga del Sol poured the water and herbs over me.

Before I had time to discover more, the front door opened behind me.

I leaped back from the sink. Mamá stepped into the living room, tired, her head hanging low. I was still in my weird clothes and had an obviously bandaged arm. I glanced around. I'd left a crochet shawl on the table earlier. I dove for it and yanked it over my shirt. Fortunately, its strings just about covered all signs of my wound.

"Mamá," I whispered.

She lifted her head and paused, like she was confused to see me up, or maybe she was blinded by the embarrassing red-and-gold pants peeking out from beneath the shawl. Either way, she smiled a little and came toward me.

She placed her hands on my cheeks, and the iron in her eyes began to melt. "Cece. Did you have another nightmare?"

Oh, right. My pretend nightmare from the other night. "Sí, Mamá," I whispered.

Papá snored loudly behind us. Mamá's mouth tensed

up, and she glared back at the curtain hiding their shared bed. She lowered her eyebrows, still covered in smudged war paint.

"You're wearing nocheztli?" I made myself ask, because I wasn't supposed to have known about it.

She stroked my face. "To keep you and every other chiquita safe, sí, I am." Her mouth puckered a little, and she pulled a hand back from my face, looking at her palm. It had come away with sweat and streaks of dust. "You're dirty, mija." Some of the hardness returned to her mouth. "What were you doing all night while I was away?"

I paused for a beat too long, and my heart sped up. Mamá's eyes narrowed.

"Herding the goats," I blurted, a little too loudly. Papá's next snore was extra noisy, and we both winced. "Um, Dominga del Sol told me that Señora Gutierrez was having hip trouble and couldn't take her goats out to graze, so I volunteered."

I was getting pretty good at lying, but it felt worse and worse each time.

Mamá's mouth tightened. "Mija, I told you to stay inside while I was gone."

I hunched over. "I know, Mamá—"

"And is that where you were earlier today, then? Speaking with Dominga del Sol?"

Lying was still better than getting caught with criaturas, but only barely. ". . . Yes," I whispered hesitantly.

She took a long, deep breath, like she was trying not to be as angry as she obviously was. I smiled, like that would help. The red streaks on her face shined like fire.

"No more leaving the house close to dusk," Mamá said. "I don't care what for, it's not worth it. *Do you understand?*"

I dropped my smile and nodded, shoulders up by my ears.

Her hand slipped away. "Go to sleep, mija," she said.

I nodded again and scrambled back up the ladder. When I closed the hatch behind me, Coyote was already asleep. I padded over, letting my racing heart slow, and collapsed into bed.

I hated disappointing Mamá. The way she looked at me downstairs, with anger and exhaustion battling in her face, made me want to bury myself away in the desert. But I knew it was infinitely better than how she'd look if she knew I was one of the brujas she may have fought just half an hour ago.

Sunday morning, I woke up to Coyote's insistent, low whisper: "Cece, wake up."

I groaned and tried to snuggle deeper into my blankets. I was so sleepy. But a hand gripped my covers to stop me. "Cece, someone's watching us."

My eyes burst open. I found Coyote crouched on the left side of my bed, staring at my window. The sun was only just starting to rise, so the outside world was still mostly made of disguising grays.

"Who?" I whispered. I couldn't imagine who would want to spy on me. I suddenly wished my parents were home, but I knew they'd probably left at least an hour ago. "I can't see them."

Coyote didn't even blink. "It's a criatura for sure." He took a deep sniff through his nose. "Female, I think. Someone older, stronger."

"Stronger than you or me?" Hopefully it was me.

"Both of us." His voice went super quiet, and he signaled for me to stay still. I froze beneath my blanket, trying to keep my breathing shallow and silent. He crawled forward, toward the window, careful to keep his head low.

Coyote stopped halfway between the wall and my bed. Slowly, he lifted a finger and pointed to the left side of the window. I rubbed the sleep out of my eyes to get a better look. Gold and black braids dangled slightly into view.

My heart bounced up against my throat. A criatura must be hanging just outside my window, on the exterior of my casa. Coyote took a steadying breath, coiled up, and sprang to the window.

"Hey!" He landed on the sill and let out a growl. "What are you—"

A long, dark arm shoved him off-balance. Coyote yelped and toppled out the window.

I leaped out of bed and dashed forward. "Coyote!"

I made it to the window just in time to see a tall, lithe figure disappear around the corner of my house. What the sunset was that?

Below me, Coyote dangled from my window frame. He held himself there effortlessly, but somehow, that criatura had been strong enough to shove him out in the first place. He scowled in the direction the spy had disappeared. "That was the Criatura of the Ocelot, but she didn't have a soul stone. A bruja must have sent her after you."

"Ocelot?" I hadn't seen that criatura at the Bruja Fights yet, from what I remembered. But maybe she'd just been in matches I hadn't paid attention to. "Wait, so you think a bruja's spying on me? But why?"

"Probably to find your weakness and use it against you in the Bruja Fights." Coyote swung himself back inside. "It's a good thing your parents are gone, or that could've been a lot worse. Ocelot's known to be a pretty strong fighter when she wants to be." He glared out the window again.

Panic buzzed in my chest. How long had Ocelot been watching us? Had she heard me say I didn't want to be a bruja last night? My palms started to sweat. No, no. Coyote would have noticed her if she'd been there. She'd probably just come this morning. Yeah. Hopefully. Because if she hadn't—

"What do you think they'd do to me?" I whispered.

Coyote turned back around, still squatting on the windowsill. "Huh?"

"If a bruja found out I wasn't really what I say I am. They'd probably report me to someone, right? Like El Silbón? Would he—come after me?" I wrapped my arms around myself for comfort. "Would El Cucuy—"

Coyote jumped inside and landed in front of me. "It

doesn't matter because you're not getting caught," he said a little too loudly. "El Cucuy doesn't leave Devil's Alley anyway. He'd probably send his Dark Saints if anything, since they're in charge of guarding the entrance. I made sure guarding Devil's Alley was top priority when I Named it—"

He cut off suddenly. I dropped my arms in surprise. Coyote's cheeks flushed, and he stood there, silent, clearly mortified, as his soul's colors bled to a stark white. That was the first time I'd heard him talk about his role in making Devil's Alley. My mind flashed back to Little Lion's words from last night.

"Can I ask you something?" I said.

He winced a little but nodded.

"Last night you said Devil's Alley is a terrible place, and Little Lion said it's a prison. So—why did you make it? In your last life, I mean."

Coyote hesitated and then looked out the window again, his eyes searching for the dawning sun. "You have to understand, Cece—I know a lot of my last life's story, but that's all it is to me. A story. It doesn't even feel like I lived the things I did then, even if I remember parts of it." He rubbed his arm. "So, if you ask me why I made Devil's Alley, I don't . . . really know. I don't have a personal connection to it. Just facts." He swallowed. "Like I read pieces of my own history book."

I stared at his profile as the white in his soul dissolved into gray. For me, he had been just a legend Mamá told me by the fire. But he'd been a legend who I'd admired. Now, I wondered if that's what he felt, too: the small, lost feeling of looking into a story for guidance to be whatever you're supposed to be.

Or maybe even for what you're not.

Standing at the window, he was just a thirteen-year-old boy learning about who he was. Just like me. Just like most of us.

He looked down at his feet. "I just know that I thought Devil's Alley would fix things." His face curled with a sudden, seething vengeance. I nearly stepped back as his scowl deepened. "I don't know *why* I thought that. All I ever did was make everything—*everyone*—worse." He kicked the wall. A sharp pop of red burst through his soul. "I was so *stupid*."

"Hey, hey." I tiptoed closer, reaching for his shoulder. "You were doing your best, Coyote."

His soul simmered down, and the color faded back to a light gray. I touched his shoulder. Slowly, he met my eyes. "You think so?"

I smiled a little. Sure, making Devil's Alley wasn't a great decision, but he probably didn't mean it to be a bad place originally. And anyway, that was his last life. "Everyone makes mistakes. Even the Great Namer, right?"

"Right . . ." He pressed his lips together. "Even the Great Namer . . . Names mistakes." He jumped a little. "I mean *makes* mistakes."

I squinted at him. He was agreeing with me, but something about him still seemed off. The gray in his soul hadn't disappeared. Was there something he wasn't telling me?

He didn't exactly seem up to sharing. So, I patted his shoulder and then grabbed a crochet jacket at the end of my bed. I signaled for Coyote to turn around, and once he had, changed out of my bruja's outfit quickly. Coyote was still looking the other way (with his eyes covered for extra insurance) by the time I was dressed for the day. "Well, this morning's been terrifying already, but I have bad news. I have to go to the Sun Sanctuary."

Coyote finally dropped his hands from his eyes as I turned to the hatch door. "Wait, you mean by yourself? Someone just sent a criatura to spy on you! You shouldn't go alone."

"I've got to. Juana used to take food to the Sun Priestesses every Sunday, and it's my job now." I started down the ladder. It was tempting, but I couldn't *not* go. If Ocelot didn't kill me, my parents would.

"Well, I'll come with you."

"Sure, if we want to get caught by the police." I hit the first floor. "Your eyes are gold, Coyote. And look at your hair!"

He peered up at the white curl dangling over his forehead. Then shook his head. "What if I shift into my coyote form? Then no one would know I was a criatura."

I squirmed a little. Would I prefer him to go with me? Yes. Yes, I would. Especially since my knees still felt shaky knowing that Ocelot and her owner were watching me for some reason.

But I wouldn't risk Coyote's life. "I'm pretty sure having a coyote tailing me through town would also be suspicious," I said. He frowned down at me. "The Sun Sanctuary isn't far, and the police would be on any criatura who tried to attack in broad daylight. I'll be okay. I think."

My stomach cramped a little as I picked up the tortillas Mamá left on the table and headed to the front door. Coyote stuck his head out of the hatch opening to watch me go, his hair dangling from his upside-down head. He looked worried.

"I'll be back soon!" I tried to sound braver than I felt as I closed the front door behind me.

Usually, I preferred to walk slowly down the familiar paths toward the center of town. But today, I ran, keeping an eye on the rooftops. Soon enough, the golden dome and steeple of the Sun Sanctuary peeked over the nearest buildings. There!

I rounded a narrow turn, and it came into full view. The morning sun shone off its gold top and lit up the stained glass windows, with Ocean goddess's mural glowing brightest in the angle of the sun. I slowed and smiled up at it, my fears dissolving with every step closer. The Sun Sanctuary was always such a cheerful, peaceful place to me. It was hard to believe anything bad could happen here.

Even if the priestess standing at the entrance frowned when she noticed my approach.

"Cecelia Rios?" Yaotl del Sol, one of the younger priestesses, asked.

I touched my hand to my shaved head. Oh, right. I'd almost forgotten they hadn't seen me with my new haircut. "Yes, it's me," I called.

"You've come to pay your respects?" She raised an eyebrow, annoyed. Juana used to joke that Yaotl del Sol's promotion to Priestess Caretaker—a Sun Priestess who was in charge of organizing daily chores—had inflated her already large head.

"Yes." I climbed the wide, brightly tiled steps even though I could tell she didn't want me to. They'd already propped the eight-foot dark wood doors open for the day, so I stopped just inside the wide archway. "Have you seen Dominga del Sol? I have her tortillas for the week."

Every familia in town had a duty to bring a certain portion of food to one of the priestesses. Mine had given tortillas to Dominga del Sol since she first became a priestess, back when my Abuela was alive.

Yaotl del Sol frowned at me. Her hard expression gave me a quivery feeling that made me want to retreat. But I took a deep breath and didn't. For the first time, I didn't run, didn't duck my head, didn't just accept her distaste.

Instead, I met her eyes and smiled.

Slowly, her gaze softened. She looked away and gestured inside. "She's in the back, doing laundry for the orphanage. Go on."

My heart rate picked up. It worked! Wow, this was so much nicer than sneaking in through the back. I grinned and thanked her before entering the sanctuary.

The front room was spacious, with three walls painted bright white and large, dark wooden rafters running lengthwise down the room. I approached the large mosaic on the far wall, passing by stained glass windows on each side, seats for meditation, and racks of candles set in front of the windows. There was so much beauty to take in at the sanctuary. But I found myself drawn to the mosaic more than anything else.

It depicted the story of creation that I loved so much. The Sun god, Moon goddess, Ocean goddess, and Desert goddess gathered in a diamond shape around a colorful center. In that center, held in place by the four deities, were sleeping animals, leaping fish, glorious stars, and dancing humans rendered in intricate patterns.

Drawn in by its beauty, I looked closer—at the center, this time. The Moon goddess's children, the stars, hovered closest to where she was positioned on the left of the diamond. Humans were near the top, hovering near the Sun god and his rays. The fish, whales, and seashells spread out from the right, where the Ocean goddess stood. And at the bottom, criaturas and animals slept in peace, just above Mother Desert. But what caught my attention most was the way the four deities reached into the center, the tips of their fingers touching one another's.

"I've always loved this picture."

I jumped and found Dominga del Sol beside me, holding a pile of starched white shirts. She chuckled and nodded to the mosaic.

"This mosaic is almost five hundred years old, you know. I think if it had been made more recently, it would be missing a lot of the truths inside it. People forget things so easily."

"What do you mean?" I asked.

She gestured to the mosaic. "How about you tell me what questions you have when you look at it?"

I turned back to the mosaic. "Well, there are no dark criaturas."

"You have a good eye. Just like your abuela."

I smiled. "And all four gods are reaching for each other."

"Very true. Why do you think the artist chose to do that?"

I shook my head slowly, taking in the ancient art. Each of the gods was depicted with a different type of stone. The Sun god with fire opal, the Moon goddess with moonstone, the Desert goddess with coyamito agate, and the Ocean goddess with turquoise. But where their fingers touched, the tiles united in brilliant jade squares.

"It kind of looks like . . ." I tilted my head, eyeing the jade. "I don't know. This might sound weird."

She nodded, encouraging me to go on.

"Maybe the gods were responsible for all creation. Together." Now that I saw the jade, I couldn't seem to look away. And it wasn't just in the center. In every creation floating around the gods' arms was a single bit of jade embedded. My mouth opened. "Like maybe there's a bit of every god in every creation. Because they . . . made us together?"

As soon as I said it, it felt right. But I was standing with a Sun Priestess in the Sun Sanctuary, the building dedicated to our gratitude to the Sun god for making us. I flushed red and looked up at Dominga del Sol, hoping she wasn't about to throw me out.

She didn't. Instead, her mouth softened in a gentle smile,

surrounded by thick wrinkles. "I think you've come to a very likely conclusion, Cece."

"Really?" I gaped.

"Well, yes. All four gods had to sacrifice themselves for the world to begin. It only makes sense that they needed their combined powers to create life as well. Even if they each chose a particular one to design."

That felt right too, as her words filled the space between us. We both looked up at the mosaic. The Sun god's face looked so soft and warm here, even captured in square fire opal tiles. Maybe it wasn't just because he was making us. Maybe it was because he was making everything, everyone, as part of a team with his sisters.

"If that's true," I whispered, "do you think the Sun god would be disappointed in me for having a soul like water instead of his fire, like everyone says?"

Dominga del Sol tilted her head as her eyes wandered over the deities. They paused on the Ocean goddess. I'd never paid much attention to her story, since we lived deep in the desert, far from her shores. Considering how much everyone hated the idea of a water soul so much, it seemed best to ignore her. But now, she caught my attention. She was dressed in turquoise rain clouds, and the hem of her dress turned into a river that faded into the ocean's vast body.

"How could he be disappointed in water," she said,

her wrinkled fingers brushing over the stones, "when he placed us in the desert, where we would learn to need it?"

No one had ever spoken of water like that to me—like it was important.

"That's something the curanderas used to teach." Dominga del Sol lowered her voice. People didn't like to hear curanderas mentioned publicly. "That every deity's contribution was important, and that we should be grateful to each of them. Some even say that's because curanderas were blessed by the gods—some blessed with the Sun god's fire, others with the Moon goddess's wisdom, a few with the Desert goddess's voice, and others," she said, looking pointedly at me, "with the Ocean goddess's strength."

My mouth opened. She spoke of water and the Ocean goddess the same way I'd always secretly believed Tzitzimitl's words to be—a blessing. A good thing. Not something to be ashamed of.

I stared up at the Sun god and his sister, the Ocean goddess, and wondered if it was possible that they could both exist inside me.

Slowly, I reached toward the Ocean goddess's depiction. As my fingers neared the stones, light flickered off them. I squinted, moving my head to try to angle away from whatever direction the sun was bouncing off them. Then I realized . . .

The light was coming *from* the stones. I went still, my

hand hovering just over their smooth surfaces. Was I seeing things again? First the water last night and now this? Next to me, Dominga de Sol straightened up. Her mouth opened. But there was no way the turquoise mosaic could really be . . . glowing, right?

Footsteps resounded behind us. I pulled my hand back, and the stones' light went out. Dominga del Sol's shoulders slumped a bit as she turned to meet the approaching figure.

Yaotl del Sol stopped beside us and planted her hands on her hips. "Dominga del Sol, you have chores to attend to."

The old woman looked exhausted. "That's true, Yaotl del Sol. Just a moment." She leaned down to take the tortillas I was still carrying. I loaded them into her arms, atop the shirts. "They don't like me to talk to children," she said. "They say I fill their heads with stories we don't like to think are true anymore."

Yaotl del Sol sighed. "It's not *that*." She looked down at me. "Understand, Cecelia, that Dominga del Sol's stories are only recorded by curanderas—"

"Which are the oldest histories we have," Dominga del Sol interjected.

Yaotl del Sol's face tightened. "When we trusted the curanderas for our protection, dark criaturas nearly took over Tierra del Sol, and we almost died out. Since the curanderas perished, we've become stronger by embracing only the ferocity of the Sun god's flame in our hearts. Clearly, it's a better way." Her eyes fell on me sharply. "We can't afford weakness."

I'd seen that look before, and I knew perfectly well what she meant.

Dominga del Sol placed a warm hand on my head. "If the Sun god, flame of our souls, were still alive to see us, I think he'd be sad to see us forget our history simply because we are afraid of being hurt again."

Yaotl del Sol stiffened. "Well, he's not here, is he? He sacrificed himself so that we could *live*. And it's our duty to do just that." She turned with a swirl of her yellow robes and disappeared out the entrance.

Dominga del Sol sighed as she watched her go. "She's not completely wrong. The curanderas weren't able to stop the flood of dark criaturas that nearly ended Tierra del Sol. But that doesn't mean they were weak." She poked the place over my heart and narrowly missed the two soul stones. My pulse fluttered.

I straightened up. "What do you mean?"

"You'll figure it out, Cece." She stroked my cheek with her free hand. "I have no doubt that you'll be the one to figure it out."

19
Hawk Hunting

"Well if it isn't the pollo who became a hawk."

I was on my way home from the Sun Sanctuary, taking a quieter route through the backstreets, when I heard the familiar voice. I whirled around, glancing across the barren street. A girl leaned against the nearest adobe house. I almost didn't recognize her, but when she turned to look at me, her nose piercing caught the light.

I stiffened. It was the apprentice bruja I'd met when I first entered Envidia. She had a serpentine smile, but her demeanor was a bit calmer this time.

"For a girl with two criaturas, you still look awfully scared." She smirked. "So tell me, how does it feel getting this far in the competition?"

I tried not to bite my lip and glanced down the street. I shouldn't stay out in the open for too long. But I didn't want to antagonize Bruja Bullring too much. When I saw the area was still clear, I turned back to her. "Are you not in the Bruja Fights anymore?" I asked.

She sighed and pulled her shirt collar back from her neck. There was no necklace. "Unfortunately not. The police caught me in the raid last night. I made it out, but they stole my criatura. She's probably dead by now."

I resisted the urge to check on Little Lion's and Coyote's souls. "Who did you have?"

"Criatura of the Tarantula," she said and shook her head. "A complete shame. I'd have loved to have seen her go against Coyote." Her smirk widened. "How did you capture a legend's soul, Bruja Cece?"

"It wasn't that hard," I said with a shrug, trying to avoid details.

She shook her head and chuckled. "Chiquita, I found out who you are, you know. You don't have to pretend."

The hairs on my arms stood on end. Had whoever sent Ocelot after me told her something?

"I've heard about Catrina, the Cager of Souls. She's a big shot in Devil's Alley. Guess it helps having some of that blood in your veins." She frowned out toward the Ruins.

I let out a nervous breath. Okay, she hadn't figured out that I was doing this to get Juana back. "My tía left me some . . . uh, tips, I guess." I cleared my throat when she sent me a dark look. "But you seemed to know a lot of stuff about the Bruja Fights all on your own. Have you entered them before or something?"

"For the past two years," she said. "Last year I had the

Criatura of the Cantil Snake. He lost in the semifinals, probably just to spite me." She sneered. "And now I've lost Tarantula. I swore this'd be the year I got into Devil's Alley."

I knotted my fingers together. "Why do you want to go to Devil's Alley?" It was hard to think anyone would want to, especially now that I knew what it was like for the criaturas.

Her eyebrows played with each other, like the question confused her. "Same reason you do, I guess. Probably the same reason Catrina did. To get out of this infernal desert." Her face hardened. "In Devil's Alley, I won't have a mamá beating me, telling me to respect people who've only ever tried to make me small." She gritted her teeth. "In Devil's Alley, I'll be the big bad bruja everyone else has to fear."

Except El Cucuy, who was the biggest bad of Devil's Alley. But she didn't mention him as she glared at the streets she'd just cursed.

If I could have turned Tía Catrina's journal into one single expression, it would have been the one Bruja Bullring wore just then—with eyes that had learned to hate more than to love. And in that same gaze, the implication that they'd been soft once. That they'd grabbed onto the wrong weapon to stop that softness from being hurt again.

"That's why I need a new criatura," she said. "How

did you find Coyote so *quickly*? I saw you that first day in Envidia. You didn't have a criatura then."

There was a change in the air. It went from vulnerable sharing to pins and needles in a moment. I didn't like it.

I stood a little straighter and scanned the area. No signs of Ocelot watching us from above. But Bruja Bullring's glare had turned on me. "I went to the old silver mine and hunted," I said. "I found him and took his soul."

"That easy?"

"That easy." I certainly wasn't going to tell her how it had really happened.

Her gaze dropped to my neck. I felt it flush. She pushed off the wall and walked toward me, slowly. I locked my legs so I wouldn't back away.

"Bet your tía's tips helped a lot, huh?" I jumped as she grabbed my wrist. "Imagine being able to power two criaturas at the same time, at your age. You got Catrina's talent too, I guess." She smiled down at me. "Two souls must be a hard weight to bear. How about I take one off your hands?"

"Don't you dare," I snapped.

Her dark eyes were framed with long, luscious lashes like Juana's, but there was iron in them. "It'll be better if you just let me have my way." She reached for my throat. "So just stay still while I—"

I slammed my skull into her face.

Immediately, pain shot through my forehead from the impact. The bruja wailed and thrust me back. I stumbled. Her mouth was bleeding, a front tooth missing.

"You cucaracha!" she cried.

I took that as a pretty solid cue to run.

I flew down the street. The bruja wasn't far behind. I pumped my legs and arms, Coyote's and Little Lion's souls thumping against my chest.

The wind bit at my skin as I threw myself into the run, faster, faster. Dust sprayed up behind my heels as I skated around a turn. I didn't dare look back. Her footsteps sounded too close as it was. I flung myself into the next street and took off. It was a backstreet, less populated, lined with trash cans and a few tubs of stored water. I weaved between them, chest heaving.

"Get back here, cucaracha!"

I threw myself behind someone's water tank. She gripped the other side, and we dodged back and forth, trying to anticipate each other. Then she lunged over it. I covered my face and screamed.

Only—a spray of water thrust her back. It bubbled over the top of the open tub and careened into her face, sending her toppling back into the dirt. Where—how? But I didn't have time for questions. The last of the stored water dribbled out on Bruja Bullring as she climbed out of the mud, and I turned to dash away.

I made it only a few steps before something metal struck my head.

The disorientation was instantaneous. My head rang like a bell, vision blurring until my feet staggered sideways. The bruja stood above me, tossing aside the lid of the nearest trash can, and tackled me.

We landed in the wet dirt. "I was going to let you live, chiquita." She slammed my head into the ground. "But now I'll take your life along with your criaturas."

I wrapped my hands around my friends' souls. She was sitting on me, her weight compressing my chest. But as hard to breathe as it was, I still forced out, "No—you—won't."

Her piercing glinted. She wrenched her fist back and aimed squarely for my nose. I gripped Coyote and Little Lion's souls tighter.

Two bare brown feet slammed into the ground in front of me. *"Get away from my friend."*

I looked up and saw Coyote glaring down at the bruja. She fell backward off me, landing a few feet away.

I took a large breath and tried to sit up, hands shaking around his and Lion's souls, when Little Lion landed beside me. I yelped, but he didn't look annoyed. He just nodded up at Coyote, reached out his hand to me, and helped me stand. He steadied me as I swayed a little.

Coyote stepped forward, his shadow crawling up the bruja's kneeling body. He gritted his teeth as he closed in on her. Her dark eyes widened, but there was no fear in them. Yet.

"If it isn't the Great Namer himself," she whispered. Her lips were bloody. "Up close, you look younger than I thought—no, I get it. You've died." Her grin spread. "What did you in? Another bruja, or was it El Cucuy himself?"

Coyote's face was stone. "You hurt my friend. You deserve everything I'll do to you."

The bruja's face slowly lost its exuberance. Coyote's upper lip pulled back to reveal his sharp canines. She scooted back, kicking up dust. He followed her, matching inch for inch, retreat for threat.

"Coyote?" I asked. He didn't even look at me as he cornered her against the nearest wall. "Coyote, please stop, she can't hurt me anymore—" I stepped forward.

Lion grabbed me. "Don't get close to him right now."

I turned to scowl at him. "What do you mean? I'm just talking—"

"And he's not listening." Little Lion looked at Coyote, and I noticed something new enter his soul. Something cold and white like fear. With a tinge of deep blue, like sorrow.

"You don't want to be close to him when he's like this."

What did he mean? I turned back to face Coyote, ready to march forward, but stopped in my tracks.

Coyote already had Bruja Bullring by the collar of her shirt, holding her a foot off the ground with only one hand. The bruja trembled in his grip, face pallid. He held her gaze, pulled her close, and growled right in her face. "You, I'll Name La Luz Mala. You'll live in a tormented mist, lost for eternity, as a prisoner of your own existence. Because you're everything I *hate* about Naked Man."

Sharp purple and white tattoos sprang up on Bruja Bullring's chest and neck, stemming from the spot Coyote held her aloft. I gasped, but Little Lion again held me back. The colors stretched like jagged Joshua tree branches up to her pained face. Tears trembled in her eyes as they neared her bottom lashes.

"Coyote, stop!" I called.

I shook off Little Lion's hold and dashed for the two of them. Normally, Coyote's soul battled between gray and pink. But in the last few minutes, the pink had vanished entirely. And the gray decayed into a roiling navy blue. It darkened into a burning, painful mess as more tattoos covered Bruja Bullring's skin.

Little Lion called after me, "Cece, don't touch him while he's Naming!"

I skated to a stop behind Coyote, reached out both hands, and grabbed his shoulders. "Coyote, please stop!"

The moment I touched him, a shock of heat rolled through me. His soul was at the center of it, nearly twice as hot as Little Lion's. I trembled as it sent images through my mind. A wide chasm in the earth, filled with darkness. Dark criaturas, flashing from Tzitzimitl to La Llorona, flickered across my mind, until the images settled on the looming, terrible figure of El Sombrerón.

The heat reached a burning peak. I fought against it, aching. I didn't know what was going on, but I had to help somehow. Somehow.

Suddenly, a wave of something cool bubbled up inside my chest and washed over Coyote's pain. The heat in his soul went out.

I opened my eyes. The air settled into a chilly peace. Coyote dropped Bruja Bullring, and the tattoos immediately vanished from her skin. She hit the ground with a loud thump but didn't pause to recover. After finding her feet, she fled down the alley, only glancing over her shoulder once to check we weren't chasing her.

Once she disappeared around the next turn, Coyote turned and gaped down at me.

"Cece!" he spluttered. "Why—why did you—?"

"You don't want to be like them," I said. "Like the dark criaturas. Do you?"

His chin trembled. Slowly, Coyote looked away and bowed his head. "No," he whispered. He sniffed and wiped his nose. "No, I don't. I'm . . . I'm sorry, Cece. I just . . . I didn't want her to hurt you."

That was—confusing, but also really nice to hear. "Well, thank you," I said. "I'm glad to have a friend like you. But what exactly were you trying to do to her?" From the feelings in his soul, it wasn't good.

Coyote didn't look at me. "I was trying to . . . remember how to . . ."

"Rename her," Little Lion finished as he stepped up beside us.

Coyote flinched.

I was stunned. "You can do that?"

Coyote's cheeks flushed. "Well, no. I tried but couldn't really remember how to finish."

"But I didn't know the Great Namer could *Re*name things," I said. "What else would you turn a human into?"

Coyote looked away again. I waited for him to say something. But as I searched his soul for some kind of clue as to what was going on, his feelings retreated again, faster this time, and he didn't speak up.

"What does it matter? You stopped him," Little Lion snapped, and his face darkened as he looked at me. "You're a *pathetic* excuse for a bruja." He folded his arms. "You weren't even willing to use Coyote to protect yourself.

That's the most basic principle of being a bruja!"

I frowned at him. "'Thanks for saving my soul from that other bruja, Cece,'" I said sarcastically. "Oh, you're welcome, Lion. You know I'd never let—"

Little Lion grabbed me by the shoulder and propelled me backward. I nearly toppled over. "If this is who you really are, then give up on this stupid fantasy! You can't be our friend *and* our bruja. You *can't be both*." He kept pushing me, a little harder each time, until he shoved me so powerfully I stumbled to a stop nearly four feet away, in front of the puddle by the water tank. "So *pick one* already. Either betray us now or just forget the Bruja Fights and scuttle back into your small, weak human life." Little Lion's face had flushed deep, cherry red, his mouth torn somewhere between a scowl and a sob. His arms trembled at his side. "Nothing good ever comes out of joining El Cucuy and his Dark Saints."

Not normally, no. Except when it came to saving Juana. Little Lion kept yelling at me, shouting at me, out of his own pain. But you know what?

I puffed out my chest. "First of all, yes, I *am* a fool who is risking her life to protect the people she loves—but I'm not a bloodthirsty bruja who *pretends* to love her criaturas and then betrays them, like your old bruja. So stop acting like I am!" I slammed my hands against Little Lion's chest and thrust him back. "Second of all, I'm only trying to win the Bruja Fights so I can get my big sister back from El Sombrerón!" Lion stumbled backward again, his eyes wide with shock. "And I will win, Little Lion! No one's going to stop me from saving her!"

I shoved him one last time. Little Lion stiffened, his face shocked and silent.

I turned from him, rage swelling. That wasn't the way I wanted to tell him I knew about his last bruja. And I hadn't planned on telling him I was faking being a bruja, especially when I wasn't sure I could trust him. But I was tired of people telling me I was a fool. Ever since my encounter with Tzitzimitl, I'd been made to think caring was a weakness. I was sick of feeling like who I was—a fool, sure, and a crybaby, yeah, and a girl with a soul like water instead of fire—was somehow not acceptable. Because if I was doing the right thing, if I was following all the goodness I believed in, that was good enough.

I didn't care how much Little Lion yelled at me or hated me, or how much I reminded him of his last bruja; I would treat him like a person. That's what I believed in. That was who I was.

I wouldn't let anything—pretending to be a bruja, my town's disdain, or Little Lion's anger—rob me of myself.

"Your . . . your sister is the Bride of El Sombrerón?"

Little Lion's voice came up behind me, low and soft.

I turned to him. We stood about five feet apart now, with Coyote between us and off to the side. He glanced at us, watching carefully. I straightened up and nodded.

"She is," I said. "And I'm getting her back."

The last remnants of anger drained from his face. And with it gone, I realized his face was soft and round, and his eyebrows weren't always heavy and scary. He stared at me, eyes large and waiting.

"You look a lot like her," Little Lion whispered. "My old bruja. Catrina Rios."

My heart jerked in my chest. Silence pulsed over us.

"Little Lion . . . ," I finally said, "*You* were my tía's criatura?"

He rubbed his shoulder. "I trusted her. And she betrayed me."

Something hot and aching bubbled up in Little Lion's soul at the admission. Hesitantly, I wrapped my fingers around it. The instant I did, the last of the aching heat in his stone ever so slowly leeched out of the quartz and into my hand. It didn't burn physically. It was a deeper fire—an old one. And for the first time, I tasted it.

He'd loved Catrina so much. Tears slid down my cheeks. I hiccupped as images and feelings flashed up my arm, panging in my heart. She'd laughed with him, cried with him, and worked alongside him. She'd promised to take care of him. She'd been his friend, and more than that— she'd become his world.

She was the one person he thought he was safe with.

And then she'd betrayed him.

My legs trembled in the shadows of the alley, holding Little Lion's soul as the old, wounded heat drained away completely. All this time, I'd thought he was just angry. But he was also sad. And deeply hurt. He'd carefully wrapped his soul in burning anger to keep everyone away from the tears he needed to cry.

Finger by finger, I dropped Little Lion's soul back onto my chest.

I wiped my cheeks. The tears kept coming, but I wasn't ashamed of them, because they were Lion's. Footsteps came closer. When I looked up, Little Lion stood there, watching me.

"I thought you were trying to trick me too. But you're not like her," he said, and offered his hand. "You . . . take care of the people you love."

His eyes were red, muted, and soft. He stared at me like I'd appeared from nowhere and might disappear the same way at any moment. Slowly, I took his peace offering.

We shook hands and looked at each other with a new understanding. I knew his pain. He knew my truth.

Coyote crossed the distance and stopped beside us. We looked up at him.

"You," he said, narrowing his eyes on me, "are no bruja."

I straightened my shoulders, ready to stand up to him too, because I wasn't going to feel bad about not being cruel any more—

"And that," he continued, his face softening, "is why you're stronger than them all."

About an hour later, Coyote, Little Lion, and I arrived at the old corn mill to the north of Tierra del Sol, well past the Ruins—the backup location for the Bruja Fights' semifinals.

It wasn't quite as large as the abandoned processing plant, but the mill was surrounded by thick boulders and stones that eventually climbed into the edge of the cerros, giving it that same discomforting feel.

Coyote and I pushed our way into the building. Little Lion had decided to stay outside, and I figured he could do with the time to think. Inside, decaying wooden crates had been cleared away and stacked against the walls, so there was space for the fighting and jeering. A fight was already underway. I didn't bother to check out the fighters, just weaved through the crowd to a more out-of-the-way spot by the wall.

Coyote fell in beside me. "We should be up next."

Fantastic. Except "fantastic" was probably the exact opposite of the feeling I got every time we had to defeat another criatura. Coyote gave me a quick, comforting smile. I smiled back.

Then Coyote's face fell.

"What?" I asked.

"There are brujas and brujos here," he whispered.

I snorted. "That's not exactly news—"

"Not apprentices, Cece." His eyebrows lowered as he stared into the crowd. "This time, there are real brujas and brujos. From Devil's Alley."

The words hardened in my gut. I followed Coyote's gaze and found the true brujas among the horde of people. There were a couple against a wall, one near the fighting ring, a few sitting on old bricks, overlooking the fights. But one brujo—the last one our eyes rested on—stood tall in the opposite corner of the building, his glowing purple eyes locked directly on me.

My heart nearly stopped.

It was the brujo I'd spoken with at the previous two fights, the one who had complimented me—and then questioned me. But there was no residue of his friendly smile today, not even an attempt at it. Now, he smirked across the room at me, and his glowing gaze was filled with shadows and hunger.

"I know him," I whispered. "He asked me why I wanted to be a bruja."

Coyote reached behind my back and took my hand. "He's definitely a real brujo, Cece. One from Devil's Alley." He glanced down at me. "Just look at his eyes. They're bright violet."

So I hadn't been imagining that. The color had really been there—and focused on me.

"But why would a real brujo be here at the Bruja Fights?" I asked. "He doesn't need to prove himself."

Across the distance, the brujo twitched two fingers. At first, I thought he was beckoning me, but then a boy came out from the shadows behind him and stood in full view.

The boy was obviously a criatura. He looked younger than me, maybe by a year or two, and had dusty white hair and tanned skin. Much lighter skin than mine, but obviously marked by the sun. I raised an eyebrow as I realized what I was seeing on his head. Ears—kit fox ears, oversized and adorable—perched on his crown. The brujo stroked the hair between them.

Coyote's jaw clenched.

"What now?" I whispered. "Do you know that criatura?"

"Not exactly." Coyote's hand tightened on mine. "I haven't met him in this life. But look at his ears—every time a criatura regrows, they get a bit weaker, right? Well, he looks around our age, but he still hasn't gotten the hang of transforming his ears away. That's not normal."

I caught on to what he was saying: the criatura's soul must be in pretty bad shape. Maybe even on its last lifetime. I met his warm, caramel eyes across the room.

"Why has his brujo brought him here?" I whispered. "He doesn't look like a fighter."

Coyote frowned. "He doesn't exactly get a choice."

The current fight ended, and El Silbón took his place in the ring again. The light swept over his black coat and boots. "Well, comadres and compadres, that was a great fight to start out our semifinal round. Now, it's time to see one of our come-from-behind favorites! Let's greet last night's interrupted fighter, Bruja Cece!"

I locked my knees so I wouldn't jump.

"And it looks like Cece's brought back the legendary Coyote! It's been a long time since I've seen an apprentice capable of carrying two criatura souls at the same time, so don't underestimate this one." El Silbón gestured at my neck. I tucked the two necklaces in my shirt.

El Silbón turned to the opposite corner to introduce the brujo and Kit Fox halfway across the mill. "And here, ready to face off against Cece and Coyote, we have a special guest."

El Silbón's voice echoed through the mill, suddenly harsh and dark, crisp and electric. Everyone turned to look at the pair. Kit Fox looked even more fragile, but the brujo's eyes flashed a bright, chilling purple. My pulse picked up. He really was from Devil's Alley.

So why was I fighting him?

This was supposed to be a contest for apprentices. In time to the beating drum, Coyote and I pressed our way through the horde of spectators. Their quick glances and churning murmurs focused on the brujo, who watched us as he and Kit Fox made their way to the ring. I swallowed. Why were they making me fight a real brujo? Was that normal for a semifinal round? Grimmer Mother had never mentioned this.

Around us, members of the crowd whispered to each other in deep, suspicious tones. They looked from me to my opponent. "That's never been done," I caught one saying. "Are they testing her?" asked another. "Is it because she can carry two criaturas?"

Coyote ducked his head to say, "I think the Dark Saints are onto you, Cece."

My blood grew cold. So this wasn't normal at all. And if it was true that the Dark Saints were suspicious, they must have sent this brujo to test me and see if I acted like a bruja. But how was I supposed to prove that to them?

"Some of you may not recognize our guest, so I'll give him the only introduction befitting someone of his station." El Silbón slipped an arm bone from his bag and used it to point to the brujo. "Criatura and Naked Man alike, look upon the third Dark Saint of Devil's Alley, Brujo Rodrigo, the Soul Stealer!"

I stopped half a foot from the ring's outer edge. My chest felt empty, like I'd accidentally left my heart behind. Brujo Rodrigo met my eyes, and his smirk widened, like he was happy that I finally knew exactly who he was.

Fear squeezed my throat. I was fighting a *Dark Saint* . . . ?

The thought threatened to turn me inside out. But I managed to raise my shaking finger and point forward. Obediently, Coyote stepped into the arena. He rolled his shoulders and scraped the dust with his bare toes. Kit Fox stared up at him, eyes wide, mouth separating in what could have been a gasp of horror.

He wasn't made for fighting. That much was obvious.

But I was supposed to beat him. My heart quickened as I look up at Brujo Rodrigo. A Dark Saint was here, in the apprentice Bruja Fights, and he'd brought the most inexperienced criatura I'd yet seen to fight? Surely he knew Coyote outmatched him. How was this a test?

Suddenly, Brujo Rodrigo pulled a necklace out of his shirt. He swung it back and forth between his fingers, making sure Coyote could see it. Coyote looked back at me and, slowly, held up eight fingers.

Eight scratches.

Kit Fox was one death away from the forever-last death.

Brujo Rodrigo lifted a single, taunting eyebrow and swung the damaged soul back and forth, back and forth. And then I knew what his test was: to see if I would kill Kit Fox—permanently.

Only then would the Dark Saints believe I was the bruja I claimed to be.

"And now . . ." El Silbón grinned as he leaped away from the circle. "Begin!"

21
The Fox Test

As expected of a Dark Saint, Brujo Rodrigo was faster than me.

Kit Fox sprang forward, looking dazed and confused, slashing his little claws. Coyote evaded easily. I gripped Coyote's soul in my hand, ready to fuel him with rage, when his emotional feedback hit me. Guilt, pain, sadness, fear—it combined with my own, and I cringed until my chest felt like it would burst.

Kit Fox tripped over himself trying to scratch Coyote. "What—are you—doing here?" he panted between swipes.

Coyote didn't answer. He just danced out of reach, never retaliating. He held Kit Fox's gaze as he dodged.

"Legend Brother," Kit Fox said, already out of breath. "What have they—done to you?"

My fingers trembled around Coyote's soul. The reverence and horror in Kit's eyes drowned out the thumping roars of the crowd. The legendary bringer of music, the Great Namer of Criaturas, and I was making him scrap in the dirt with the criaturas he'd created.

The moment the thought went through my mind, Coyote's eyes cut across the ring to meet mine. I knew he needed my fury. Without me blocking out the reality of it all, he couldn't bring himself to end Kit Fox.

But neither could I.

Sharp emotions twisted in my chest. I did my best to keep them from Coyote as I considered my options. If Brujo Rodrigo had organized this to test my resolve—then I had to pass it. For Juana.

I closed my eyes to block out the sight of Kit Fox's scratched soul and gripped Coyote's stone. Rage, heat, pain, fear—I sifted through them and settled on the picture of El Sombrerón in my head. Of his hand wrapped around my sister's waist. Of her voice screaming for me to run even though she was the one in danger.

Rage swelled up in my chest and into my fingers. Coyote let out a roar and punched Kit Fox clean in the face.

A snap echoed through the ring. My stomach twisted as Kit Fox stumbled backward, clutching his nose and mouth. Coyote winced.

But I couldn't lose my grip. Even if Kit Fox was on his last lifetime, Brujo Rodrigo was watching, and my sister needed me. That had to be more important, right? Mamá would say so.

Coyote looked away as his foot connected with Kit Fox's jaw, and the young criatura flew through the air. He rolled, streaked with dust, to the opposite end of the ring.

Brujo Rodrigo didn't even glance at Kit Fox as he landed on his side of the circle. The brujo's dark stare stayed pinned on my face. I could feel him cataloging every nervous glance, every emotion I struggled to keep from surfacing. He cocked his chin upward once, Kit Fox's soul swinging leisurely. In response, Kit Fox lumbered to his feet. Bruises already purpled his nose, but Brujo Rodrigo made him face me as Coyote backed him against the side of the ring.

Brujo Rodrigo didn't even make Kit Fox attack this time. He stared, waiting for me to deliver the final blow. Kit Fox threw his arms up around his head, shaking as Coyote loomed over him. Excited cheers rose from the crowd. People chanted my name. My guts tangled up, and just as Coyote readied another blow, I thrust a feeling into him:

No.

Coyote's hand froze as the word rolled through both of us. No. I couldn't—wouldn't—end this criatura. There had to be another way.

Brujo Rodrigo's eyes thinned to dark, amethyst slashes at Coyote's hesitation.

I looked at Kit Fox's soul, where it swung from Brujo Rodrigo's fingers, just within the boundary of the arena— and fed his soul a new target.

Immediately, he dove forward, claws extended. The spectators bellowed with anticipation. El Silbón leaned forward eagerly. As I had hoped, Coyote swerved just past Kit Fox, plunging his hand into the darkness at the edge of the ring.

His claw reached past the side of Kit Fox's head, toward Brujo Rodrigo, and cut the leather strap swaying between his fingers.

A single, rugged pebble fell into the ring.

The floor started to crumble. But Coyote snatched up the stone before it could return to the desert, turned with a flourish, and threw it to me.

I caught the soul and held it close. "I win."

Concrete silence. All eyes turned to me. Brujo Rodrigo's mouth tightened, but he said nothing. I knotted Kit Fox's leather necklace back together and placed it around my neck.

Kit Fox's soul lit up inside my chest like stray sunshine and a freshly caught breeze. I placed my hand over his soul. This criatura should never have been in the hands of a Dark Saint.

"Can you believe it, comadres and compadres, brujas and brujos, criaturas and humans—" El Silbón's arms shot into the air. "Cece Rios has just defied all expectations, stolen the Dark Saint's criatura—and won the match!"

A deafening cheer rocked the mill. The sound almost made me jump after the stony silence. Everyone, even El Silbón, was leaping, whistling, shouting, their faces awed and ravenous at the turn of events. Everyone except Brujo Rodrigo.

His expression remained cold, calculating. He lifted a single hand and snapped his fingers.

Out of nowhere, two criaturas descended around him. The moment their feet hit the floor, the applause died. Terror gripped the room. No one dared look away from the Dark Saint. Not me, not Kit Fox, not even Coyote.

Brujo Rodrigo's criaturas came into view. Criatura of the Gila Monster crouched directly in front of him, long claws already gouging out lines in the dusty floor. On his right hovered the Criatura of the Golden Eagle, his hair lined with telltale blond streaks and his talons twitching.

"Where did the cheers go? Everyone looks so frightened." Brujo Rodrigo scanned the silent attendees, but there was a satisfied glare in his question. "You haven't even seen the third one yet."

Third one? He had another criatura that wasn't with him? Brujo Rodrigo surged across the space between us. I locked my legs as he cut between Kit Fox and Coyote, his feet disrupting the chalk circle, his two criaturas following closely.

My breath faltered. I'd won the match by making his criatura incapable of fighting back, hadn't I? I'd followed the rules. But his face was all the anger of winter and the bite of hunger, and it sharpened with shadows as he closed in.

Just when I was about to cower, a hand touched my back, and Little Lion stepped up beside me, his face hard and ready. He must have felt my fear and come inside.

"What have you done, Cece?" he asked quietly.

I didn't have time to answer before Brujo Rodrigo stopped in front of me.

Behind him, his criaturas leaned forward, their eyes glinting. My gut clenched so hard I felt sick. Lion growled low in his throat. Brujo Rodrigo's hand whipped out of his pocket. I winced and closed my eyes. There was a beat of silence. Slowly, I peeked an eye open.

Brujo Rodrigo held out a single white card. My hands shook as I took it.

The end of the canyon in the cerros, at the southern edge
of Iztacpopo.
Just after sunset, when the moon is full.
The Binding waits.

"Congratulations, Bruja Cece," Brujo Rodrigo said, though there was no celebration in his voice. "You've made it to the finals."

I started to sweat as I read the card over again. This was what I'd been waiting for. But why did it feel like a threat? Brujo Rodrigo tapped the edge of the card, his smirk cold. Slowly, I turned it over to check the back.

See you soon, mija, was handwritten there.

Lion stiffened next to me, but I couldn't look away from the writing. I'd been reading it in a red leather journal for the past week. My stomach folded over itself. Brujo Rodrigo knew my Tía Catrina. What did that mean for me?

Brujo Rodrigo's lips pulled up in a slow, stiff smile as I lowered the invitation. Everyone was still watching us, but no one knew whether to cheer or not. In that uncomfortable silence, he put his hand on my shoulder, giving it a hard squeeze and then rocking it.

"We look forward to seeing you there tomorrow, Cecelia Rios." His lashes came down heavy on his eyes. "So be careful on your way home."

He released me, and he and his criaturas pushed past us for the exit. I couldn't move. Somehow, I wasn't dead. I'd won. And I'd even made it into the finals. So why did I feel like I was in more danger than ever?

Brujo Rodrigo and his criaturas disappeared through the front entrance. El Silbón stepped into the chalk circle.

"The third Dark Saint of Devil's Alley, everyone." His electric, scratchy voice didn't stir excitement from the crowd the way it had earlier. "Good luck, Cece Rios. Let's hope you handle the finals as well as tonight's match." He turned his shadowy face toward me, and everyone's gaze followed.

The warning wasn't lost on me. El Silbón served the Dark Saints. He'd probably been the one to tell them about me when I had first signed up, the little girl who looked out of place, the Rios chica whose sister had been stolen by El Sombrerón only a few days prior.

Lion stood on my left, and Kit Fox, staring at me with his mouth slightly ajar, stopped on my right. Coyote stood in front, and turned me around to face the exit.

"Let's get out of here, Cece," he said. "You're one of the five finalists. That's what matters."

The sounds of another fight starting up trailed behind us. Kit Fox kept glancing sideways at me as we headed for the exit. He'd looked so small in the ring with Coyote, but he was actually an inch taller than me. We stumbled out of the door into the fresh, sharp air of the cerros. Coyote offered his back.

"Here," he said. "I'll carry you home."

Wordlessly, I accepted the ride. Fear tailed us as Coyote carried me across the cerros. The dim lights of the mill faded behind us, and the tiny specks of Tierra del Sol's lights grew brighter as we made our way home. Little Lion and Kit Fox ran on either side of us. But even surrounded by my new friends, I couldn't help but think of the way Brujo Rodrigo had looked at me when he'd congratulated me. With barely contained anger. What would he have done if others hadn't been watching?

"What if this isn't really an invitation?" I asked, gripping the small card in my pocket, as Coyote jogged us toward Tierra del Sol. "What if it's a trap or something?"

Kit Fox came up beside us. "The invitation is real. I watched him write them all."

Well, that was a relief at least. I tried to smile at him through the darkness. "That's good to know. How's your nose, by the way?"

Kit barely had any eyebrows, but they climbed up his small forehead in surprise. "It'll be better by morning," he mumbled shyly.

That was comforting. I touched my hand to his soul. Now if only I could figure out why Brujo Rodrigo's last look still hung on me like icicles.

Lion rushed up on our right. "Do you hear that?"

Coyote slowed. I glanced behind us, but the scenery still moved too quickly at this speed for me to spy anything. Suddenly, all three criaturas stopped running. I nearly lurched over Coyote's shoulder.

"What is it?" I asked, coughing.

I couldn't see his face, but Coyote raised his nose and sniffed. His shoulders tensed beneath my hands.

Kit Fox bristled. "The third one."

Lion gestured wildly at us. "Get Cece out of here!"

Wait, what?

A lithe shadow sprung out of the darkness. I didn't have time to gasp. No time to scream. The dark figure swooped in from the left, taking out Little Lion and Kit Fox in a single tackle, and sending them sprawling into the desert. Coyote swung around, and that too-late scream finally came out my mouth.

"Hold on, Cece!" he yelled and soared into the sky.

His jump had us nearly flying over the desert. The wind scraped the tops of my bare ears and chilled my cheeks. Coyote's arms clenched my legs in place, and the edges of the Ruins came into view. I threw my head back to look behind us.

"Lion, Kit!" I called out.

There was no answer. But just as we started falling back toward the ground, a tall, dark figure appeared in the sky behind us.

I froze. The moonlight broke through the tattered clouds above and lit the criatura's face. It was long and sharp, with a strong nose, and yellow eyes that were bright as the sun. Long braids of black and gold hung around her head as she closed in on me. My stomach clenched into a dozen, suffocating knots. I recognized that hair.

Ocelot.

She twisted in midair and thrust her arm between Coyote's back and my stomach. I screamed. Coyote called out, but his words were distorted in the wind. In a simple, elegant move, she shoved us apart, gripped me tightly by the middle, and kicked Coyote down into the ground.

He plummeted hard, face-first, into the desert directly below us.

"Coyote!" I screamed as Ocelot flipped backward. The blood rushed to my head, and I had to squeeze my eyes closed to shut out the nauseating, tumbling scenery. Finally, we stopped. My head was swimming. When I opened my eyes, Ocelot held me by the front of my jacket, pinning my shoulders to the back wall of an abandoned house at the edge of the Ruins.

Ocelot looked down the bridge of her smooth, prominent nose at me. I trembled, searching for the ground with my toes, but there was nothing. She must have had me at least a foot off the ground. My mouth was too dry to speak. Ocelot was nothing like the criaturas we'd fought so far. She'd taken out Coyote, Little Lion, and Kit Fox in less than three moves, without getting a single scratch on her dark brown skin. She was older. She was wiser.

Coyote struggled to get up a distance away, gasping and

breathless. Lion and Kit were still nowhere to be seen. It was obvious she knew exactly how to take us down.

Ocelot's long brown fingers wrapped deeper in my jacket collar and hiked me farther up the wall, so I was level with her face.

"You may have beaten me at my own game tonight, but I know your name, your familia, and your sister, the Bride of El Sombrerón," she said. I stared at her in confusion. Beaten her at her own game? But I hadn't even fought her—no, wait. Her eyes caught the light, and they were unfocused, filmy. Like she wasn't awake. Was Brujo Rodrigo talking *through* her?

"The Dark Saints would have destroyed you before the first round was over if your tía hadn't persuaded us to wait and see what you would become," she continued with her master's message. "So here is your last warning, a gift Catrina's words have bought you: do not attend the finals tomorrow if you intend to rescue Juana Rios. The finals are for those who swear loyalty to the Dark Saints. If you come, we expect devotion. We demand your life."

She dropped me.

I bit my tongue when I landed. Hot, coppery blood spread through my mouth. She stepped back, gaze still glassy. I trembled as I took in all five feet, ten inches of her. Her plaits of gold and black hair swayed in the light rustle of wind.

When I finally dared to blink, she was suddenly, inexplicably, gone.

About ten feet away, Coyote had finally climbed to his feet. I ran over, still shaking, and offered him help as he straightened up. We held on to each other.

"Are you okay?" I whispered.

His mouth dropped open "Me? Cece—she nearly—if she'd wanted, she could have—" His voice cut off in a squeak.

I looked off into the desert, as if I might catch another glimpse of her. My knees were still knocking together. And I couldn't calm the tremors in my hand, even as I tried to comfort Coyote. But I knew she wasn't the one who threatened me. Ocelot was just a powerful pawn.

"Brujo Rodrigo's been using her to track me all this time," I whispered. "But Tía Catrina convinced him, El Sombrerón, and El Cucuy not to remove me from the competition." I wrapped my arms around myself. "And that was the Dark Saints' last warning. *My* last warning."

Coyote looked at the ground, his gaze darting back and forth in a frenzy. His soul boiled with heat, but it was gray through and through.

"What's wrong?" I asked.

He lifted his head, chin trembling. "I couldn't protect you, Cece. She—she really could have hurt you."

His soul's heat shuddered through me, and I reached out to try to calm it down. But as I did, his feelings retreated until his soul went cold.

"Hey, it's okay," I said.

"No, it's not," he said. He didn't meet my eyes.

Oh, Coyote. I reached out for him, hands still shaking.

Footsteps came up to us. Coyote and I turned to see Little Lion and Kit Fox approaching.

Lion frowned. "Well, we just got our butts kicked."

22
The Tale of the Great Namer

"I don't think I've ever been defeated that fast," Kit Fox mumbled. His nose was still purple from Coyote's blows earlier, but surprisingly, he didn't look too much worse for wear.

Lion rolled his eyes. "You're a baby fox, that's no surprise." He slapped his hands to his chest. "But I'm a *black lion*! And she—she wiped the floor with me. This is the most humiliating day of my life." He folded his arms and scowled at the three of us. "Let's just get home before another Dark Saint sends someone to kill us." His body blurred, and suddenly he was gone.

We watched him leap over the nearest building and disappear into the Ruins. I let out a strangled laugh. Leave it to Little Lion to be embarrassed that he'd gotten beaten up, not frightened that he could have died.

"Do you think it's safe to go back home?" I asked.

Kit tilted his head. "Brujo Rodrigo's already had Ocelot

spying on you at home for a while. It can't be more dangerous now than it was before."

Right. My guts churned. He could have taken me out
using Ocelot anytime he wanted. I pulled the invitation
out of my pocket and read over Tía Catrina's crimson writing again.

It was strange to think that the tía I'd never met had
somehow saved my life.

"You carry her back," Coyote spoke up, nudging Kit's
side. "Maybe you'll do a better job."

"Coyote?" I stuffed the card back in my pocket and
reached out for him.

He leaped away into the dark sky, and my hands hung
empty. I lost sight of him quickly. Kit Fox came up beside
me as I sighed.

"You're not mad at him?" he asked quietly.

I looked at him, bewildered. "What? Why would I be?"

"Well, he failed you."

"He didn't *fail* me," I snapped. Kit flinched, and I softened my voice. "Sorry. It's just—Ocelot is so much more
experienced. He couldn't help that." I frowned. "I guess
I'm just glad she didn't hurt any of you too much."

He tilted his head, like he wasn't sure what to make of
my response. "She was definitely holding back, but she can
only fight Brujo Rodrigo's control so much." His heavy

statement weighed down on me as he looked at me with a curious smile. "Ready to head to your home, bruja?" he asked.

"You can call me Cece," I said.

"Cece," he said, testing out the name. He nodded and offered his arms. I climbed into them. One of his ears bent sideways seconds before he sprang, and we were practically flying through the air.

His arms secured me against his chest, and I bounced but never fell free, even as he stepped onto boulders and walls, eventually finding roofs. We shot through town. The wind blew over my shaved head and against my skin until the stress and pain were swept away.

Kit was slower than Little Lion and Coyote, but after the wild chase we'd just been in, I was grateful for a calmer ride.

Eventually, my home came into view and Kit slipped in through my window shortly after Coyote and Lion. Inside my room, Coyote sat on the floor, in a corner by my bed, looking at his hands. The candlelight cast deep shadows across his dull frown. Lion sat a distance away, stacking a small pile of pillows.

The moment Kit let me down, Lion gave me a look. I wasn't exactly good at deciphering his not-angry expressions yet, but this one was pretty clear: *Can you talk to him?*

Quietly, I padded over and sat down beside Coyote. He looked up.

"You know tonight wasn't your fault, right?" I whispered.

Coyote's fingers tightened into fists. He dropped them into his lap. "Do you know why the four gods had to sacrifice themselves to create the physical sun, moon, land, and ocean we know today, Cece?"

Kind of a weird way to answer my question, but okay. "Because life couldn't begin until the world began, and the world couldn't begin until all the gods sacrificed themselves to bring it about."

He nodded. "When Mother Desert breathed life into me, the world hadn't begun yet. She wasn't supposed to have created me, but she was lonely and wanted company. That's why I had to stay hidden away in a cave. She was afraid the other gods would destroy me if they found me, so they wouldn't have to sacrifice themselves for the world to begin." He took a quiet breath. Little Lion and Kit Fox shuffled around, trying to act like they weren't listening in, but they glanced frequently in our direction. "Eventually, the Moon discovered me. She told Ocean, who comforted me when I was afraid. She convinced Mother Desert to tell Sun about me. And Sun was kind." His eyes softened as he spoke of the gods. "They each promised that they would do everything in their power to keep me happy and safe. So together with Mother Desert, they decided it was right for the world to begin. So that I could have a true life. That's when they sacrificed themselves. And they each left a creation to populate the world."

I wasn't sure where this was going, but I did love the creation story. So I nodded. "The Moon goddess made the stars, and Ocean goddess made the sea life. Desert goddess made you and the animals, and Sun god made us, Naked Man."

"Out of every creation the gods had made, I thought humans were the most—beautiful." Coyote's mismatched eyebrows tugged together, and he didn't meet my gaze. "They were beings like me. Not exactly like me, of course. But more like me than the gods or their other creations were. So I watched Naked Man from afar. I saw their struggles and ached for them. I—loved them."

My heart swelled with Coyote's feelings; warmth, but followed by something colder, darker.

"Before Mother Desert sacrificed herself, she gave me her voice, the power to create—she made me the Great Namer." He lifted his head slowly and looked at me. "And once she was gone, I was all alone. I loved humans so much that I—I wanted what they had, too. I wanted a familia." He pressed his lips together. "That's when I Named the criaturas. I modeled them after humans, but gave them teeth and claws like Mother Desert's animals, so when hard times came, they could protect themselves. I called them my brothers and sisters. They were the familia I'd always wanted."

The floor creaked. I glanced over my shoulder. Lion and Kit sat by makeshift beds, their stares focused on their Legend Brother in silent salute.

"But one day, Naked Man came across us. I was excited to become friends, so when they arrived, I welcomed them into our camp. But Naked Man was afraid." Coyote's voice reverberated against the stone walls, and the candles on my desk shivered as if in remembrance. "And they slaughtered my familia."

His soul's colors evaporated into blankness. Nothing painful, nothing joyous. Just numb. My heart ached for him.

That wasn't the way our legends went at all. I wondered, silently, what other history we'd rewritten.

"Because of me, each criatura soul bears a scar. And no matter how much time passes, a part of them remembers that they were killed because of my love for Naked Man." His Adam's apple jogged. "I can never seem to protect anyone I care about."

My room grew quiet as Kit, Lion, and I stared at Coyote. I reached hesitantly for his hand, but he stood and cleared his throat. "Anyway. We should get to bed. The finals are tomorrow."

"Coyote, wait—" I started.

Footsteps echoed below. All of us looked at the floor. I froze, surrounded by my friends' makeshift beds, jerky crumbs, and dirty footprints.

"Out, out!" I whisper-shouted, waving wildly.

In a blur, the three of them dove for my window. Kit was nearly too slow, but Coyote snatched him by the collar and pulled him out right before Papá lifted the hatch.

Then it was just me and Papá's weary, glowering gaze.

"Hola, Papá," I whispered. "Perdón, ¿te desperté?"

His heavy eyebrows crushed downward. I winced. He took another step up, so his arms were above the floor, and grabbed my wrist. I froze.

"After all I do to put you through school, you waste your time, make a mess, and wake me up in the middle of the night? Do you know how early I have to get up? Are you ever grateful?" He threw my arm back at me, so I nearly fell backward.

I scrambled up from the floor. I almost retreated to the far part of the room, but at the last second, something stopped me. I'd stood my ground against one of the Dark Saints tonight. I'd survived a confrontation with Ocelot. I should be able to stand up to my papá too.

Normally, I would've just shrunk back and continued to let him yell. But for the first time, I lifted my head and spoke back: "I *am* grateful for what you do, even if you don't think I am." He scoffed. I clenched my fists. "I didn't wake you up on *purpose*—"

"Enough," he spat. "Enough, Cece." He clenched his jaw, and water rose in his eyes.

This time, I did take a step back. I'd never seen Papá cry—not even the night Juana was taken.

"If only El Sombrerón had taken *you*," he hissed. "Instead, he left us with the child cursed by Tzitzimitl."

Silence suffocated the room.

My already sore throat tightened again. Deep down, I'd been waiting for him to say it. A part of me had known that he'd wanted to all along.

He held a hand up. "Go to sleep, water child. You wake me up again, and I will show you how hard a papá is meant to be . . ."

The hatch door cut off anything else he might've said.

There was nothing left to do but blow out the candles. In the darkness, I curled up in my bed, silent, as Coyote and the others crept back inside like shadows. I tucked my face under my blanket and concentrated on keeping the stirring pain in my soul out of Coyote's, Lion's, and Kit's.

The three of them went to bed silently. But as tears

finally slid down my cheeks and spotted my mattress, the pitter-patter of water rang off the roofs outside.

"Rain?" Lion whispered. "In winter?"

Coyote's voice was soft and low: "I've never seen it rain in Tierra del Sol at this time of year."

The small nocturnal storm waged on and lulled my friends to sleep. With time, the rumble of thunder lessened. The downpour slowed to a drizzle. Slowly, the quiet and the coolness eased open the knot of my hurt feelings.

Let Papá think whatever he wanted about me. Dominga del Sol believed in me. So did Coyote, and Lion, and Kit.

And I would cling to the hope that they were right.

Kit Fox and I were the first to wake up after Mamá and Papá left for the day.

"Keep still," I whispered, dipping my rag back into a small bowl of water.

Kit Fox ceased his restless shifting. I took the wet corner of my cloth and scraped at the trail of blood that had dried from his nose to the turn of his chin. I'd gotten his nose clean already, and now I was washing his mouth.

The early morning brightness streamed in through my window. It made it hard to see, especially when staring at Kit Fox. His hair and ears were so light that when the sun hit them, they were blinding.

Finally, I managed to get his face clean. "Does that feel better?" I asked.

"Yes," he said. "Thank you, Bruja Cece."

"Just Cece," I said. "And is your nose all better?"

"It healed overnight," he said.

I sat back, rag in hand, and perused his face. He smiled, brown eyes lit by the morning, hair shimmering like strings of sunshine pinned to the earth. He looked so content and small. It made me glad we'd gotten him away from Brujo Rodrigo.

"How old are you?" I asked.

Kit raised his eyebrows. "This lifetime or all together?"

"Oh. Um, this lifetime I guess."

"About eleven years old."

I smiled a little at his molasses-sweet face. That seemed about right. "I guess that means I'm not the youngest out of my friends anymore. I'm twelve—almost thirteen."

His thin eyebrows tugged together hard, just for a second. The look disappeared quickly, but I leaned forward.

"What?" I asked.

He bowed his head and shook it. His ears flapped a little. "It's nothing."

I folded the rag and placed it on the floor. "You can tell me, Kit. I—I know you probably weren't treated very well in Devil's Alley, but you're safe here."

"You called me your . . . friend." He lifted his head. His gaze bore into mine, sudden as the intense splash of flavor you get when biting into a caramel candy. "I don't understand. Brujas don't *make* friends with criaturas."

Oh. Of course I seemed suspicious to him. The same way

Lion hadn't trusted me until he knew why I was doing this.

"Well," I started. "I should probably tell you—I'm not really a bruja."

Kit gasped. "So, it's true!" Well, that made me feel self-conscious. "Brujo Rodrigo said he thought you might be pretending, so you could go after the Bride of El Sombrerón."

I'd almost forgotten that he'd been living in Devil's Alley until last night. I straightened up, beaming. "Have you seen Juana? Is she okay? Where do they keep her—"

"I don't know." Kit shook his head. "I'd just heard whispers of her coming to live in El Cucuy's castle. That's all."

My throat tightened. Oh. Right. My chest ached with unanswered questions and fragile hopes. I just wanted to know she was okay. I wanted to see her again and run to her. I wanted to bring her home so she could be safe and happy.

When I looked up, tears traced down Kit Fox's cheeks.

"Sorry," I burst out and wiped my running nose. "I'll try to pull my feelings back, give me a second." I started to rein the emotions in, but Kit's hand touched mine before I could get anywhere.

"Don't," he whispered. "I want to understand. I want to believe you."

He was so sweet, the tears burning my eyes dropped

onto my cheeks. Most people told me not to cry. No one had ever offered to cry with me before. I laughed even though my throat was knotted.

"Thank you," I said.

"You love her a lot. How can you bear it?" More tears gathered on his eyelashes.

"Sometimes . . . I can't," I whispered. "I think about how scared she must be. And I feel like I'm turning inside out because it's my fault she's gone." I gripped the front of my shirt, chin quivering. "But that's why I have to win the Bruja Fights, so we can enter Devil's Alley, and I can rescue her."

Kit Fox stared at me.

"So, I guess love isn't easy to bear. But that's why it's also worth it." I wiped my cheeks clean. "She's my sister. And I miss her this deeply because I've loved her that intensely."

I brushed his cheeks dry, and he smiled.

"You really aren't a bruja," he said quietly, with certainty. "You give power instead of taking it. I guess that makes you more of a curandera."

"You think so?" Curanderas kept coming up, but each time, they felt more important. Now, even just hearing the word sent a comforting ripple through me, and my skin prickled. "Have you ever met any curanderas? In your past lives?"

"Probably. But each time I regrow, it's harder to remember my old lives. And curanderas haven't been around in over two hundred years, so I don't have any solid memories of them." He shrugged.

"Yeah, I guess that makes sense. It's just—everyone in town thinks they were weak because they let Tierra del Sol fall into ruin. But a friend of my abuela's, Dominga del Sol, talks about them like they were really important. I just wish I knew what they did. Or maybe what they didn't do." I put my chin in my hands.

"Well, I may not remember any one of them specifically, but I can tell you what their powers were." He leaned toward me. "Each curandera had a special bond with one of the four creation gods. *That's* what made them curanderas."

Well, that didn't sound like me—I was supposed to be a daughter of the Sun god, but I couldn't even make a fire opal glow. My mind floated back to the Sun Sanctuary, at his mosaic looking so warm and tender. But I found myself recalling the turquoise that made up the Ocean goddess's outstretched hands and the way it had glowed with peaceful blue light.

"If you really want answers, you should go to the curanderas' sanctuary." Kit Fox stretched his back.

"There's a curanderas' sanctuary?"

"Sure." He paused his stretching to eye me. "There are actually four, but only one of them's in Tierra del Sol."

There was one here? I gasped and plastered my hands to either side of my face. I'd grown up here all my life, and I'd never known there was a curanderas' sanctuary! My chest tingled with excitement. Where was it? Hidden in the Ruins, maybe?

I stood up. "Can you tell me how to get there?"

An annoyed grumble stirred to our right. We turned as Little Lion sat up, his black hair sticking straight up. He glared at me with one open, still-sleepy eye, frowning.

"Do you have to shout so early?" he mumbled.

"Sorry, Lion." I stooped down and grabbed my bag. "I'm going to head out for a bit, okay?" I turned to Kit Fox. "Do you know how to draw a map?"

Little Lion scrambled to his feet. "Wait, hold on. Where are you going?"

"Kit says there's a curanderas' sanctuary in Tierra del Sol!" I grinned.

Lion folded his arms and glared briefly at Kit. "And you think it's a good idea to just head out there, alone, when Ocelot attacked you last night?"

I pouted. "I mean, when you say it like that . . ."

Lion rubbed the side of his face. "Ugh. Let's just wake up Coyote. With the three of us together, you stand a better chance."

"Wait, but what if people see you?" I asked.

Little Lion ignored me and rolled over to Coyote's blankets, which were piled up next to him. I crossed the room, ready to argue a bit more, as Lion stripped the covers back.

But there was no one there.

We stared down at the spare pillows and blankets that had been stuffed there to make it look like Coyote was sleeping. Little Lion leaned back, confused. Kit Fox peeked around my shoulder.

"He's gone," Lion said.

My pulse quickened in my ears. Lion rubbed his forehead. Why would Coyote leave without telling me? Slowly, I took his soul in my hand, but it was cool to the touch like any rock from the desert. There was no quiet rhythm like a heartbeat. No colors—no pink, not even gray. It was like his soul was gone too.

"I can't feel him," I whispered. Lion's and Kit's worried faces turned to me. "Do you think he's hurt? What if he's—he's—"

"You'd know if he were dead," Lion said. "He's probably just pulling his feelings back from you. Maybe he's worried about something and wants to be alone."

"What could worry him enough to make him leave?" I bit my lip. Was it the finals? Brujo Rodrigo? Both? I was definitely nervous, but Coyote was more than capable in a fight.

Kit placed a hand on my shoulder. "Cece—you were in danger last night, remember? And he couldn't protect you."

I rounded on him. "That wasn't his fault!"

"You heard him. He thinks it is," Lion added.

I paused and pictured his face the previous evening, and the way his soul had twisted with so many tormented colors.

Lion's expression softened as he walked up to me. "Cece, remember what he said? Coyote couldn't protect us all those thousands of years ago." He tapped his soul through my shirt. I pulled it out, and his soul's scars rotated into view. Oh. I looked up and met their gazes. Lion sighed. "I think he hoped he could change that with you. And he probably thinks he's let you down."

"But—but he hasn't," I said. "How do I find him so I can tell him that?"

Little Lion ran a hand back through his hair in aggravation. "I don't know—you're the bruja."

I let my arms fall to my sides. I was the bruja. I was Coyote's friend. I should know where he'd run off to, shouldn't I?

Wait a second—I was the bruja!

I wrapped my hand around Coyote's soul. The quietness of it still made me shiver, but I closed my eyes and tried to feel for him. I'd pulled back my feelings from Coyote before, and he'd done the same with me. But if I could press ideas and feelings into him during battles, couldn't I do it now, too?

I summoned all my worry and let it slip into Coyote's soul. *Where are you?* I tried to ask using memories of when I first met him, of losing Juana in a crowd once and looking for her. *Are you okay?*

At first, his soul felt as cold and calm as the desert at night. Then, short flashes of images resonated from it through my mind. A brilliant mosaic with all the most precious stones. Candles set nearby. Carefully washed stained glass windows. Tiled floor. Quiet and peace.

I opened my eyes. "The Sun Sanctuary?"

Why would he go there of all places? He was born of Mother Desert, not the Sun god. What significance would it hold for him? I nibbled on my bottom lip. Well, whatever the reason, I had to go find him. He was out in broad daylight, and especially if he was in the Sun Sanctuary, he was bound to get caught.

"I'm going to go get him!" I dropped my bag and headed toward the hatch. Lion and Kit fell in beside me, but I stopped them. "Hang on, you two aren't coming with me."

The two of them opened their mouths to argue.

"Lion, your eyes are bright red. And Kit, you have giant fox ears on your head. You both *look* like criaturas. You can't come with me."

They pouted in unison.

"It's bad enough that Coyote is out there somewhere, possibly getting discovered. I don't want something bad to happen to either of you as well." I tried to soften my worried tone and smiled. "I'll be back soon. And if I do get into any trouble, I know we'll work it out—together."

Lion sighed and folded his arms. "Just—be careful, Cece. And call for us if you need help."

Kit smiled. "We'll be there for you."

24
The Will of Cecelia Rios

When I arrived at the Sun Sanctuary, Dominga del Sol stood at the front entrance, ready to welcome visitors. She smiled as I padded up the steps.

"Are you here for your friend?" she asked.

I stiffened. "Um—what do you mean? I don't really have—"

"Coyote." Her smile spread wider as I tried not to have a heart attack. "He came before the sun rose, so I let him in. The Great Namer hasn't been seen in Tierra del Sol for a very long time. I had a feeling if anyone was responsible for his return, it would be you." She stroked the stubble on my head.

I stared up at her. "But how did you—" I glanced at the closed doors. "So he *is* here. And you're not going to tell anyone else?"

"Of course not." She winked and pushed the entrance open. "The Great Namer has always been a friend to Naked

Man when we have been a friend to him. And young and lost as he is now"—she turned to face inside—"it looks like he's sorely in need of one."

I ducked beneath Dominga del Sol's arm and stepped indoors. The sanctuary was quiet. No one was here yet, not even other priestesses. Just a small figure on the other side of the room, standing in front of the mosaic, his head inclined back to take it in.

At first, I didn't recognize Coyote. He was wearing a wide, straw hat that covered his multicolored hair and a bright red poncho over his usual shirt. Wait—those were my papá's clothes. Coyote must have taken them off the drying line this morning. I came up beside him, and despite the disguise, his gold eyes were as obvious as ever. The tension in my chest eased.

"Coyote?" I said.

He didn't look at me. His gaze traveled over Mother Desert's image. Her eyes were closed, her mouth open, her arms stretched up to touch the world and all its creatures. A coyote slept closest to her, nestled in the ends of her long black hair.

"Do you know what I'm most scared of, Cece?" he asked.

"I'm guessing it's *not* giving me a heart attack when you suddenly disappeared." I pouted. "Because you nearly did."

His face fell. "Sorry. I just . . ."

I glanced behind us. Dominga del Sol had shut the front door and stood lighting candles beneath the farthest stained glass window. Coyote was lucky it was her he'd run into this morning. At least it meant we were safe for now.

I turned back to face his question. "What are you most scared of?"

He took a breath. "I'm scared of . . . disappointing her."

We both looked at Mother Desert's depiction. Her deep brown skin, her soft smile.

I glanced at Coyote. "Why would she be disappointed in you?"

"Because she gave me her voice," he said. "She trusted me with her power to create. And what did I do with it?"

I waved up to all the animal criaturas in the mosaic. "You made the criaturas. Like Lion, and Kit—"

"Yeah," he interrupted. His chest suddenly rose and fell faster. "Like Little Lion, and Kit Fox, and La Llorona, and—" He stopped and looked at me, unshed tears hanging on his lashes. "And El Sombrerón."

Oh. I stared, wordless.

"Juana being taken was never your fault, Cece." He looked down at his hands, and I realized they were shaking. "It's all *my* fault."

His soul drowned in deep, cold gray and chilled my

ribs. I shuddered. This is where it came from, then. This is where his soul was stuck battling.

"Is that the real reason you agreed to help me?" I asked. "Because you feel bad about creating the dark criaturas? I understand why you made them. You were just trying to protect animal criaturas from humans—"

He pressed his hands over his face. "I didn't make dark criaturas *just* for that. I was angry. I think I—*wanted* to hurt Naked Man. To make them suffer the way they and their brujas made my familia suffer." He bowed his head, still speaking through his fingers. "And the worst part is that I don't even know why I thought that was a good idea. If anything, it just made things . . . worse. Just like Devil's Alley. Just like everything I ever did."

I thought of the cycle I'd pictured a while back, with criaturas, brujas, and Naked Man all hurting each other.

Something needed to enter that circle and disrupt it. Then, no one else had to end up like Juana. Then, no one else had to carry the pain Coyote, and Lion, and Kit did in their hearts.

"You hate me now, don't you?" Coyote's voice cracked. "But I just want you to know that—that I'm sorry. I thought I could fix everything if I could protect you and help you get your sister back. But—but just like always, I couldn't protect you. I couldn't even stop Ocelot. I'm just going to fail you like I have everyone else." A fresh wave of tears hung on his dark lashes.

I looked up at him. "I don't hate you, Coyote."

To have made a creature like El Sombrerón, he must have been so incredibly angry, so full of rage. And he was right—what he'd made those creatures to do wasn't okay.

But I'd already learned that when people are in pain, they do terrible things to try to bandage their broken hearts. Like Papá and his drinking. Like Tía Catrina and her desire for power.

"Making the dark criaturas was definitely a mistake," I said. He rubbed his teary eyes. "It did make things worse. But Coyote, you've been trying to make up for it." I smiled up at him. "I forgive you. You don't need to feel guilty anymore."

The pink in his soul started to trickle back. The sun flashed through the nearest stained glass window and sent rainbows over his cheeks, the rays dancing over his straw hat.

"And I guess you have just as much reason to get my sister back as I do, huh?" I extended my hand. "What do you say? Let's make up for our mistakes together. For Juana?"

Slowly, his shoulders relaxed. The pink swelled, and the gray and navy blue in his soul bled away. The warmth rose back in his soul stone and reached out to touch my own.

"For Juana." He slipped his hand into mine.

We shared that solace for all of a minute before a deep pang rang through Kit Fox's soul at my throat.

I touched the stone. Coyote dropped his hand. "What's wrong?"

I let out a slow, shaking breath. There was a distant, muffled sensation ringing through his small pebble. I didn't know his soul too well yet, but it buzzed with something yellow—almost like panic.

I looked up. "I think Kit is in trouble."

His face hardened. "Let's go."

Coyote and I landed in front of my house soundlessly. I looked up at it. Kit Fox's soul stone still throbbed with frightened yellow, but it didn't feel as urgent. Was he okay?

Coyote's ear twitched. "I think I hear him and someone else downstairs."

That couldn't be good. I slid off his back. "You should go upstairs, before anyone sees you." My street wasn't exactly a busy one, but we'd already risked a lot traveling here in broad daylight.

"Are you sure?" Coyote asked as I approached the front door.

I took the doorknob in hand and smiled at him. "Yeah. I'll let you know if I need help."

He hesitated. A distant figure turned onto the street, so far away they were the size of an ant. I pointed urgently. With a short sigh, Coyote sprang into the air and disappeared into my room.

I turned back to the door. My hands were shaking a bit. I had a bad feeling about what waited on the other side, but there was only one thing left to do.

I pushed the door open and walked inside.

Mamá stood in the living room, holding Kit Fox by the scruff of his ragged blue shirt.

"You have to tell me sooner or later," she yelled, shaking him slightly. Kit's fluffy ears twisted back against his head. He cringed. "Why are you here? Where is your soul?" She shook again, and he let out a short yip. "Were you trying to hurt my daughter? Who sent you?"

I gaped, and the door clicked shut behind me. Mamá looked up.

"Cece, you're safe!" Her mouth upturned with relief before she rounded a burning look down at Kit, who flinched again. "I found this criatura in your room, and I thought you were taken." She tightened her grip on his collar. "Now, I can turn him in without worrying."

"Mamá, no! Let him go! Please!"

Mamá jerked up her chin. I froze under the intense heat of her gaze. For a moment, I was seven again, begging for

Tzitzimitl to be set free. And Mamá's disappointment, her anger, her fear—it was just as palpable now as it had been then.

I swallowed hard. Kit Fox looked at me across the room, gripping his shirt so the collar wouldn't choke him. He was strong enough to hurt Mamá, but he hadn't. He hadn't even fought to get away. He trusted me. Slowly, I straightened up. Faced Mamá. And stepped forward.

Her eyebrows tugged together. I knew it was time. There were no lies that could untangle all the others, no words that would salvage this, except the truth. I grabbed Kit's, Lion's, and Coyote's soul necklaces and pulled them out of my shirt.

Mamá's eyes widened in horror.

"I'm a bruja, Mamá," I whispered, small and waiting.

Her fingers fell open. Kit stumbled toward me, and I opened my arms to him. He came and snuggled into my side, his right ear flopping against my head.

"Cecelia," she whispered. "No. Not you too."

"It's not what you think," I rushed on. "I'm doing this to get Juana back, I promise!"

She reared up, and even though she was only a few inches taller, I shrank from her. Kit slid behind me, and I blocked him from her view. "Do you think that calling down the wrath of the Desert goddess will bring your sister back?" she boomed. "Do you think that these criaturas have power that can fill the hole she's left behind? They cannot!"

"No, Mamá. I'm not like Tía Catrina! I don't want what she wanted." I gulped down air, stepping slowly, shakily toward her. She stiffened, looking down on me without a word. "The Bruja Finals are tonight, and I have to win if I want to get Juana back." I reached out my hands, even though I wasn't sure she would take them. "I'm not afraid anymore, Mamá. I will fight for my sister, and I will bring her home. Then, our familia won't be so broken."

I stopped in front of her. At some point in my speech, her chin had started quivering. Slowly, her hands reached out for mine. Inches before they touched my skin, she flinched back.

"The curse," she said, and there was no more anger in her voice. Her hands shook and dove into her thick hair. She pulled at the strands, face crumpling. "It has drowned the flames of your soul. Oh, my little girl, my daughter, they have taken you *too*."

"That's not it!" I said, voice high. "It was a blessing, Mamá, not a curse—"

Footsteps sounded behind me. I turned around. Kit scampered back, toward me, as Papá filled the doorway. I locked my knees. He was mostly shadow, his face blocked out by the lowering sun behind him. He stepped forward, stare darting from Kit Fox, to me and my necklaces, to Mamá's broken expression. His heavy stare veered back and landed again on me.

"Papá," I whispered.

He crossed the room in three wide steps and slapped me across the face.

I hit the ground with a spin and landed on my back. The air disappeared from my lungs. Kit ran to my side. Papá bore down on me, his hand still extended. Kit wrapped himself around me, but through his hair, I saw Papá's flared nostrils and heavy, raging chest. I trembled. For all of his mistakes, he'd never hit me before.

"Miguel!" Mamá cried.

"She is a *bruja*!" Papá's teeth gritted. "I will not allow her to humiliate our familia—"

Wind suddenly rushed over Kit and me. Kit pulled back and helped me sit. My face stung, and I was sure it would be as purple as dusk by tomorrow. When I finally straightened upright, Little Lion stood between me and Papá. And Coyote had Papá by the wrist.

His growl rumbled through the air. "If you ever hurt her again I won't hesitate to *break—your—arm*." He twisted my father's arm until his face filled with pain.

"Coyote!" I yelled. "Don't. Please."

Coyote stood over him, taller and younger, stronger and more protective of me than my papá had ever been. Mamá leaped forward between Coyote and my father. Her body was wide and stout, and she shoved both of them back, away from each other.

She turned a glare on Coyote. "Do not touch my familia, criatura." She rounded on Papá as he caught his footing. "And you—I have forgiven your many sins against me, but I will not forgive your hand against my daughter's face."

I froze as she spun to face me. "And you, you are confused, Cece. Tzitzimitl's curse has made your mind weak and trusting." Her breath shook. "Please. I cannot lose you too." Her eyes melted into warm brown pools.

I stood with Kit and Lion's help, my face and heart aching, watching my mamá shatter slowly in front of me. I knew she didn't want to lose me. I knew I probably seemed selfish. But still, I shook my head.

"I've got to go," I whispered. "Adiós. And if I never see you again—I love you." I smiled at Mamá. Then I turned a hard frown on Papá. He nursed the wrist Coyote had twisted, his face torn between a glare and a look of panic. "I even love you, Papá." A knot formed in my throat. "And I forgive you. That doesn't mean what you've done is okay. It doesn't mean *anything* you've done is okay." I touched my cheek. "But it does mean that I hope you'll change, and even if you don't—I'm going to be okay. I can be okay. The rest is up to you, Papá."

Despite my brave speech, I wasn't really sure I was ready to forgive him yet. My eye was already starting to close up. But if anything did happen to me while rescuing Juana, I didn't want to die hating him. I didn't want to be captive to him like that.

I wanted to be free to love him. He didn't have to be right, or have power over my life, for me to do that. So I'd work on forgiving him—just far from where he could hurt me.

I turned away from my parents. Coyote, Lion, and Kit looked at me, their soul stones pulsing with sadness. Were they—sympathizing with me? I smiled a little to give us all courage. Coyote leaned down so I could wrap my arms around his shoulders.

"Let's go, Coyote," I whispered.

The three of us left my home in a rush. A quiet, lonely place in my heart wondered if it would be for the last time.

The wind's chill soothed my swelling face. The sun was a heavy orange orb now, turning hot pink as it touched the edge of the horizon. Houses streaked into small, distant caricatures as Coyote carried me away, dancing across the roofs, whisking me into the afternoon.

Kit ran up on our right side. "I'm sorry, Cece," he said,

just loud enough so I could hear him. "I heard your mamá coming and tried to run, but I wasn't as fast as Little Lion."

Lion swooped up on our left. "Don't be too mad at him." He stared off into the cerros, where we were headed. "I should've grabbed him when I left." He pouted. "Instead I had to wait outside the kitchen window to make sure he was okay, since I was pretty sure you didn't want me to beat up your mamá."

"Yeah, good call. I definitely didn't want that," I said with a small smile. The wind quickly brushed it away. "And I'm not angry. This . . . had to happen eventually."

Coyote's grip tightened on my legs. I rested my head against his shoulder. It was an effortless ride in his arms. The safest I'd felt in a long time.

25
The Sign of the Binding

By the time we reached the cerros, the day had gone, and clouds had blocked out most of the night sky. They hung low overhead as we approached the spot Brujo Rodrigo's invitation described. I pulled the card out of my pocket as Coyote and I closed in on a tall pile of boulders at the entrance to the canyon. The volcano, Iztacpopo, cast a sharp shadow over us.

Coyote, Lion, Kit, and I stopped at the rock outcropping. We were the only ones there.

I looked at my invitation again. "Maybe . . . we got the wrong spot?"

"No." Coyote looked up to the other side of the gorge. "We didn't."

The canyon expanded like a gaping mouth before us. The rugged path between the hulking slabs of rock inclined up sharply to the base of Iztacpopo—and at the top, two shadowy figures watched us.

Brujo Rodrigo and El Silbón.

They both stared down the path at me. I tried to swallow my fear, but my mouth was so dry, I nearly choked on it instead.

"Tonight's the final round of the Bruja Fights!" El Silbón crowed across the distance. His voice had the same grainy, electrical quality, even out here in the open. "And finally, our last contestant has arrived. Will she be able to prove to the Dark Saints that she is worthy to enter the kingdom of El Cucuy?" He traced the brim of his hat. The bones in his bag rattled against each other and echoed through the canyon. "This criatura will be waiting in Devil's Alley to see."

El Silbón turned and faded away into the desert's darkness. Panic crawled up my back. Everything about this felt different from what I'd expected.

I blinked, and the moment I opened my eyes again, Brujo Rodrigo stood before me. I stumbled back. Coyote grabbed my hand to steady me. I straightened up and met Brujo Rodrigo's purple-black stare. He said nothing as he looked down his nose at the four of us.

"Where are the other finalists?" I asked.

"They've already come and gone by now," he said. "You, Cecelia Rios, are the last to be tested. We'll see if you'll join the other four winners in Devil's Alley tonight."

"But I thought I was going to face off against them."

His lips twisted up on one side. "No. You've already proven your power—you're here to prove something else."

"Prove . . . what?" My knees shook.

"Above all else, Cecelia Rios, a bruja must be loyal to El Cucuy and his Dark Saints." He smiled. I almost stopped breathing. "You've made it to this final round because your tía vouched for you. But today, her word will no longer be enough. Today, you must prove that you are a bruja worthy of entering Devil's Alley—or face the wrath of the Dark Saints."

I struggled to keep my fear from flowing into my friends' souls. "So I have to prove my loyalty?" I finally found my voice. "How do I do that?"

His smirk widened. "For your final test, Cecelia Rios, you will take the Mark of the Binding. If you're successful, you'll be allowed to enter Devil's Alley. And if you fail, the Mark of the Binding will reduce you to ash."

He spread his arms. His three criaturas dropped around him, first Ocelot, then Gila Monster, then Golden Eagle. Coyote and I jumped back, and Kit and Lion stepped up on either side of us to form a united front. My friends each glared at one of the criaturas. Brujo Rodrigo's gaze narrowed on me.

"Are you ready to begin your last test, Cecelia Rios?" he asked.

I'd been lying a lot lately. But saying yes might have been my biggest lie yet.

Brujo Rodrigo's smile tightened. Carefully, he and his criaturas stepped to the side.

Out of the darkness cast by the stones behind him, a creature rose. It towered high above my head, straightening out to loom over and consume me in its shadow. My heart froze. The hulking, terrifying being stepped forward. El Sombrerón finally stood above us all.

His presence swallowed any moonlight foolish enough to shine through the clouds above. My breath died on my tongue. He was here. Colors flashed through my chest—all of my criaturas' emotions and my own—in a messy cloud of confusion and fear. He was part of the final test?

Brujo Rodrigo stood next to him. I'd thought he was tall, but the top of his head barely reached El Sombrerón's shoulder.

"Kneel before El Sombrerón," he said.

At first, I couldn't move at all. Brujo Rodrigo's face hardened. I quickly forced my knees to kneel in the dirt before the two of them. Coyote frowned, but he, Kit, and Lion followed suit. El Sombrerón tilted his head. His face was impossible to see, but I could tell he was watching me closely.

He extended a finger toward me. I held my breath. Every instinct inside me said to run. But I didn't. The finger came to hover over my forehead. It twitched, and a claw extended from the shadows into sharp clarity.

"For you to become a true bruja who can enter Devil's Alley, you must repeat after me the vow of the Binding," Brujo Rodrigo said.

My breaths came faster now. But it was hard to calm down with El Sombrerón's claw leveled between my eyes.

"Today, I leave behind who I am for who the Dark Saints want me to be," Brujo Rodrigo recited. "I will shed my familia's name. Tierra del Sol will no longer be my home. I will obey the laws of the Dark Saints above all others."

I hated everything about this vow. But if I didn't say it—who would save Juana?

"T-today," I started, "I leave behind who I am for who the Dark Saints want me to be. I will shed my familia's name. Tierra del Sol will no longer be my home. I will obey the laws of the Dark Saints above all others."

El Sombrerón's red gaze caught the moonlight as he extended his claw to my skin. I closed my eyes. His nail pierced the skin on my forehead, and the pain made me hiss.

Brujo Rodrigo continued: "I, and my soul, and the souls of any criatura I own, will belong to the Dark Saints from this point on until the day I perish. I, Cecelia Rios, abandon my old name to the one now given me by El

Cucuy and his Dark Saints—Cecelia of Three Souls."

Tears welled up in my eyes until I could feel the water in my soul, always so much stronger than the fire I was supposed to have been born with. I hated this. They couldn't own me. They couldn't own my friends!

"I—I—" My mouth wouldn't form the words.

El Sombrerón began to draw a line down my forehead. He waited halfway, for me to finish the oath. But I couldn't. I wouldn't.

The criatura who had stolen my sister was right here—what was I waiting for?

I shoved his hand away. Before his nail even left my skin, the pain vanished. El Sombrerón jerked backward. Brujo Rodrigo stared at me, mouth open.

Were they really that surprised?

"What?" I asked.

"Cece," Coyote said. "You're—glowing."

I looked down at myself. Blue light shone from my deep brown skin and glowed from my nails and veins. I placed a hand to my forehead. The wound El Sombrerón had just carved on me was completely gone.

Brujo Rodrigo glared. "What is this?"

El Sombrerón pulled his silver guitar forward. "The Binding knows when someone is lying. She's a fraud."

"But no one's ever *glowed* like that before," Brujo

Rodrigo spat. "And the mark didn't make her burst into flame like the other failures. The wound just healed!"

I stood on shaky legs. The blue light soaked deeper into my skin, reaching past all my nervousness and worries, beyond my fears, and touched my heart. My knees strengthened. I lifted my chin to the arguing Dark Saints with all the boldness of a storm at sea.

"I'll never swear allegiance to you," I said. "Now—give me my sister!"

I lunged for El Sombrerón. He dodged back. Kit Fox and Little Lion launched forward with me. Coyote leaped the opposite way, aiming for his back. But Brujo Rodrigo's criaturas jumped forward and grappled with my friends. I didn't pause. Didn't wait. The blue light filled me up, strengthening me, and poured over into my friends. Their eyes flashed with turquoise light, just like the stones on the mosaic in the Sun Sanctuary.

I could do this. I kicked off the ground and reached high for El Sombrerón's soul. This time, I wasn't going to—

He strummed his guitar. Sour music filled the air. My body froze just inches away from him. Coyote, Lion, and Kit stopped moving too. The notes crystallized around us, thick and irresistible, until everything felt so cold that I thought my blood would turn to ice. It was just like when he played for Juana, only this time, he was looking for revenge, not a bride.

The music shook the dust, shook the boulders, the canyon. As he strummed, his guitar notes morphed into rampant words that crowded my skull.

You can't do it, carried through the notes. They scoured my soul until I buckled over. *Your mamá is disappointed in you. Your papá always hated you. Your sister is gone because of you.* El Sombrerón's eyes flashed red. *You're weak. Your water will boil away in the heat of fires more powerful than you. And you were wrong to ever believe otherwise.*

The words drilled through my skull and drowned out the blue light inside me. The glow around my skin vanished. I was on my knees again, shaking as the music pressed down on me.

"As I suspected, this was all a ruse to steal back her sister's soul." El Sombrerón stopped beside Brujo Rodrigo and tilted his head down at him. "You let yourself be tricked, Soul Stealer."

"It was a calculated risk," Brujo Rodrigo spat, glaring at El Sombrerón. "Catrina said—"

"Your weak-minded attachment to Catrina has muddled your thinking. Now, I trust I can leave the child to you—or do I need to tell El Cucuy to replace you with the Cager of Souls?"

The anger in Brujo Rodrigo's face drained away as he looked at me. "I know my duties."

My body wouldn't move. *You can't do it. You're worthless.* The words still echoed in the air, paralyzing and sharp. El Sombrerón strode away into the distant nighttime. Brujo Rodrigo headed for me.

He crouched down and grabbed my three necklaces. My chest tightened. "Don't," I said. "Please."

Brujo Rodrigo smiled, as if I were an amusing, inanimate *thing* instead of a human being. But Coyote was recovering from El Sombrerón's song faster than I could. He stood behind the brujo and shakily swung for him.

Ocelot caught his fist before it could interrupt her master's work.

Her yellow eyes met Coyote's. But her gaze was dull, and her face was slack. Everything inside her was Brujo Rodrigo.

The man's smile curdled. "I think it's safe to say you've *failed* the Bruja Finals."

He ripped all three souls from my neck.

My raw scream blended with Coyote's, Lion's, and Kit's. Almost in unison, the three of them collapsed. My chest ached deep and wide, like an open wound. I hadn't realized how accustomed my soul had grown to theirs after all this time. It was an attachment immediately mourned.

Gila Monster grabbed the back of my jacket and held me aloft. I dangled there, cold and trembling and alone. Coyote, Lion, and Kit lay in the dirt beneath me, completely unconscious. Gila Monster moved me so Brujo Rodrigo and I were face-to-face.

Brujo Rodrigo glared at me. "Do you know why the Dark Saints are so feared, Cece? El Sombrerón and El Cucuy have a power greater than all other criaturas. They have the power to steal and transform the souls of Naked Man." He pulled back his arm like he was preparing for a blow. His hand tensed, the fingers curled. "And when I became the third Dark Saint, they endowed me with the same ability. That's why my title is the Soul Stealer."

"*No!*" I yelled with all the air in my lungs.

"For daring to defy the rulers of Devil's Alley, Cecelia Rios, I will be your judge." Brujo Rodrigo aimed his hand at my chest, just above my heart. "I take your soul to avenge your disrespect against El Sombrerón, guardian of Devil's Alley, and for breaching the greatest law of all: El Cucuy's will and pleasure."

His hand sunk into my chest.

It was the most invasive thing I'd ever felt. It was all the tears I'd ever cried, all the feelings I'd ever had, squirming between the claws of a stranger. Brujo Rodrigo's fingers tugged backward, and his hand emerged from my chest.

A stone, small enough to fit in his palm, sat like a light greenish-blue teardrop in the cup of his hand.

A piece of turquoise. My soul stone?

The heartbeat filling my ears began to fade. I couldn't breathe. The world felt as if it were falling down around me.

Brujo Rodrigo held up my soul. It flashed frantically between his fingers. "Turquoise," he breathed. "An unusual color for a human born in Tierra del Sol. Usually, it's a ruby or a fire opal, filled with fire from the Sun god. But you're touched by the Ocean goddess, aren't you, Cece?" He smirked at me. "That explains the glowing light from earlier, at least. You're no bruja at all. You're a sniveling little *curandera*."

He nodded. Gila Monster dropped me.

The impact rattled my bones, but I didn't feel it. I struggled to cry out as Brujo Rodrigo and his criaturas walked toward my friends' unconscious bodies. His criaturas each picked up one of mine, hauling them onto their shoulders.

Brujo Rodrigo lifted my soul up to the sky, his back to me. "A curandera. Who could believe it, in this day and age. So that's why people say you were cursed by Tzitzim-itl." He looked at me over his shoulder. "I'll tell you a secret, Cecelia Rios. Curanderas may have been touched with the power of one of the gods, but they died out for a reason. They always chose life instead of death, respect over dominance, and in the end, they were too weak to use the gods' powers to their fullest. And you're just the same. Wasted potential." He bared his teeth. "Tzitzimitl didn't curse or bless you. She was just the first to tell you the truth—that you're as weak as spilled water in the heat of the desert, and you'll evaporate just as easily."

Between his fingers, my soul flashed with fragile light. I—was a curandera? All along, a part of me had hoped I could be, and that there was some great, ancient power and truth waiting inside me. But now?

I was going to end up just like they had, wasn't I? Broken and forgotten. Letting everyone down.

My fingers went numb as my soul's light died out in the distance.

Brujo Rodrigo chuckled. "You're probably feeling it already. Unlike criaturas, humans can't live long after being separated from their souls. First, you'll lose your sense of touch. Then your sight. And, right before the end, you'll forget who you are." He paused a few feet away. "I had high hopes for you, for Catrina's sake. She'll be angry with me for a while after this. But at least I'll get to enjoy watching your soul crumble into dust, little curandera."

He turned his back and strode away.

His criaturas followed with my friends dangling from their backs. Tears filled my eyes, but I couldn't keep my head up any longer. I dropped my face into the sand. The numbness crawled up my cheeks, just like he said it would, as their footsteps trailed away.

I had really thought I could do this. I was supposed to be braver, and stronger, and able to get Juana back.

But I guess I always failed when it mattered most—just like the curanderas before me.

The numbness burrowed deep into my skin, and my vision went white. Everything was falling away. The desert, my senses, and any hope I'd had of getting my sister back.

"Child of Naked Man," a voice said.

I wasn't sure how, but by some miracle, I separated my eyelids. Drops of cold sweat ran down my temples. Everything looked gray and blurry. Something stood over me. It was white and thin, barely catching what light I could still see.

"Cecelia Rios," it said.

Something cold locked around my hands. I wasn't sure how I could still feel it at all, but the touch was familiar— like fingers made of stone.

"How have you come so far from your home again, your soul stolen by a Dark Saint?"

My lips parted. I could barely feel them, but I knew this voice. And if this was my last chance to speak, I had a question I needed to ask.

"Tzitzimitl?" I said. "Did you curse me to be a curandera?"

Her other hand fell over my cheek. My vision began

swimming with shades of gray.

"I am . . . weak as water," I said. Stolen soul or not, feeling surged back into my heart, and tears welled up in my eyes. "It's my fault Juana and Coyote and Lion and Kit . . . are suffering."

There was so much more to say, but I could barely stay awake. I had lost everything. I might as well drain away into the sand.

Tzitzimitl's hand stopped over my heart. "Water does not have the same strength as fire, so why should you compare them? Water gives life. Without it, there are no animals, no criaturas, and no Naked Man. How can you say that water is not strong, even if it does not burn?"

Through the numbness, I felt something push against my chest—Tzitzimitl's other hand. My chest compressed and then expanded under Tzitzimitl's guidance. A sharp breath filled my lungs.

"Water and fire are not enemies. The Ocean goddess and the Sun god are sister and brother. I blessed you to know that, Cece Rios. To know your soul is *as strong* as water," she said. "So that you would not lose yourself as the Cager of Souls did."

Her hands pumped my chest up and down. I almost told her it was pointless, but the hopeless words fell away because I wanted to believe her.

"Your soul has been taken, but it is still yours. The Ocean goddess blessed you with her power, but you made it into your strength. Find it now, Cece. Find your strength, and this time, do not doubt it."

I dragged in air. I had to breathe. I squinted at the white blur of Tzitzimitl's face.

"Because I will tell you the greatest secret of all, Cecelia."

My hands finally twitched. I managed to force them up to my eyes and rubbed them hard with my floppy fingers.

"You already had a soul as strong as water, even before I came to you. You were blessed by the gods from the beginning."

When I opened my eyes again, the world was sharp and clear—and Tzitzimitl was gone.

Sensation rushed back into my body. I knew what I had to do.

I had to keep fighting.

Because now I knew who I was. I was Cecelia Rios, Cece, sister of Juana, pretend bruja, best friend of Coyote, ally of Little Lion, protector of Kit Fox, and last of the curanderas. I was the blessed of the Ocean goddess. I was—I was *strong as water.*

I slammed my hands into the dirt. My feet slipped in the

dust, but I commanded them to hold their ground. Slowly, awkwardly, I stood.

Because I wasn't weak. I looked down at myself. My body was bruised, my clothes stained, and tears smeared my cheeks. Whether or not I had just hallucinated Tzitzimitl's words, she was right.

My soul was strong.

So I had to get it *back*.

I lifted my feet. I lifted my head. And I started along the trail Brujo Rodrigo had left behind.

27

Brujo Rodrigo the Soul Stealer

The closer I got to Brujo Rodrigo, the more sensation returned to my body. I could feel a distant pulse in my wrists and chest. As the feeling returned, I sped up my pace. I had to close in on him soon, before he returned to Devil's Alley.

Fortunately, I spotted a shortcut across the top of the canyon. It was a difficult path, but I hiked without ceasing, and this higher position would give me the advantage I needed. The whole way up, I looked down on the trail Rodrigo's party had left behind in the loose dirt.

Soon enough, I caught up.

They were near the end of the canyon where the cliff and the land narrowed into each other. I knelt on a stone shelf, just ahead of them. Slowly, Brujo Rodrigo and his criaturas moved closer. It was tempting to dive straight for Ocelot—she carried Coyote's body over one shoulder, his unconscious head swinging with each step. But then I spotted Brujo Rodrigo heading right beneath my rock shelf.

He tossed my blue soul stone up and down in his hands pensively. I followed his every movement. He passed under me, and I crawled to match his pace. Just as his hair appeared beneath the ledge—

I tumbled off.

I meant to leap more, um, *purposefully*, but my body was even more clumsy and awkward than usual. So, I belly flopped ten feet down onto his shoulder and sent us both slamming into the ground.

When we sat up, his purple-black eyes widened as he spotted me.

I grinned. "Did you miss me?"

"How are you *alive*?" He stood and aimed a kick at my ribs.

I rolled away just in time. "I am the caretaker of my soul," I said. My arms wobbled as I pushed up and stood to face him. "*I* am. *Only* me." The blue stone in his fist started to buzz, vibrating his hand. He looked down at it in alarm. "Now give it *back*."

He jerked his head toward me, sneering. "I was being merciful when I said I'd leave you to die. But you continue to defy the power of Devil's Alley." His face twisted. "Now, I'll punish you the way I punish my criaturas when they question me."

He slammed both hands over my soul stone, and I felt it—a dark, hissing pain worming its way through me.

"No!" I belted.

I'd witnessed this before. The pain Grimmer Mother had inflicted on La Chupacabra. The pain she'd wanted me to use against Coyote. But this time, it was directed at me—and it was as powerful as the desert was large.

Ravenous heat pushed up my throat and reached for my mind. Or, attempted to. I could feel his eagerness to burn me like a bonfire.

But I was made of water.

"I. Said. *No.*" My voice rattled the stones around us.

At the sound, Brujo Rodrigo stumbled, and his criaturas rocked back and forth, their faces flashing between alertness and the dullness of Rodrigo's control. I narrowed my eyes when his furious gaze met mine.

"You want to master my soul?" I cried. Fluctuations of hot and cold battled in my chest. I gathered all of my feelings. Brujo Rodrigo's forehead wrinkled. "Go ahead and try!"

I shoved the strength of all those emotions forward.

My love for Juana. My mourning for Coyote's pain. My sorrow at Lion's past. My grief at imagining Kit's deaths. My love for Mamá. My worry that I'd never live up to her expectations. My fear of Papá. My love for him all the same. I pushed it all forward, into my soul, up Brujo Rodrigo's veins, careening all the feelings of a lifetime into his chest.

Let him try to ignore *that* emotional feedback.

At first, his face just tensed up. Then one by one, his criaturas fell to their knees. My friends tumbled off their shoulders and flopped to the ground. Brujo Rodrigo's hands shook.

"What are you doing?" The veins on his face stood out. "Stop!"

"You wanted my soul, didn't you?" I asked. "This is what it takes to bear it."

I thrust the memory of what had just happened—of going numb, of crying, of being almost nothing—into his heart. He let out a guttural cry and stumbled sideways, falling against the canyon wall. I stopped in front of him, looming over him.

I paused there, watching him tremble and falter. For the past two weeks, I'd experienced all these feelings. I'd experienced Coyote's, Lion's, and Kit's feelings too. But the same feelings that had made me want to be stronger, to be better—they were tearing this Dark Saint apart.

"Please," he heaved out. His left hand opened. My soul slipped from between his fingers.

I snatched it back and grabbed his criaturas' souls from around his neck for good measure. They fell free with a sharp, hard tug.

I came back with four souls—mine, Ocelot's, Gila Monster's, and Golden Eagle's. The moment I touched mine, skin to stone, warmth flooded back into my veins. My chest filled with certainty and peace. I stepped back and couldn't help smiling. Whole again.

Brujo Rodrigo's three criatura souls buzzed lightly and distantly up the leather straps I held them by. I couldn't feel them the same way I did Coyote, Lion, and Kit, but that was probably because I hadn't accepted them by placing them around my neck.

"No!" Brujo Rodrigo's cry interrupted my reverie.

Ash suddenly crept over his face, like mold spreading through his skin. I stiffened as his smooth cheeks pitted and sizzled. His body began to crumble into the dirt, and when he opened his mouth, it was only to gargle a few words:

"Fool," he gasped. "No human can stand against . . . El Cucuy's rule." His hands shivered away into dust. His head slapped against the stone, the skin wearing away. "If El Sombrerón doesn't end you for this . . . El Cucuy . . . will."

In mere seconds, the third Dark Saint was nothing but a pile of dust and bones—a skull whose empty eye sockets still stared at me.

I backed up a couple of steps. "What . . . ?"

I'd never heard of this happening to a brujo. I glanced between his criatura's soul stones and the ash he'd left behind. The wind smeared the soot across the desert stone.

When I looked up, Ocelot, the closest of Brujo Rodrigo's criaturas, stood before me.

I met her yellow stare. Without his influence, she wore a sleek, adult confidence that was at once intimidating and comforting. I glanced from her to Gila Monster and Golden Eagle. The last two, older as well, stared at me without blinking.

Then I spotted the souls she was carrying—Coyote's, Lion's, and Kit's. Hope made my soul sparkle blue. The color lit up my fingers.

Ocelot stared down at her old brujo's remains. "They never warn the apprentice brujas about this before they enter the Bruja Fights. That when your soul learns to feed off the power of others, and it's suddenly stripped of its sustenance," she said, kicking his skull to the side, "you'll find yourself empty, your own soul stone hollowed out."

A chill ran through my skin. She was right. No one had mentioned there was a drawback to becoming a bruja, especially not one as bad as Brujo Rodrigo just endured. But it made sense. How could anyone not destroy their own soul in the process of torturing another's?

"This monster has feasted on criatura souls for over a hundred years. It's no wonder his own soul was nothing but dust without us." Ocelot turned to me. Calmly, she offered my friends' soul stones to me.

"I propose a bargain," she said. Her expression was clear and sharp now without Brujo Rodrigo's interference. "Let Gila Monster and Golden Eagle free, Cecelia Rios. I offer your allies—and my own soul—in return." Her face was stoic but not unkind.

I stared down at her soul stone and the three scratches across its back. She was willing to give it to me to set Gila Monster and Golden Eagle free? That was so—kind. My soul stone gave a sharp spark of blue light, and the three criaturas took a step back.

I grinned sheepishly and slipped my soul into my pants pocket. I guess I needed to get a necklace for that soon. Pretty inconvenient.

"Thank you." I faced Ocelot. "But you don't have to bargain." I placed the three souls into her palm. "I just want my friends back."

Gila Monster and Golden Eagle surged forward and snatched their stones out of Ocelot's hands the moment the trade was done. I stumbled as they rushed past me into the night. They left Kit and Lion dozing on the ground behind Ocelot, next to an unconscious Coyote.

Gila Monster and Golden Eagle vanished down the canyon, while cheering, laughing desperately, and even crying out, "Merciful curandera!"

I smiled a little and turned back to Ocelot. I reached for Coyote's, Lion's, and Kit's stones. She pushed them *and* her own into my palm.

"Keep it," she said. "Not in exchange for Gila Monster and Golden Eagle's. But because you destroyed my greatest tormentor. For that, I owe you, young curandera."

Her pledge made me think back to the first time I met Coyote. "I don't want you to do this just because you feel like you have to. I'm going to fight El Sombrerón, and it's going to be dangerous."

Ocelot watched me for a moment. "This is my choice," she said. "You freed me. And if you are going to fight El Sombrerón, I will stand with you all the more."

Well—who was I to argue with that?

"Thank you," I said. "I could use all the help I can get."

She didn't smile, not really. But her eyes implied one. "I imagine someone as strong as you could take him down all on your own."

I let out a single laugh. "Well, I don't know about that. But maybe I'm strong enough to know it's *okay* not to be strong enough to do it alone."

And with that, I placed their soul stone necklaces around my neck.

They rushed inside my heart like the feeling of coming home. I placed a hand over their stones. Each settled in my chest differently—Coyote like a warm fire, Lion like a hot storm, and Kit like sunshine on a windswept day. And now this new ally, a friend in the making: Ocelot was untilled soil crusted over with winter's hail. Their souls filled my chest with the intensity of an earthquake and the peace of morning sun in the springtime.

It was a lot to take in at once. I swayed and fell backward, so my rear hit the ground. The world swirled for just a moment.

When it settled, Coyote was sitting in front of me.

"Coyote!" I said. In a rush, I threw both arms around him and laughed. He bent his head down, so his nose touched my crown.

"You're okay," he whispered.

He squeezed me and hugged me back. I smiled into his shoulder.

"If you two are . . . done . . ." Ocelot sounded uncomfortable about our open affection. I guess being stuck with a Dark Saint for so long would do that to a person. "We're on a tight schedule from here on out. El Sombrerón will probably already be looking for Brujo Rodrigo."

Coyote's head whipped around, noticing the older criatura for the first time. He growled. Ocelot's eyebrows lowered just a tad in response.

"Hey, it's okay." I placed a hand on his shoulder. "Ocelot's on our side now. You were asleep for a bunch of important stuff."

As I struggled to explain, two pairs of footsteps approached. I glanced around Coyote and saw Kit and Lion staring at me.

"You're awake!" I said.

Lion stiffened. "What did Brujo Rodrigo do to you?"

Kit stepped forward hesitantly. There was a soft pulse from his soul. It rang through my chest and buzzed in my pocket. The three of them—four now, with Ocelot looking distinctly awkward—made a semicircle around me. Oh, could they feel the change in my soul? I plucked it out my pocket and lifted the turquoise tear drop. Lion's breath caught. Kit took another step forward.

"That's the Dark Saints' power," he said. "El Cucuy and El Sombrerón always give their third in command the title Soul Stealer after they give the Third Dark Saint the ability to tear souls from bodies."

Ocelot crossed her arms. "He's trying to say that Brujo Rodrigo stole our curandera's soul."

A small flare shot through Lion's stone. Coyote's face fell.

"But I got it back!" I waved it at them.

"But are you going to be okay?" Coyote looked me up and down, like he was checking for wounds. "Humans aren't supposed to have their souls on the outside."

He was right. It was strangely vulnerable to have my soul outside of my chest. No wonder criaturas feared brujas. To have someone be able to reach out and snatch at who you are—it was so easily misused.

I smiled all the same. "My soul is strong as water. I think I'll be all right."

Coyote's, Kit's, and Lion's faces all lifted with surprise, but before I could explain further, Ocelot stepped forward, placing her hand on Coyote's shoulder.

"Legend Brother," she said. "We have a mission to attend to."

"Uh—yeah. Right." He cleared his throat and looked back at me. "Cece, you don't have the Mark of the Binding, so you can't go into Devil's Alley. Maybe if we can force El Sombrerón—"

"You don't need to enter Devil's Alley to get your sister back," Ocelot interrupted. "El Cucuy and El Sombrerón rule because they have the same power—to transform humans and their souls into whatever shapes they please. It's why their power is unopposed even by brujas. Whenever El Sombrerón leaves the castle, he turns his brides into braids of hair so he can carry them with him in his pocket. It's how he controls them. A braid of hair cannot exercise its will even if it tries."

Juana. My mind filled with my sister's smile. If everything Ocelot said was true, and El Sombrerón was still in the human world, then—

"We have to take down El Sombrerón," I said. "Before

he returns to Devil's Alley."

Lion folded his arms. "It won't be easy, Cece. He's the second most powerful dark criatura in existence."

Kit shrank a bit. "I'm not even sure it's possible to defeat him."

"We can do it." I stood to my full height, my chest puffed out, and looked at my four companions. "If we're together, if we fight with everything we have, we can bring my sister back."

Yes, I was afraid. Like when I'd jumped out the window of my bedroom, and when I'd first gone hunting for a criatura, and when I'd first entered the Bruja Fights, or like just minutes ago, when I'd thought I would die soulless in the desert.

But I wasn't going to let fear hurt the people I loved anymore.

And that went for me too.

A rumble moved through the ground before we had time to bask in our renewed determination. We all turned to see a presence appear from our left.

The canyon ended there, about twenty feet away. The slice between the walls of rock created a window out to the cerros, now blue and gray in the moonlight. El Sombrerón's tall, shadowy figure stained the view.

Coyote looked from the figure to me. "Time to fix our mistakes, Cece."

28
The Braided Sister

El Sombrerón stood facing us, silent and still, as the atmosphere around him changed. The sand felt like glass. The canyon turned into an open jaw. The moon slid behind clouds. I held my breath as Coyote, Lion, and Kit tensed up, and a primal instinct screamed for me to run the other way.

But I didn't.

"We need to steal his guitar," I said instead. "If we take it, he won't be able to defeat us like he did before."

Coyote brandished his claws. "We're with you."

I nodded. Kit, Lion, and Ocelot stood at my side. I gripped my fingers into fists. Juana was just a few steps away. This was it.

Ocelot leaned forward. "When there's an opening, we aim for his robes," she whispered to me. "He'll have her braid in a pocket inside them."

Another footstep shook the ground. We all shivered and looked up.

"Cecelia Rios." The air warped around El Sombrerón's

voice. "You've defeated the Soul Stealer and taken your spoils of war." His hat swiveled to Ocelot. She held her ground. "To think the pathetic younger sister of my new bride now bears more souls than any of the noble brujas in Devil's Alley. It's a shame I must kill you."

He shifted, and his silver guitar peeked out of his cloak. There. If I could just get that away from him, we stood a chance. My skin prickled as the breeze picked up, and clouds brewed in the sky overhead. The smell of moisture entered the air. I held on to it, for comfort, for hope, for strength. I still didn't know how curandera powers worked exactly. But I wasn't going to let that stop me.

"I've come for my sister," I said. "And I'm not leaving without her."

"Your kind has never been strong enough to defeat me, little curandera." His hand whipped the guitar out of his cloak and struck its silver chords. "You will fail."

The notes hit the air like a flock of birds taking flight. Instantly, my knees went wobbly, like my body was turning into atole. I sucked in a hard breath. No, the world couldn't really be rocking left and right. El Sombrerón's song was playing tricks. I stepped forward, stomach churning. No more wasting time.

I dove straight for him.

"Cece, what are you *doing*?" Little Lion's voice called to me.

My criaturas surged after me—most likely because they thought I was about to get myself killed. Which was possibly true.

El Sombrerón readied his guitar to strike me, as he'd done the night he'd stolen Juana. He swung, aiming straight for me—but I braced myself, caught it with my chest and arms, and used the momentum he'd knocked me back with to carry the instrument straight out of his grasp.

I fell back, clutching it to my chest. "Now, Coyote!"

Coyote scooped me up and ran. I held the guitar as he carried me out of El Sombrerón's reach. The dark criatura followed us away from the canyon's mouth, out toward the rocky cerros surrounding Iztacpopo's base. Ocelot leaped up behind him, raised her claws, and slashed them down his back.

The blow made him stumble, but only slightly. Kit and Lion joined her, and the three beat down on him from every side. He slowed under their constant barrage. Coyote stopped to catch his breath about twenty feet away from him. I slipped out of his hold, my hands shaking around the neck of the guitar.

"Now what?" Coyote asked over the din.

I grinned shakily. "He can't use this against us if I break it!"

Coyote gave me a firm smile, nodded, turned, and jumped into the fray. Together, the four criaturas battled

El Sombrerón, tearing at his cloak and at his smoke skin, barely dodging his powerful blows. Now, it was time to level the playing field. I dug my feet into the crags of the rocks and tried to heave the guitar onto my shoulder. But I must have misjudged its weight, or my footing, or my clumsiness, because in midair its weight pulled me sideways. The two of us toppled off the rocks.

The guitar hit the ground with an unearthly clang, but the silver itself was unharmed. I wasn't as lucky. Sharp pain erupted all over my body as I pulled my head up from the sand. But I couldn't stop. Large, thundering footsteps echoed through the cerros. I reached for the guitar. I had to destroy it—

A shadow blotted out the moonlight. I looked up as El Sombrerón surged above me, throwing Ocelot off him and reaching down for me. I screamed. He wrenched me into the air.

His red gaze burned from beneath his hat's brim. "You foolish child. Even if your criaturas were strong enough to defeat me, my guitar would only heal me. I am El Sombrerón, the Bride Stealer, the Undying, Guardian of Devil's Alley's gate. Thus, I was Named. Thus, I will be."

So the guitar was even more important than I thought— we had to break it for sure now. But I couldn't help fixating on his robes, on what I knew hid within them. This was my chance. "Well, I'm Cecelia Rios!" I thrust my hand into his cloak. "The curandera who will defeat you!"

El Sombrerón made to rip me away from his robes, but just then, Coyote and Lion pounced on his back. He whipped around, trying to shake them off. The scenery swirled with his rough movements. I scratched at his cloak. Come on. Ocelot said Juana's braid had to be here some-where! The clouds gathered overhead. My fingernails and soul started to glow with a rush of determination that made my chest swell and the hair on my arms stand on end. Thunder began rumbling above us. Suddenly, a rush of air whipped up behind me, and Ocelot's and Kit's claws swiped down El Sombrerón's robes on either side.

Everything slowed. A crash of lightning struck not far from where we fought and illuminated El Sombrerón's smoky cloak. It split into fraying pieces of smoke, solidi-fying into fabric as the strips fluttered away. Items spilled from his torn clothing. A couple of bones. A few ribbons. A guitar pick—and a long braid of thick black hair.

I caught the braid just before it fell. It was warm, puls-ing with something electric. El Sombrerón roared as my criaturas attacked him from every side, their swipes just precise enough to miss me. His grip tightened on me, and his other hand swung to rip the braid out of my hand.

I clutched her braid to my chest in one hand. "I won't let you take her again!"

I threw my other arm forward, to block his approaching

blow. My fingernails reflected a brilliant turquoise. Sapphire light surrounded my skin.

A great deluge of rain suddenly poured from the sky, directly over El Sombrerón's head.

The criatura months were usually dry, but rain came down heavier now than I'd ever seen even during the storm-prone summer. It swelled like a waterfall, and soon even El Sombrerón's tight grip wasn't strong enough to resist the stream. He dropped me to the desert ground. It was already flooded, and the water cushioned my landing.

I looked around desperately for El Sombrerón's guitar, but it had vanished under the sudden flash flood. El Sombrerón stumbled as the rain hit him, hammering him down and slowing his ability to fight back against my undeterred friends. Coyote whooped. "You're doing it, Cece!"

Me? My heart jumped as the storm rose. My soul glowed in my pocket, even lighting up the water. The rain's roar echoed in my ears and chest and tingled against my skin. Wait—was I really doing this? This—this water was here for me?

Was this the power of a curandera?

El Sombrerón thrashed through the water and rounded on me. "Return my bride!" he roared.

Well, there was one way to find out. *Help me*, I reached

out to the water with my soul.

My soul's light grew almost blinding. The water around me pulled, and the current dragged me steadily out of El Sombrerón's reach. I gripped Juana's braid close to me as the water kept me just a few steps ahead.

El Sombrerón dove for me. The rain kept following his movements, but the current wasn't fast enough to keep me safe.

"Lion!" I cried, because he was the fastest.

El Sombrerón's hand aimed for my head. I squeezed my eyes shut and let the tingling power of my soul flood over, into Lion. Footsteps splashed through the water, and Lion reached me just in time, dragging me out of El Sombrerón's grasp.

Lion landed on a cluster of rocks a short distance away. His eyes flashed turquoise just for a moment, and he nodded to me. Behind us, Coyote dove on El Sombrerón, fighting to keep him back. Ocelot and Kit joined him, all three of them and the rain barely enough to hold him at bay.

"*Juana.*" I clasped the braid.

I wasn't sure this would work. Just because criatura souls could be communicated with using feelings and memories didn't mean that whatever El Sombrerón had transformed my sister into would react the same way. But if I had a soul stone, and I had been able to control mine, surely I could call to hers.

I pressed the braid to my turquoise stone. *Come home,* I pleaded with her, pushing those feelings through my stone and into her hair. The braid pulsed with static electricity. I held it closer and closer. "Come home, hermana," I whispered.

Despite the rain, the braid caught fire. I thrust my head back, away from the scorching heat, as the flames licked up between my fingers. Somehow, they didn't burn my skin, but I tucked my soul stone back in its pocket for safety. Was it working? Could Juana hear me? The braid of hair in my hand crumbled—and then something exploded out of my grip.

"No!" El Sombrerón cried.

I fell back from the fire, shielding my face. The fire roared and raged, screaming, screaming—until it was an actual voice.

Juana shrieked as her body formed from the flames.

It wasn't like her scream of terror on Noche de Muerte. It was the scream of a wounded creature on the edge of vengeance.

The heat vanished. My jacket steamed and the edges smoldered. Slowly, I dropped the hand I'd been using to shield my face.

A couple of feet away, Juana swayed lightly on her feet.

Great shadows stained the skin beneath her eyes. Her hair was shorter than before, hanging in thick waves just above her shoulders, curling in the rain. She was still in the Amenazante dress I'd sewn. Its hem hung in tatters, stained with dirt and riddled with holes.

Her gaze targeted El Sombrerón before she could see me. Her hands coiled into fists. Her stance was caught somewhere between predator and prey.

"*You*." Juana gritted her teeth until she looked as animalistic as any criatura. "This time, I'm not going to steal your soul. I'm going to *shatter* it."

"Juana!" My shoes sloshed through the rising water as I came up behind her. "*Juana*." I caught her arm and spun her around.

Her face lit up. "Cece?" she whispered, and her voice was the one I remembered again.

I laughed and threw my arms around her, tears gushing.

She grabbed me desperately. "Cece," she said again. Her hands darted over my shoulders, fingers caressing my shorn hair. "Holy sunset, Cece, it's you. But you're glowing. And your hair! Am I—?"

I squeezed her closer. She was cold and shivering, but the harder I held her, the more her skin warmed. She flickered like a candle nearly blown out, but she was still fire, my sister.

"You're home, Juana," I said.

El Sombrerón's feet shook the earth and sent waves through the water at our ankles. I jerked out of our embrace as he materialized above us, his cloak hanging in strips, his skin furious smoke. But most importantly, his guitar was back in hand. How'd he find it?

"You've earned your death well, Cecelia Rios." He lifted his silver guitar.

Juana shoved me behind her and spread her arms protectively. Coyote plowed into El Sombrerón's side and drove him to the ground. Lion and Kit caught El Sombrerón's feet while Ocelot struggled to pry the guitar out of his grip.

Just then, El Sombrerón rose to full height and lifted his guitar so Ocelot dangled from its neck. He kicked her off it and stomped her into the ground. Ocelot gasped. El Sombrerón rose again, grabbed Coyote and Kit Fox in one hand, and crushed them into the ground beside her.

Their pain reverberated through me. I lunged forward, hand out. "Stop! Don't hurt them—"

"No!" Juana screamed as she rushed past me, her hair whipping around, wild strands sticking to her face. She leaped for El Sombrerón's guitar. "*No, no, no!*"

Lion dove in with her and kicked El Sombrerón's elbow. The dark criatura grunted as the impact sent him stumbling. Juana grabbed the guitar. Ripped it straight from his hands. El Sombrerón reached for her again as she turned her back.

"Juana, watch out—" I made to run for her.

As always, Lion was faster.

El Sombrerón caught him in the gut. Little Lion's body bent with the impact, and he flew straight into a rock wall. He collapsed at its base and lay motionless. Pain rocked his soul. Coyote lumbered to his feet and ran to him.

Halfway between me and El Sombrerón, Juana planted her feet and heaved the silver guitar over her shoulder in one swing, despite how easily it had sent me tumbling. Rain ran down its silver edges, and fell like tears down its strings.

"No!" El Sombrerón's command rolled through the ground.

"No?" Juana roared. She looked back at him, her eyes wild. He started to come after her, but Ocelot and Kit scrambled up and clawed onto him. Juana hefted the guitar up and slammed it into the ground. A hot crack of lightning cleaved the sky as stones pierced through the guitar's sides.

El Sombrerón winced.

"No!" she repeated, like she was taking the word back from him. She kept slamming the guitar down again and again. It shattered, strings flailing, until only the useless neck was left. "*No, no, no!*"

I wondered what she was saying no to. No to him hurting me, no to him hurting her, or no to whatever he'd already done.

Rain dripped down the broken neck as she tossed it away. "I've wanted to do that for ages," she said.

El Sombrerón made to charge at her. But Coyote leaped up and grappled with him, their hands locked in a deadly push and pull. "Your guitar is gone—you're not indestructible anymore!" he yelled. "It's over."

"Over?" he rumbled. El Sombrerón's fingers closed over Coyote's trembling wrists. "You have been tamed by a pollo who believes herself to be a hawk. And mortal or not, I will make sure you fall with her when her wings *break*."

He snapped Coyote's arm with the last word.

Coyote's scream echoed around me. My heart froze. El Sombrerón shoved Coyote to the side. The energy coming off him was different now. It wasn't the calculated, mysterious monster anymore. Now that his guitar was gone, he was a hulking, burning beast, and his gaze shone like fire as he came toward me.

Juana seized my shoulder. "Run, Cece!"

Coyote's broken arm dangled uselessly by his side. "Cece, run!"

But El Sombrerón, even injured, was faster than their

words or my reflexes. He knocked Juana aside, sending her rolling through the floodwater that was now two feet deep. I lurched after her, but El Sombrerón's hand caught my neck and hauled me into the air, above his head.

Nine feet off the ground, I stared down at El Sombrerón's faceless darkness. My heart thundered. His fingers dug into my skin and began to burn.

"What should I transform you into?" he asked. As he spoke, crimson marks crawled out from his touch, each one a pattern of heat and pain. Tears blurred my vision as his magic sizzled against my skin, and I gasped and struggled.

Coyote found his footing below. "Cece!" he cried. "Remember! You're not just a human!"

El Sombrerón tipped his head. "How about . . . a pile of ash?"

The burning marks wormed up my face as smoke rose from his hand.

"You're a *curandera*!" Coyote yelled.

The heat spread over my friends' soul stones. I saw the moment it hit them. Each of them collapsed into the water, writhing. Coyote held his broken arm and fell to his knees. My lungs trembled as we shared the destructive power of El Sombrerón.

No. Juana's word reverberated through me and interrupted the heat, stopping just beneath my eyelashes. My heart shuddered with my refusal to burn, and my soul's light surged upward. Something shot up inside me, a geyser, a crescendo, a wave that drowned out the fear. Thunder boomed again overhead. Slowly, the light around my skin evolved from a low glow to a stunning turquoise *shine*.

I grabbed El Sombrerón's wrist with both of my wet, trembling hands. The last time he'd held me like this, he'd beaten me and stolen my sister. He'd broken my familia. But things were different now. He might have wounded us, might have broken Coyote's arm, might be able to throw me around, but—

"You have no power over me!" I yelled into the storm.

The blue light of my soul spread, overflowing into my criaturas. Their soul stones started glowing blue around my neck. Coyote looked up at me, and his eyes shone like blue suns. Kit and Ocelot raised their heads from the ground, their eyes sharp and turquoise.

I squeezed El Sombrerón's hand at my throat, and the red streaks on my cheeks suddenly shattered like glass off of my skin. Rainwater dripped down my face and cooled over any pain. His red eyes widened. A dark shudder moved through his arm as I pushed my water's strength toward him. Glowing blue streaks, wound together in intricate patterns, appeared on his hand and spread down his sleeve.

El Sombrerón shook his head and stumbled back, but

didn't let me go. "What is this?" His other hand grabbed at his smoky skin, trying to push the blue lines away. They only wound up his shoulder, spreading faster as my soul stone pulsed. "No curandera has done this before."

I dug my nails into El Sombrerón's hand as a spiral blossomed down his throat and washed over the soul stone hanging there.

"You don't get to hurt *anyone*! Not anymore!" I yelled.

The moment my blue light encircled El Sombrerón's soul stone, his body froze. His arm locked, paralyzed. I willed his fingers to open. They lifted like a hinge and set me free.

Coyote and Kit Fox lunged forward. Kit Fox somersaulted and caught me as I fell. Coyote raised his good hand's great, sharp claws, jumped into the air, and twisted above El Sombrerón's head. Their eyes met, dark criatura and Great Namer.

Coyote delivered the final blow.

Kit and I hit the ground. The rain overhead slowed to a trickle. El Sombrerón swayed on his feet—and then fell to the earth in a great, thundering slap of water and mud.

His soul swung up in the air, trailing his fall. The large black stone caught the moonlight. I watched a single scratch dig its way through its surface. And as it finally dropped next to El Sombrerón, the water and desert ground parted for it. Together, his newly scarred soul and body disappeared instantly into the sand.

Everything fell finally, serenely quiet.

The rain petered out. The flood began to recede. Coyote straightened up next to where El Sombrerón's body had fallen. He stared at the ground as the gray in his soul seeped away, and a peaceful pulse moved through his stone. His soul filled with the words *it's done*. He closed his eyes. Finally, the pink could shine brightest of all his feelings.

I sighed as relief settled over us. My body slowly stopped glowing. Kit lowered me to the ground, and he, Ocelot, and Coyote went to check on Lion.

Sloshing footsteps sounded from my left. I turned and found Juana standing there, a little scuffed, but no worse for the blow she'd taken. The water had nearly drained away. She approached hesitantly, eyes glancing between me and my criatura friends gathered around Little Lion.

She stopped in front of me. "You're a bruja," she said.

"A curandera, actually." I said. "But also kind of a bruja? Maybe both. I don't really know. Either way, these four are my friends." I placed a hand over the four souls at my throat. "They won't hurt you."

That should have been obvious considering Little Lion had saved her earlier, but I still found it helpful to say aloud. Ideas become more powerful when you give them words.

"Cece," she whispered.

Her hand reached for mine. I took it and then took her, and we were holding each other, desperate and sopping wet in the cerros. I buried my face in her shoulder as she clasped me to her chest.

And then, for the first time since she erupted from the braid, she gave a light, shivering laugh. "It's really over," she whispered in my ear.

I beamed into her collarbone. It was a weak chuckle, almost a sob, but it sounded a lot like hope. I squeezed her as tightly as I could, and the aching parts of me began to heal.

We were still hugging, almost laughing, almost crying, when Coyote, Kit, and Ocelot helped Lion limp over to meet us.

29
La Casa de Familia

Juana stood before the door to our house, looking up at it as if it were a foreign entity.

"What's wrong?" I whispered. I tried to stay as quiet as possible. The police would probably be patrolling the street soon, though we hadn't encountered any on our way back through town. Either way, I didn't want to be banished before I could see my familia put back together.

Coyote's soul stone warmed my ribs, and I glanced up at him. He sat on the edge of my roof, nursing his arm. Ocelot, Kit, and Lion were there too—but only Lion's feet were visible, since he was resting. I was glad his wound had closed so quickly, though he'd need to rest for another day before he was back to his old self. Kit swung his legs off the edge of the adobe and chatted to Ocelot between frequent checks on Lion. Ocelot focused on him, clearly listening carefully, even if she made no reaction outside of the occasional abrupt nod.

Coyote was the only one watching me. My chest warmed with the pink in his soul. The gray had vanished for now.

I hoped it would stay that way for a while longer. After all he'd done for me, and after all the battles he'd waged inside himself, I thought he deserved to bask in hope.

I smiled up at him before looking back at Juana.

"Mamá and Papá have missed you," I said.

She nodded, slowly. The light from inside the window shone in her eyes. They seemed fuller, now, than they had when she'd first unraveled from the braid.

"I missed them too," she said. "It just looks so much smaller than I remember."

There was something unsettling in the way she said it. Like our adobe house, our home, was a distant memory she had returned to unexpectedly.

I stepped closer. "Do you . . . not want to go in?"

I'd never considered that she might feel uncomfortable coming back here. But I understood the expression on her face. I'd only been gone for a few hours, and the house felt less like home than it had earlier that day. Maybe because I wasn't sure whether I'd even be able to stay.

Juana didn't answer my question right away. Her eyes ate up the light, and she took a hard breath. "Cece?"

"Yeah?"

"I'm scared." She took another breath, this one shuddering. "I'm scared, and I hate it."

In all my life, I'd never heard Juana admit to being afraid.

Juana had always been iron, a mountain, a fire, just like Mamá. And she'd been so angry with me for not being the same way. She'd yelled at me to hide my tears. She'd scoffed like she thought I should be above it.

But there was something I had finally learned that she hadn't yet.

I stepped forward and took her hand. It was calloused but warm. She looked at me like a candle on its last bit of wick.

I squeezed her hand. She squeezed back.

"It's okay to be afraid," I whispered. "As long as you don't let it stop you from being the best of who you truly are."

Her lips tipped upward, just slightly. She glanced up, then, at the edge of the roof. Coyote waved at her when she spotted him. Her hand twitched, like she might return it. But then she let it fall limp to her side, like she was too tired to finish the gesture.

"How long was I gone?" she asked. "Here, for you?"

"Just about a week," I said.

She winced, like there was an ache in her chest. "Only a week?"

Only? Those seven days had been agony. But if it seemed short to her—how much time had passed in Devil's Alley?

She dropped her gaze to the front door. "Cece?"

"Yeah?"

"You became a bruja in just over a week," she said. It wasn't a question.

When she said it like that, it really did feel like a short time. I nodded. "Yes."

She swallowed. "And you did that . . . for me?"

I glanced at her. She didn't meet my stare. "Yeah, Juana," I said. I wrapped my arm around hers to keep her warm. "You're my big sister."

She cracked a weak smile. "You're unbelievable." Her next inhale came in shaky. "Cece—will you stay with me?"

She stared at our front door like it was the entrance to El Cucuy's castle. I looked at it with her and couldn't help feeling the same way.

"I'll stay with you," I said. "I promise."

And yes, I was frightened. I was worried about what Mamá would say when she saw me, when only five hours ago I had broken her heart. I was afraid to see Papá again— afraid to let him see the way he'd bruised me, and afraid that he would try to do it again. But I also knew I had a choice in how all of this turned out. So for now, I would choose to walk in with Juana, and be by her side, and share in this all-important moment. The rest I'd figure out later.

"Good luck," four voices whispered above us. I looked up and found my friends cheering us on.

Coyote sat in the middle, smiling softly, as he propped up Little Lion on his right. Lion, looking tired but peaceful, nodded toward us. Kit Fox beamed on Coyote's left, leaning against Ocelot. And Ocelot's eyes implied a deep, gentle encouragement that I could feel all the way through her soul.

"Thank you. All of you. We wouldn't be here without you," I said back.

"That's for sure," Lion mumbled. Coyote snorted and gave him a look.

Juana stared up at the four criaturas like she still wasn't sure what to make of them.

I laughed a little and looked at my big sister. "Ready?"

Slowly, she nodded, and we approached the door together. The closer we came, the more courage built in my chest. Juana's eyebrows were drawn, and I saw the fear there, but there was also excitement in her eyes. We held each other tightly—

And stepped forward together into our familia's home.

Glossary

abuelo—Grandfather.

abuela—Grandmother.

adobe—A building material made by mixing sun-dried earth with organic materials like straw. Adobe is particularly well-suited to sunny, dry environments like those in northern Mexico. My abuelo told me about the time he watched his papá and tíos (uncles) build their first adobe house. It took a lot of time and work but had a beautiful result.

Amenazante—Threatening or menacing. So, in Cece's world, it's the Threatening Dance.

atole—A sweet, cornmeal-based beverage served hot with cinnamon. When thickened, it resembles rice pudding or porridge. Typically eaten for breakfast or as dessert, but it can be eaten for any meal. Fun fact: My familia has always prepared atole like a soup, only with rice instead of cornmeal.

Axochitl—Cece's mamá's name comes from Nahuatl, the ancient language of the Aztecs, which is still spoken today in parts of Mesoamerica. It's pronounced, "Ah-shoh-cheet-tl." The "tl" sound isn't one that exists in English.

bruja—A female witch. In traditional folklore, brujas used dark magic to curse others by casting spells using intricate ingredients. My abuelo told me that his mother was once cursed by a bruja when the family wouldn't sell her a goat for a cheaper price. Fortunately, he said a curandera came along a few days later and healed her.

brujería—Witchcraft or the practice of dark magic.

brujo—A male witch. In traditional folklore, stories with brujas are more common than those with brujos, which is why the fights in Cece's world are called Bruja Fights.

buenas noches—Good night.

buñuelos—Fried tortillas covered in cinnamon and sugar and served as a delicious snack or dessert. Fun fact: I love buñuelos almost as much as Cece does.

burro—Donkey.

cantos—Songs, poetry, or stanzas of an epic poem. In Cece's world, the *Cantos de Curanderas* means songs of the curanderas and contains ancient instructions about the magic and techniques they used.

coyamito agate—A type of agate native to northern Mexico, known for its gorgeous red, brown, and sometimes even purple layers of color.

charro (pantalones de)—Close-fitting pants that, together with a cropped jacket, white shirt, and high-crowned hat, were worn by Mexican horsemen ("charros") in the seventeenth century. They're designed to fit snugly to avoid getting caught on brush and typically feature embroidery, buttons, or another type of related decoration in a vertical line down the outside of each leg. From the 1900s on, the charro style has evolved into a way to express national pride despite its humble origins and became the colorful, classic Mariachi outfits we know today.

chica—A girl or young adult woman.

chiquita—Typically used to refer to a female that's physically small and translates to little lady or small fry. It's usually an affectionate term but can be condescending depending on the speaker.

La Chupacabra—The Goat Sucker. Usually called El Chupacabra. This legend surfaced in the 1990s and describes a reptilian, hairless creature that drains goats of all their blood in the middle of the night. In Cece's world, La Chupacabra's gender is female.

criaturas—Creatures. This term is also used to refer to babies or children. Thus, in Cece's world, criaturas are both legendary creatures and the children of Mother Desert.

cucaracha—An insult that means cockroach.

El Cucuy—The coconut or the skull. A dark, frightening bogeyman with red eyes who hides in closets, stalking children and kidnapping the badly behaved ones under the cover of night. His origin story changes according to who's telling it, but some say he locked his children in a closet because they were so much trouble. While he was out running errands, his house caught fire and his children died. From then on, he wandered the world in denial, searching for his children in other people's closets and then stealing children to fill the hole his own had left behind. In Cece's world, he is the most powerful of the dark criaturas and king of Devil's Alley.

curandera— Spanish term for native healer, or a priestess who uses magic to heal physical and spiritual ailments using ingredients taken from nature. Also, curandero (priest).

dulce de leche—Literally translated to "sweet of milk," this delicious food is made from heating sweetened milk slowly until it caramelizes. When I came to visit, my abuela would let me eat some right out of the container. Because I'm a good girl.

Envidia—Envy. In Cece's world, it's the town where Grimmer Mother and other brujas and brujos live.

Etapalli—Cece's abuela's name, pronounced "eh-tah-pah-yee." The name comes from Nahuatl, but this pronunciation is based on Spanish phonetics.

familia—You might've already guessed this one, but it

means family in Spanish.

Isla del Antiguo Amanecer—The Island of the Ancient Dawn. In the novel, this is the country Cece lives in.

Juana—Cece's sister's name, pronounced "hooah-na."

limpia—Cleansing (ritual). Curanderas perform limpias on people to cleanse them spiritually or physically and protect them from evil spirits. These ceremonies often incorporate sacred items taken from nature, like basil and eggs. In Cece's world, the limpia has a similar function, but it focuses on preparation and strength using elements of the world's four gods instead.

La Lechuza—Screech Owl. In legend, screech owls are often supernatural beings of some sort—like witches who have transformed themselves to wreak havoc, the angered spirits of dead women, or possibly even shape-shifting vampires. In Cece's world, La Lechuza is a dark criatura.

La Llorona—The Weeping Woman. In legend, she is always depicted wearing white. Her origin story differs depending on the region, but many stories say she's a ghost who drowned her own children and now haunts waterways, waiting to drown others. My great-abuelo once thought he saw her when he traveled along a river on his burro at night. Fortunately, it was just the white strap of his hat floating in his peripheral vision. That story still makes me chuckle to this day.

La Luz Mala—The Bad Light. This legend originates from Argentina, Chile, and Uruguay. A glowing ball made of gas that lures lost people into the countryside. When a person reaches it, the toxicity of the gas will kill them.

mija—My daughter, my child. A contraction of mi and hija, sometimes spelled m'ija. This term is often used by people who aren't necessarily the parents of the person they are addressing. It is considered a sign of affection and denotes closeness. For example, my tías, abuelo, and abuela call me mija when I visit.

Noche de Muerte—Night of Death. In Cece's world, this is the night when Devil's Alley opens.

nocheztli—A Nahuatl word meaning the blood of the prickly pear, it is a dye made from the cochineal parasitic insect that lives in cactus nopal. Gross? Maybe. But the color is beautiful.

ocelot—A small wild cat native to the southern United States, Mexico, and Central and South America. Usually nocturnal, this feline has rounded ears and a long body with a tawny-yellow or grayish coat dotted and striped with black.

Perdón, ¿te desperté?—Sorry, did I wake you up?

pollo—Chicken.

señor—Mister or sir.

señora—Mistress or madam, denotes a married woman.

señorita—Miss, denotes an unmarried woman.

sí—Yes.

El Silbón—The Whistler. His story originates from Colombia and Venezuela but has spread across large parts of Mesoamerica. The details change depending on the region, but many stories say he killed his father after his father killed his wife. El Silbón's abuelo then cursed him to carry his father's bones in a bag on his back for all eternity as punishment. Some say that hearing his whistle foretells your death.

El Sombrerón—The Man with the Big Hat, also known as the goblin, depending on the region. Likewise, the exact details differ depending on where in Latin America you're from, but many stories say he lures away young, beautiful women with his guitar's siren song. He's also known for being obsessed with braiding hair, even to the point of braiding horses' tails in the middle of the night.

tía—Aunt.

Tierra del Sol—Land of the Sun.

Tzitzimitl (singular), Tzitzimime (plural)—In Nahuatl, these names are pronounced "tsi-tsi-me-tl" and "tsi-tsi-me-meh," respectively. The Tzitzimime were, according to Aztec mythology, skeletal female deities who lived among the stars and protected children—unless there was a solar eclipse. The folktale differs slightly from region to region, but some stories say the Tzitzimime warriors would come down from the stars and kill people en masse during a solar eclipse because of their war against the sun. In Cece's world, Tzitzimitl is the only one of her kind.

Acknowledgments

I've been writing since I was ten years old, and writing with the aim to become a published author since I was fourteen years old. It's hard to quantify how many people have helped me in that time and how many of their small acts have contributed to the creation of *Cece Rios and the Desert of Souls*. But I'll do my best to showcase their love at work.

To start, a huge thank-you to my lovely agent, Serene Hakim, whose quality editing feedback, determination, and support have been a stabilizing influence during my publishing journey. Thank you for loving Cece so much and for understanding both her and me. I'm blessed to work with you.

To my fabulous editor, Stephanie Guerdan, who loved Cece and was always willing to listen to my thoughts, knock ideas back and forth, and fight for my novel's entrance into the library of HarperCollins. Thank you for your patience and encouragement as I learned to be a better world builder. Your feedback, sound-boarding, and passion have been essential, and I've deeply enjoyed working with you.

And another huge thank-you to the entire HarperCollins Children's team. To the marketing team who saw my book's potential, to the copy editors who have carefully helped me get the timeline in place (your small catches always add up to a big, positive effect), to the wonderful design team, and to everyone who helped bring this book to life. You are essential, and I am grateful for what you do.

Now, for some personal thank-yous. To my mom, whose battle to forgive and stay kind ended up giving Cece her soul. Thank you for being a wonderful mother who I treasure, a great teacher, and even my first editor. I'm so grateful you never let my impatience get in the way of telling me the truth. You're the reason I learned to grow.

To my abuelo, who shared his memories of Mexico and helped me graft one of my cultures into my heart, so I no longer had to feel so detached. Cece's story is filled with the background you gave me.

And to my granddad—I wish you could have lived to see the day Cece was published. But I'm so grateful you got to hear the news that it would be, and for the support and encouragement you gave me, even all the way across the Atlantic. To my darling nanny (my grandmother, for my non-British readers): thank you for the way you supported me and read my novels growing up. You didn't let an ocean stop you from being there for me, and I'll always remember that.

To my sisters, who are fires and waterfalls in their own way. You let me read aloud my stories (for way too many hours, sorry) and (sometimes reluctantly) read through entire manuscripts for me on your own. We've never been good at saying heartfelt thank-yous. But I want you to read it, to see it, immortalized here: Thank you for being my familia. Thank you for loving me in whatever way you can. Thank you, hermanas. I love you both.

And to my dear, close friends Magnolia, Loleata, Kate, and Laura. You are sisters of my heart, and I'm so grateful for the many ways you've supported me and my writing over the years. You are far above rubies.

An acknowledgment wouldn't be complete without savoring the contributions of my writing family. Thank you to the Table of Trust, the PW '14 and PW '15 groups for their beta reading, support, and helpful advice. Thank you to the entire PitchWars community, for existing and fostering growth. And a particularly heartfelt thank-you to the 5th Wind Writing Group, for sincerely cheering me on and giving me authentic, thoughtful feedback. Reading and eating treats with you once a week is an honor.

And above all else, to my Heavenly Father and Jesus Christ, who are my comfort and solace, the gold that fills and reseals the wounded cracks in my soul's pottery. I hope to be as kind, loving, righteous, and truthful as you teach me to be. I'll keep growing and being joyful; I promise, above all else, I won't quit.